Advance Praise for *Terry Brankin Has a Gun*

Malachi O'Doherty draws from a wealth of professional and lived experience. He crafts characters and plot that are plausible and unsettling in their moral complexity and ethical duplicity. In a society endeavouring to make sense of its bloody past, *Terry Brankin Has A Gun* reaffirms that no one gets out of this imperfect peace unscathed.

Thomas Paul Burgess, author of *Through Hollow Lands*

A deftly spun tale of dreadful intricacy and bewildering insight into a paramilitary world in denial of its own duplicitous logic. O'Doherty is a gifted storyteller – here is a wholly believable cast of modern-day imposters – as ordinary as they are sickening, as selfish as they are chilling. We learn that the effects of the Troubles are still rippling and karma is the only true compatriot. I left this book feeling I knew Northern Ireland a lot better than when I lived there in peace times.

June Caldwell, author of *Room Little Darker*

It's payback time in this tense and gripping novel shot through with wicked humour, because the past is never dead, especially not in the world of Terry Brankin. I sat up late into the night to finish this brilliantly thrilling tale of responsibility and guilt.

Wendy Erskine, author of *Sweet Home*

This is a marvellous book – part-thriller, part-portrait of a marriage, part-anatomy of a dysfunctional society: it is clear sighted, totally unsentimental and it steadfastly refuses to avert its gaze. It tells a horrible truth about our damage but with style and panache.

Carlo Gébler, author of *Confessions of a Catastrophist*

This novel fires a truth-telling bullet into the heart of things. A fast-paced joyride through the backstreets of Belfast and bogs of Donegal, it reveals the danger of delving into the past and brilliantly skewers the corruption, lies and hypocrisy in Northern

Irish society through its perfectly observed cast of characters. O'Doherty's sharp-shooting pen effortlessly illuminates the shadowlands of modern-day paramilitarism.

Rosemary Jenkinson, author of *Catholic Boy*

A compelling and gripping story. The subject is a timely one as people in Northern Ireland who experienced the Troubles continue to seek closure with regard to family tragedy and, in some cases, their own guilt. This is not only an exciting story but is a must-read for anyone who cares about what the Troubles did to people and wants to better understand it. There isn't a false note in this book.

Annie McCartney, novelist and playwright

Terry Brankin goes from warfare to lawfare to be-careful-what-you-wish for. This punchy, highly filmic, pacy post-Troubles novel is a prescient warning that truth and reconciliation are not always mutual, and can even be murderous.

Henry McDonald, author of *Two Souls*

A tense and fast-paced political thriller that switches effortlessly between Troubles-era Belfast and the present day, dealing en route with the fallout from what was done. A compelling insight into the workings of the paramilitary machine, the challenges of policing the state, and the far from clear-cut relationship between the two.

Bernie McGill, author of *The Watch House*

The past might be a foreign country but not in Northern Ireland where the secrets of the past complicate the present in unexpected and devastating ways. In Malachi O'Doherty's tense and compelling new thriller nobody is as they seem, or claim to be, but one thing is certain; there will be consequences for their actions. O'Doherty's prose is taut and suspenseful, shot through with gritty humour that keeps the reader guessing and turning the page until the very last twist.

Nessa O'Mahony, author of *The Branchman*

TERRY BRANKIN HAS A GUN

Malachi O'Doherty was born in Muff, County Donegal, and grew up in Belfast. He was a teacher to Libyan soldiers, a ghostwriter for an Indian guru, a contributor to BBC Northern Ireland and a regular writer for the *Belfast Telegraph*. Much of his writing career coincided with the Troubles. He has written numerous books about that period, including *Fifty Years On: The Troubles and the Struggle for Change in Northern Ireland* (Atlantic Books, 2020) and *Gerry Adams: An Unauthorised Life* (Faber and Faber, 2018).

TERRY BRANKIN HAS A GUN

MALACHI O'DOHERTY

First published in 2020 by
Merrion Press
10 George's Street
Newbridge
Co. Kildare
Ireland
www.merrionpress.ie

9781785373107 (Paper)
978178533114 (Kindle)
9781785373121 (Epub)
9781785373138 (PDF)

British Library Cataloguing in Publication Data
An entry can be found on request

Library of Congress Cataloging in Publication Data
An entry can be found on request

This book is a work of fiction and while it draws parallels with the political context in Northern Ireland it should not be taken to imply any allegation, or to disclose information of any kind, about any living person.

Typeset in Sabon LT Std 11.5/15 pt

Cover design by Fiachra McCarthy

For Maureen

ACKNOWLEDGEMENTS

Several people have influenced the writing of this book and deserve a mention. At an early stage my then agent Jonathan Williams offered valuable guidance. So did my niece, Katie O'Kelly, particularly in relation to Kathleen's shopping expedition. David Torrens of No Alibis Bookshop contributed as a friend and ally. My later agent Lisa Moylett was a huge help, as was the editor Maria McGuinness. Other helpful readers of early drafts include Stephen Walker, Niamh Gormley and Darragh MacIntyre. The Arts Council of Northern Ireland assisted me at one stage with a SIAP grant and the finishing work was done during a period in which I was a recipient of a Major Artist Award from the Arts Council, funded by the National Lottery. My wife, Maureen Boyle, a writer herself, was an unfailing support and astute critic.

PROLOGUE

Back Then

He was driving to his death and didn't know it. The death itself would be so sudden and decisive, he wouldn't even have a second to anticipate it – nor would his wife and daughter beside him. They would all be torched in an instant. Horrible to think about, if you are a bomber with a conscience, but reassuringly brief.

It had been a long day. The light was dim, and the wipers slashed rivulets across the windscreen. The lights from oncoming traffic seemed brighter than usual and stung his eyes. He was tired and the drive was boring. In the back seat, his daughter switched between fidgeting and moaning. She had a little doll that one moment she was hugging close to her and the next, flopping carelessly onto the seat beside her. He checked on her occasionally in the rear-view mirror, afraid that she would slide out of her seat belt again.

Beside him, Libby selected *Black Beauty* from a stack of tapes in front of the gear stick and slotted it in, wishing she hadn't to hear it through again. Paddy reached across to press the rewind button, keeping one hand on the wheel and an eye on the drab, wet, familiar road. Two hours from home. Seconds from death.

Approaching the border, he hoped that the checkpoints would not delay them. There should be a decent motorway between Dublin and Belfast but, he supposed, security took first claim on budgets. There was no point in yawning or complaining.

Men who knew all about security were waiting for a bottle-green Rover just like Paddy Lavery's. Theirs had been a long day too, meandering around mountain roads to evade detection, crouching between gorse bushes in combats that could guard the skin against thorns but not the backs of their necks against the rain that dripped on them from the low trees they manoeuvred through. They knew that there were soldiers in hill-top towers who had cameras that could check the hair in their ears.

Clever and painstaking enough not to be seen, not even to raise a suspicion, they had collected their package, placed it and primed it and unrolled a wire to the shelter of bushes. The lookout guy would know the target by the make and colour of the car, by the number of passengers: a man and a woman – the chief constable and his wife – and their child behind them. Pity about the child. Probably grow up to be as bad as the da anyway.

The man with binoculars would signal from a rise; the other would trip the switch.

Was his daughter dozing? Paddy wasn't sure. He'd thought wee Isobel would enjoy the drive; he'd wanted her brother Seamus to come too but knew now that two would have been double the distraction and the worry. He'd be back down this road in a couple of weeks for the All-Ireland and could make it up to the boy then.

The one with the binoculars wasn't sure at first, but he had only about a hundred yards of road in which to make up his mind. The make was right: it was a Rover. The colour? In this light? Yeah, it was green, yes, bottle green. Do you mean wine-bottle green or beer-bottle green? But he held back because he could only see two heads. No, there was definitely someone in the back seat. Now his heart was pounding. This was on. He'd be far enough back to be safe from the blast but the suddenness of it and the noise always got you anyway. He waved a signal then lowered himself flat on the cold wet ground. He turned his face away from the car as it passed close below him.

And the blast punched his heart.

God knows what that was like for the people in the car. In the moment it had taken him to shudder and recompose himself, they had been obliterated. Then the car's wreckage was tumbling on the road, screeching and rattling, thankfully away from him.

He'd have looked silly if it had fallen on top of him. Surely they felt nothing as fire tore through them. He couldn't help imagining it though, being scorched and torn from below. But even if there was a fraction of a second of the worst possible pain, there would be no recall of it now, in Heaven or in Hell. And he believed in neither. The Chief Con and his wife and sprog were beyond all grief and suffering. As well for them.

In an hour, he and the others on the team would be scrubbed and in a pub in Newry. The first pint would take the bitter taste out of his mouth. The second would settle him. In time, he would be warm again and among friends, who would let him sit close to the fire. And if they had to, would swear he had been there all day.

One

'Hello, love.' Terry Brankin had a tone reserved for his wife when her number showed up on his phone. When he had taken calls from her more brusquely, on other lines, she had accused him of coldness.

'There's a policeman wants to come to the house tonight.'

'What's that about?' It was as well to pretend he could have no idea.

'He didn't say.'

'Well, sure you go out like you planned, and I'll deal with it.' He had a half-memory that this was her night for the book group.

'No way, Terry.' She'd want to support him and didn't understand how he would manage better without her there.

Kathleen knew that Terry had been in the IRA, back then. They had told each other everything, she supposed, had made a point of it. A month into their relationship they had sat together at the dining table in her Camden Street flat and unfolded their lives to one another. She had told him about Ciaran Simpson, a lad who fished for mackerel around Rathlin Island and courted her by leaving a massive dogfish on her mother's step. She had told him about a German man called Tomas who had camped near her home one summer and brought her into his tent. He had told her about Lynne Doniger, a girl he'd met in Lancaster who'd left him for another woman. And about a couple of other lovers. She had felt that they had bonded with this show of honesty. They presumed now that they wouldn't infect each other, so they could stop using condoms and she could go on the pill.

'How long were you in the IRA?' she had asked him then.

'A couple of years.'

'And don't they shoot you if you try to leave?'

'No.' He laughed. 'Loads of people left.'

They had sat silently together, toying with teacups. He knew there'd be another more probing question.

'Did you kill anybody?'

'The honest answer is that I killed hundreds of people – dozens of peelers, some shop girls and farmers, even a wee nun driving home. I had a part in every killing the IRA did in the time I was in it. That's what membership means.'

'But, up close?'

Up close the way their friend Tom Donnelly was shot? He sighed deeply. 'I never shot anyone dead. I shot a few in the legs, wee hoods. The kneecappings. That was my job for a time. But then I got out. I'm not proud of everything I did, but then is anybody?'

She had left it at that and when thunderous echoes of a waning war reached their door or rattled their windows at night, they might grimace but say nothing, for trouble as messy as in Northern Ireland ultimately implicated even herself in its secrets. If you lived in Belfast, you saw men move in back alleys; you should have called the police and thought it wiser not to.

***

Another call cleared up part of the mystery. Terry was walking along Bedford Street, past the Grand Central Hotel where the building's height, or something, magnified the wind.

'Can you talk?' said Ig, expecting Terry still to know his voice.

'Have you not been shot yet?' said Terry, lapsing into the old humour.

Ig liked that too and said, 'The peelers are coming to see you – the Cold Case crowd.'

'Which cold case have they in mind?'

Ig was one of the few people on earth who knew how many old cases Terry could help with if he was minded to.

'Magheraloy.'

They were silent together for a moment.

'You'll keep it tight, won't you?' said Ig.

'Why Magheraloy?'

'That journalist mate of yours, Hardwick, did a big doc on it for Channel Four. Have you not seen it? That's what's got people demanding something be done. I hope you didn't tell him too much.'

Terry watched the lunchtime crowd moving round him. Familiar faces from the local BBC, solicitors and shop girls, weary men in suits drudging towards retirement, snappy young people brisk with ambition and purpose, and he wondered which of these he might have been himself if he had not been the man he was, what stories they carried that were as grim as his own. He didn't bother to wonder how Ig knew what the police were planning. He'd learnt not to ask.

The Cold Case Review team was a branch established for political reasons to review the files on paramilitary killings. They were never going to just let the bloody Troubles be over. Still, it was work for him too. Solicitors were making good money out of unfinished business. An amnesty for old killers would not put him out of work, but it would shift the balance towards more domestic stuff: divorces and conveyancing, claims against the Housing Executive for people who'd fallen down steps. And he got to fight some of these old murder cases with the confidence that his clients wouldn't suffer too much if he lost. If the organisation they had been part of was on ceasefire and the offence dated from before the peace deal, they only did two years. That was a concession in the big Agreement.

When he got back to his office, he nodded to his receptionist without breaking his stride. At his desk, he eyed some files disconsolately then braced himself and picked up the phone to call Nools.

'My past is catching up with me.'

'The Unbearable Lightness of Being.'

So she was not alone. He put down the phone. He'd call her again later. Terry then searched his computer for news of the most recent political developments, to see if there was any suggestion why the police were concentrating now on the Magheraloy bomb. Over 3,000 people had died in the Troubles. The Magheraloy bomb accounted for just three of them: 0.1 per cent.

He scanned the morning headlines. It all looked familiar. The parties were agonising over education reform and hospital closures. A unionist had launched a tirade against the Republican Party leader, Dominic McGrath, saying he had the blood of innocents on his hands and that he was the spawn of Satan. It was the sort of thing somebody or other said about Dom every week in life. He was surely used to it. Another dour unionist, trying to make a name for himself, challenged McGrath to name republican dissidents who had been disrupting traffic with bomb hoaxes and petrol bombing Orange halls. 'You know these men; you trained them.'

Terry knew it was many years since old Dom had trained anybody. He had known McGrath as well as anyone ever had – *if* anyone ever had. Then he dipped into the Northern Ireland blogs and found a comment on the Cold Case Review. It read: 'Let's face it – the last thing anyone in power wants is another political crisis, so even if the Cold Case team was to find McGrath's DNA or prints on a gun that killed a peeler twenty years ago, they would do nothing about it.'

He couldn't resist typing below it: 'I don't know. The deal's done so Dom is expendable now. Letting him go down now would do less harm than a cover-up being exposed.' Then he changed his mind about posting it. He'd be tempting fate. By the same logic he was even more expendable himself.

***

Kathleen tidied the living room, vacuumed the carpet, pushed armchairs aside to check under them, dusted the mantelpiece and wondered if they really had to have a gauche piece of prison art on it: a Celtic harp made with matchsticks and signed 'Boomer', whoever the fuck Boomer was. She cleared the fireplace and reset it, picked up newspapers and magazines, and wondered how much a policeman would tell about them by spotting *Mojo*, *The Literary Review* and *Modern Woman*. She wanted to be finished before Terry got home because she knew it would annoy him that she was tidying up for any visitor, let alone for a peeler.

She moved on to the kitchen. She lifted up the hinged top of the hob and wiped round the hotplates, took out the little metal dishes that gathered grease, wiped them, then replaced the tinfoil she kept padded under them to be doubly sure. There was a smell from something. She'd find it. She worried less when she kept working, scrubbing as vigorously as if she was angry, trying not to be angry with Terry.

***

Terry had just one meeting that afternoon, with the loathsome Benny Curtis. Benny was an Ulster loyalist who worked to a simple theory: his men would have a better chance of getting off in court if they were represented by Catholic lawyers like Terry Brankin. It didn't always work. Benny wanted to talk about that.

A tall, lean man in a silky grey suit, Benny didn't look like a thug. He hadn't the muscles of the hard men who pumped iron in the gyms nor had he the bulbous gut of the men in pubs and drinking clubs who mostly slabbered and bragged but could be put to use for pickets and mob violence. He was more like a salesman, with a front of plastic charm. Terry had seen his type in other paramilitary groups. McGrath was one of them. Benny walked into the office, disregarding the receptionist. Men like Benny didn't ask permission to talk to anybody.

'Do sit down,' said Terry, confident that the loyalist would recognise the sarcasm in his tone, not that you could rely on subtlety with men who were used to solving problems by the most direct route.

'That case was a fuckin' waste of money. I'm wondering whose side you're on.'

'I'm a lawyer. I'm on the side of whoever is paying me.' Then Terry played for time by fetching the case folder from his drawer and poring over its loose pages.

'It was open and shut,' said Benny. 'We opened it and they shut it.'

'He wasn't going to get off.' Terry thought that had been obvious from the start and was tired saying it.

'Because some half-blind Fenian bitch swears it was him she saw in the dark across a street and with a mask on?'

'She used to babysit him. It's a killer detail.'

'It was your job to make her look stupid.'

'The judge in the end believed her because he couldn't accept that a woman would send down a man she had nursed on her lap if she wasn't sure,' Terry said.

'That's precious little he knows about human nature then, isn't it?'

Despite this outburst, Terry trusted that Curtis would moan then make no real difficulty for him. They had sat across from each other at this desk many times and though they had never discussed their own backgrounds in detail, each knew that the other understood the paramilitary world, and had killed. One good reason to be wary of detail was that they might find out things about each other they would be more comfortable not knowing.

Terry said, 'Are you guys getting any grief from the Cold Case crowd?'

'Fuck's sake, don't talk to me. It's worse than having nits.'

'So how do you deal with them?'

'Mostly we just tell them to fuck off. Otherwise you'd be getting a lot more business, wouldn't you?'

'Is that the way of it; they're just ticking the box?'

'Mostly. Why, what have you done?'
'Nothing. Whacked a couple of loyalists, that's all.'
And they laughed.

***

If Kathleen just sat on the sofa and thought about the police coming, she would fret. If she sprayed the surfaces, scrubbed and brushed, dusted and tidied and emptied the bins, checked the bathroom floor for discarded underwear and damp towels and put books back on their shelves, she would be able to contain the thoughts of what might happen and not be unhinged by her fear. 'Yes, fear!' She had said it, at last, though only to her clean, empty kitchen. 'Fear.' And yet more anger with Terry for bringing this on them.

***

Terry had learnt in the IRA – and remembered still – that children and fools evade their fears and a soldier faces them. He resisted the impulse to push from his mind the contemplation of the worst that could now happen. Did the police have new evidence against him? Was it possible that an informer had exposed him? There had been plenty of those. Mick Harkin, who had worked with him on the Magheraloy ambush, was dead now, and the dead don't speak. He had spent five years in the Kesh in the early 1990s for a bank robbery and then, after a couple of weeks out, had blown himself apart with one of the new Semtex drogue bombs they were working on. So, if there was an informer behind this new investigation, it wasn't Mick. It was someone else who had known him back then and remembered him still, after nearly twenty years. He doubted there was anybody talking now, which meant he was safe, but you could never be sure.

Terry understood the informers. He understood them better than he'd ever admitted because he had nearly become one. After

Magheraloy, he and Mick had been arrested, held separately and interrogated. They had both been trained to resist the pressure and had both got through it. The lesson was: say nothing. Just sit still for seven days and say nothing. Then, if they had the evidence they would use it and if they didn't you walked.

It was embarrassing to think about it, even after all those years. Back then, the police had devoted much of that seven-day holding period to kicking Terry about the interrogation room for trying to kill the Chief Con, as they called him.

In the republican mythology, the police were said to operate in pairs, with a good cop and a bad cop, one being genial and offering to help, the other, during his turn, kicking the shite out of you. Alternating treatments played on your fear and coaxed you to hope. That was maybe how they dealt with the younger ones, the ones who might respond to a little psychological manipulation. They didn't even bother trying to soften up Terry, which was a compliment in a way. They just hammered him.

It is hard to sit still when your balls are swollen and your arse is bleeding. It's hard to think when you've been slapped about the head so often that your ears are ringing constantly and you can't even relax your face into an expression that doesn't ache. He had assured himself then that he was weeping with the physical pain, not the fear. It hardly mattered. The kicking had touched on the tenderest nerves in his body and they were pulsing in the weirdest way inside him, and he had hardly trusted that he would be put back together again as a coherent human being. When they let him go, he went to Dom McGrath and told him he couldn't face doing any more jobs.

Dom was good about it. What Terry remembered now was how the republican leader had handled him so much more gently than the police had done, and filleted him more neatly.

Two

Dominic McGrath was poised and thoughtful when Terry went to see him the day he was released from interrogation – eight days after the bomb. He lived, even then, in the large house on the Glaslough Road, that he occupied still, when he wasn't abroad at political conferences or meeting heads of state. It was the sort of house a priest or a doctor might live in. From the outside, back then, it was a fortress, with grills on the windows and cameras over the front and back doors. A security man inside had a look at you through the camera as you waited between two gates, in a kind of airlock. Perhaps there were metal detectors. No one knew just what Dominic McGrath had, but they knew he had the best.

Then there was another buzz and the second gate opened. Dominic was waiting for him in the hallway, in jeans and a sweater, a mug of tea in his hand.

'Turlough, a chara!' He always addressed him first in Irish. 'Stand where you are now and Oweny here will frisk you – nothing personal. Then come through to the kitchen.'

Terry let Oweny frisk his body as closely as any soldier or peeler had ever done. He emptied all his pockets and Oweny ran clenches of his big fists along his arms and legs. Terry winced at the clasping of his sore balls, but neither made any remark.

'Open your shirt,' said Oweny.

'Uh?'

'Open your shirt.'

Oweny ran his fingers through the curls between his pectorals and brushed his belly with his knuckles until his fingers were deep inside the band of his trousers.

'OK.' Oweny cleared him.

Terry walked through into the kitchen. Dominic was sitting at a pine breakfast bar. 'Sugar?' he asked.

He took the stool facing Dominic and raised a hand. 'Fine as it is.'

They sat quietly for a moment, Terry warming his hands on his mug.

'You had a hard time with the peelers, but the training helped, right?'

'They nearly broke me, Dom. Because I don't feel good about that operation. If I felt OK about it, I'd be impenetrable. I'm not.'

'What is it worries you most?'

'That they could turn me, Dom. I swear to you – there were long nights when it seemed only right that they should. I can't do this any more.'

'It's not for everybody,' said Dominic, 'but the way things are going, there'll soon be a lot less of the dirty jobs and more political work. You'd be good at that.'

'Dom, we killed a kid.'

'It's what happens in a war, Terry. Do you think Maggie Thatcher was squeamish about killing kids?'

'So that's what makes a good warrior – not being squeamish about killing kids?'

'That's certainly part of it. And you only deal with it by comprehending the full context, by seeing that this is an evil that is not of our making and that when we are free, we'll create a world in which the children of the nation are safe.'

Maybe Terry just didn't believe that stuff any more.

Oweny put the morning mail and a few newspapers on the counter and Dom glanced down at the headlines. There was a photograph on the front of *The Irish News* of a boy with a plastered leg in traction after a punishment shooting.

'He looks all sweet and innocent now, doesn't he?' said Dom. 'Look, it's clear you are not ready to go back to this, and maybe you are leaving us. That's OK, a chara. No problem. Nobody's going to hold that against you, believe me. You've made a big contribution.'

Terry felt immense relief at that. He had always trusted that if things went bad, he could turn to Dom and Dom would sort it out. So they drank their coffee and talked about other things: 'Have you heard the new Christy Moore album?' said Dom. 'Has he found religion or something?' They laughed.

Then Dom said, 'The way we'll work it is this. You'll go away for a year. That will help you clear your head and remove you from any operations. If the Special Branch think you can be worked on to tout for them, then it's best you know nothing of day-to-day stuff. Come back in a year and then if you want to get involved again, there'll be a place for you. That's a promise. OK?'

Terry was wrestling to comprehend this. Dom, in the gentlest way possible, as if it was a kindness, had just ordered him out of the country. Where would he go? He had nowhere to go.

'You won't be under army orders. OK? But I've asked Ig and Dan to debrief you on your time in Castlereagh. It's just to help other guys going through the same thing. They'll take you away for a couple of days and help you talk through it all. It will help no end with our training. You'll be obliging as you can, won't you, a chara? You will surely.'

Ig and Dan were on the internal security team. These were the men who killed informers.

'I am not an informer, Dominic.'

'Turlough, I know you're sound. This is just to help the lads understand the newest methods the Brits are using to break them. You just be as open and honest as you can be and you'll come to no harm at all. OK?'

'OK.'

'They are in a small white van at the corner of the street. Oweny will walk you down. Sin é,' he said and got up and walked out of the kitchen.

***

It was amazing for Terry to think now that that was nearly thirty years ago, for the taste of his fear returned when he recalled the moment that Dom McGrath handed him over to the nutting squad.

Oweny had led him out through the airlock and into the street. It was a beautiful bright early spring day and Terry feared he might never see another like it. He followed Oweny down the hill to the corner. He almost needed to tell his legs what to do. They were within sight of the cemetery, and about as far in another direction from the dark, shielded police station. Oweny appeared to have no fear of being seen. The white van was parked outside a doctor's surgery. Oweny opened the rear door and waited for him. Terry could have made a run for the police station. If he was sure he was going to his death that would have been the sensible thing to do. But he gambled on the margin of possibility that he would survive this, so he did as he was told. He stepped up and wobbled a bit with his head down. Then the door closed behind him. He would not escape now. Dan, the driver, started the engine and drove off.

Ig was in the front passenger seat. Terry had seen Ig at meetings in the early days, at teen dances earlier still. He'd had that nickname at school. It was short for Ignatius, from St Ignatius Loyola. And Dan had been one mean hurler for the parish team – short and fast. The big lumps of fellas that got picked for backs fell over each other when he wove through them.

'Put this over your head,' said Ig.

He threw a black cotton bag over his shoulder without turning round. Terry picked it up. So they didn't even trust him to see where they were going. He drew the bag over his head. It smelled of other people's sweat and sick. You'd think they'd clean these things, if only to get rid of forensics on them. He settled himself as comfortably as a man can in the back of a moving vehicle with a low ceiling and a ribbed floor.

Ig spoke again. 'Here's the deal, Terry. You are ours now, to do with as we wish, and you are safe if you give us nothing to worry about. The next few days are going to be the worst of your life. That's the way it is. Nothing we can do about that and nothing personal. So just sit there and be quiet, and if you pray, pray into yourself.'

They *would* be the worst days of his life. However much he had feared the police or his own conscience, before he let him go, Ig would make sure Terry feared the IRA more.

They drove for an hour, much of it at speed on a long open road, probably the motorway, with the radio on. The chirpy music now sounded sarcastic. Ig and Dan talked about football, occasionally lapsing into a thoughtful silence as if remembering their mission. Terry tried to think through what he would say to them later, when they had him tied to a chair. He'd already told Dom he had weakened; he could hardly brag now that he had stood up to the Special Branch and braved their interrogation without flinching. Was there any small detail they would be able to work up into a real suspicion of him? He couldn't think of one, but he knew that if there was one they would find it.

The last part of the journey was up a stony country lane and Terry heard distant cattle, sheep and a dog running breathlessly alongside the van, then the darkness deepened, the acoustics softened. They were inside. Dan opened the rear door and he stumbled out onto rough ground and into the smell of stale peat, straw and damp wood. Hands gripped his arms.

'Have you shit yourself yet?' said Ig. 'They all do.'

They took him to a corner room and made him sit on a chair.

'Don't look round. Take the bag off.'

For a moment, he breathed the smells of the countryside and heard sounds that might otherwise have cheered him: birdsong and a breeze. He felt a rush of ease and relief from the stifling filth of the bag. There was a table beside him with a cassette tape recorder on it, one of the single-speaker models with a built-in microphone. Ig and Dan sat on chairs behind him. It was a dirty room with bits of straw and filth on the floor and unpainted plastered walls that exuded decrepitude, lack of care. This was a place put together by someone without any feeling at all.

Ig had a small cooking pot with a wooden spoon in it on the floor beside him. Dan had a pistol in his hand, an old Webley. The slicker guns were kept for more urgent work. It hardly mattered if this one jammed occasionally; there would always be time enough to take another shot.

'Right,' said Ig. He stood and switched on the cassette recorder and went back to his chair. 'Just tell us what the cops did that was so clever that you nearly broke. And don't be giving us the silent treatment; it won't work here.'

'They just went on and on about the wee girl.'

'Not like that. Tell it as a story. Start from the beginning. No details of the operation.'

'How can I talk about it if I don't talk about the operation?'

'No details about the operation.'

Then Terry realised that this could be for the ears of people who weren't in the movement. It was to be the confession that justified them shooting him. He soon discovered what the pot and wooden spoon were for. Ig used them to signal when he was to start speaking, so that his own voice never appeared on the tape. Then if he didn't like what Terry said, he would rewind, find the last recorded bong on the pot and start again from there.

Terry hadn't broken for his Special Branch interrogators, but he told Ig and Dan stuff that endangered him. All IRA members had been ordered simply to sit still and say nothing, not even to ask for the toilet or a cigarette, just to brave out the haranguing and the abuse in the certainty that they would walk free if they provided no evidence against themselves.

'I told them I was nowhere near Magheraloy. I told them I was drinking all day in Cullyhanna, that I was nowhere near the bomb. Once I asked them for water, just once. Once or twice I asked to go to the toilet. I told them nothing.'

Ig stopped the tape and said, 'So you broke the rule. Say you broke the rule and you are sorry. Wait.' He pressed the record and play buttons again then tapped the pot with the spoon.

'I had been properly trained in how to resist torture and interrogation by state forces. I regret that I did not put my faith in that training. I have let myself down and let my comrades down.'

Ig stopped the tape. 'That'll do.'

He was left to sleep on the floor and they went through the whole thing again the next day.

Even years later, no matter how often he replayed the horror in his head, he still didn't know at what moment they decided not to shoot him. One thing was for sure – his pleading had had nothing to do with it. When, finally exhausted and broken, he had gone down on his knees, weeping and cringing, begging them not to kill him, humiliated like a baby, his trousers soaking and cold against his skin, his pants full of cold shit, he knew even as he crumpled and moaned that they had seen many other men and women in the same state, and had spared some and killed some. And that each decision had been cold and logical. It had not really been in Terry's power to save himself at all.

Three

It was a frustrating drive home. The traffic on the Lisburn Road moved slower than walking pace at six every evening. The radio news said that the Republican Party president, Dominic McGrath, had called for full disclosure about the dirty tricks the British had used in their war against the Irish people. As well he might, thought Terry. The British had won their war by placing agents all around McGrath, bugging his office and his car and turning people who worked for him. It wasn't Terry that Dominic should have been worrying about back then; it was Oweny the security man and Dan the driver of the white van – both informers. A year before, Oweny had been whisked out of his home by MI5 and taken on an RAF flight to somewhere in England for his own safety. Even his wife wouldn't accept calls from him now. And Dan was dead. The poor man had foolishly thought that the peace process enabled him to go on living in Belfast after he had been outed. He couldn't bear to live anywhere else. Then somebody – probably Ig – had rung his doorbell one night and shot him in the face with a double-barrelled shotgun: the most thorough and least traceable of weapons.

Think how much worse things could have turned out, Terry said to himself. Had he stayed in the IRA and been loyal to McGrath, he would have been surrounded by the same spies. The Brits would have known his every move and they would have kept him in place for as long as they had judged him to be a useful fool. His least unpleasant fate would have been to spend most of the 1990s in jail making Celtic harps out of matchsticks for Irish Americans to raffle in bars – like Boomer, whoever the fuck Boomer was. And that would have been hell.

***

Kathleen was in the shower when the thought came to her: how much do I know? How much do I want to know? She had lived in Belfast through the closing years of the Troubles, when the bombs were bigger than they had been before and the sectarian killings had multiplied and come close. She wasn't naïve. She was sure she wasn't naïve.

She had lost a friend to loyalist killers. She had learnt that you keep your sanity if you stop asking questions, stop wondering what impact even your own words might ultimately have. Then she turned up the heat to try to make her skin hurt enough to clear her mind of bad memories and big fears.

What would a bullet do to a skull? She had often thought about that, thought about how a person might feel in the last moments of mental and physical torment before being finished off, usually when fearing for Terry. She had only ever seen people shot dead in films, and she assumed that in the real world it was bloodier. If Terry had shot a soldier from a distance, without seeing his fear, or if he had shot someone in self-defence, she could forgive that more easily, but she knew that IRA men had shot people in the face, had emptied pistols into them as they lay on the ground, that they had shot women. Over the years she had seen the coverage of all their doings on the nightly news and had often blanked it out and turned to something else rather than ask herself: would Terry have done that if they had ordered him to?

But she knew that Terry was a good man. She knew that, like hundreds of others, he had got swept into a war that was not of his making; that he had found his personal, even moral bearings in the depths of that war, and that he had saved himself from death and imprisonment though not from guilt.

As she dressed in the bedroom, she heard him come through the front door. She brushed her hair and studied her face in the mirror, recognising the gravity in her own expression. She would have to ask him.

He had dropped his briefcase on the floor and was planted on the sofa, bent over and rubbing the day's stress out of his brow. The room was already untidy again.

'Hi.' She leaned over and kissed him on the head.

'Sorry about all this.'

'We'll manage – but tell me everything before they get here. Don't leave me exposed.'

He swallowed hard. 'OK. Sit down.'

She sat opposite him so that she could see his face. 'What are they going to ask you about?'

'The Magheraloy bomb. It was one of the famous ones. Did you hear about it?'

'Where the frig is Magheraloy? No, I never heard about it.'

He sighed. 'It was on telly the other night. Magheraloy is in County Louth, touching the border. We did a lot of ambushes down there. This one went wrong.'

An accident. Good, she thought. An accident would be easier to live with. Anyone can have an accident.

'The plan had been to blow up the Chief Constable. We were into big, high-profile targets then – spectaculars, the media called them. Remember the whack at Downing Street. So that was the thinking: do something big and stay in the news. We had set up an ambush. The Chief Constable of the RUC was coming back from holiday with his wife and kid in the car.'

'Oh, no!'

'We were happy to take the kid and all, so long as we got him. It wasn't us that coined the phrase collateral damage. You've seen it on the news yourself, missiles hitting bridges in Iraq and some poor fucker driving a trailer of melons or something goes up in flames ... but what the hell.'

'It doesn't make it right.'

'It was worse, love. Much worse. We hit the wrong car.'

'And?'

'And three people died for nothing. Father, mother and daughter.'

She hadn't taken it all in yet. 'Who were they?'

'They were called Lavery. They were from somewhere in south County Derry. You don't watch the funeral or read the stories when you do something like that. You don't want to know.'

'Oh God.' She had to try and comprehend this. There had been a girl in her class at school called Lavery, and there was a lecturer at the university called Lavery.

'Oh God, Terry. A whole family ... just killed.'

'You rationalise. You tell yourself they could have crashed into another car or a lamp post; they just happened to run into our bomb.'

'Fuck.' This was different from what she had expected, from what she could excuse, had excused. She was stunned. She had imagined Terry as an IRA man shooting at soldiers and policemen who were armed and alert to the threat, who were defending the political set-up that had produced the Troubles in the first place. She had imagined him attacking people who expected to be attacked, who were paid to take the risk. But, if she was honest, she had always known too that children had been killed. From the very start, children had died in ricochets and bombings. She suddenly felt stupid for never having asked Terry if he had been implicated in the least defensible things that the IRA had done.

'What was your part in it?' she asked.

'I set the bomb at the side of the road and laid down the tripwire for another guy to trigger it. Mick Harken. He's dead now. Then I did lookout for the car and for anyone that might come near us.'

'Whose mistake was it?'

'Mine. I signalled to him to hit the wrong car.'

It seemed a small relief to her, that he had not actually pressed the button, or whatever it was they did. Shit! Fuck; she was screaming inside herself. Something like panic was building up in her. A child! Fine little limbs, soft smooth skin, hair in bows, eyes as bright as jewels.

'You saw the car coming. Had you got the number wrong or something? The colour? What?' She hadn't worked out the worst of it yet.

'It was the right colour and the right make.'

'Did you not see the child?' Then it dawned on her what a stupid question that was. Of course he had seen the child. The car was the right colour and the right make and there were three people in it and one of them was a child. That's what made it the right car.

'Ah!' she gasped. The breath would not come to her. When she could speak she said, 'How old? The child – how old?'

'A wee girl. Ten.'

At least Terry's frankness helped. She'd be nearly forty now.

'Oh, dear God. To take that much away from people.'

Kathleen was perplexed by the enormity of her husband having killed a child. Every time her mind tried to grasp it she recoiled. She was almost wheezing now and she left the room without saying more. Words felt false.

Terry knew not to follow her. She would be waiting for the feeling to match the thought. She'd be dreading the clarity that would overwhelm her. In the IRA he had mixed with people who could absorb shocks like this, who could manage with black humour. He had known men who had done dreadful things and he had stood at bars and drunk with them, never questioning them, always trusting that it wasn't easy for them. But Kathleen was not out of the hard culture. She had cried for the whale stranded in the Thames when it was on television. Ig would have said, all that for a fucking fish!

Kathleen came back into the room and her face was streaked with tears and her hair dishevelled. She practically spat at him. This was worse than he had feared. There was a logic in it he had not foreseen.

'For years we tried to have a baby and we couldn't. Well that was justice. That's what that was. And I never knew.'

He said, 'You'll have to compose yourself before the police come. Don't give them the satisfaction, please.'

'I don't care what they think. I don't care what they do.'

***

21

Inspector Basil McKeague believed in God and he believed in Hell, and that made his job easier. He didn't depend on the corporeal and temporal world for justice. He visited Terry Brankin's home that night with the fullest information to be had on the Magheraloy bomb that had killed Patrick and Elizabeth Lavery and their daughter, Isobel. He knew who had provided the intelligence that the Chief Constable and his wife and child would be driving up from Rosslare, crossing the border at Magheraloy after returning from a holiday in France. He knew who had mistaken the Lavery car for the Chief Constable's. He knew who had made the bomb and set it by the roadside. He knew everything. He knew that Dan Leeson, who had debriefed Terry Brankin for the IRA, had been a Special Branch agent. He had the transcripts and the tapes of that debriefing. He had everything but admissible evidence, and he could manage without that because he had faith in God. So he rang the Brankin doorbell that night assured that he was about to meet a man who would burn in Hell.

'Mrs Brankin?' The woman who answered was in her fifties, trim and healthy with it. She had been crying. That didn't surprise him.

She led him into the living room, where Terry Brankin was sitting on the sofa. He had turned on the television while Kathleen answered the door. Terry did not rise to shake hands with this man who had come to ruin their lives.

He looked the cop over. He was tall and fat in a jacket that was too tight for him and a trouser belt that supported his paunch. Good skin, though; didn't smoke or drink. Red cheeks, so he was either nervous or angry or had bad circulation. Terry would outlive him. This was a burnt-out ould peeler, not someone they'd have sent on a serious job, either to face danger or even make an arrest. There was nothing to worry about.

Inspector McKeague said, 'Would you mind turning the television off? I am going to need your full attention.'

Terry was surly in the face of authority and did nothing, so Kathleen picked up the remote and stabbed the air with it three times until she had pressed the right button.

'Thank you,' said Inspector McKeague. 'You both know why I am here?'

'Yes.'

'Then you'll excuse me if I sit.' The inspector sat on the armchair by the fireplace and set his thick brown briefcase on his knee.

'Do you want a cup of tea?' said Kathleen, not knowing what else to say.

'He won't trust us not to poison him,' said Terry, so Kathleen sat down.

'Well?' said Terry. 'You may begin.'

The inspector took his business card from his top pocket and set it on the table, and then he spoke in the soft measured tones of someone who might have been selling insurance. 'Mr Brankin, you were a suspect in a bombing incident in Magheraloy in March 1985 in which three members of the Lavery family were killed. Isn't that right?'

'I was questioned about it in Castlereagh.'

Kathleen sat back with a stunned look on her face, amazed that conversations about murder and guilt were routine for both men.

'Well, let's be plain about our understanding of that incident. You were part of the bomb team. You were the lookout rather than the trigger man. That was Michael Harken, who met his just deserts later. Are you content to proceed with this conversation on that understanding?'

'No.'

'For God's sake', blurted Kathleen, 'what's the point in playing games now?'

'I have not cautioned you, and none of what we say has any value for evidential purposes.'

'So,' said Terry, 'you have no expectation that you will get to that point.'

'Not really. But I have procedures to follow, largely for the sake of Seamus Lavery, the son of Patrick and Elizabeth Lavery, the twin brother of Isobel. I am instructed to review files of old killings and to offer the families of victims the best possible prospects of prosecution of the guilty. You are guilty. That is why I am here. Unless you actually choose to confess I can, of course, do nothing.'

'Well, I am not going to confess.'

Inspector McKeague opened his briefcase and, before the Brankins could move, he dropped a large colour photograph onto the floor where both could see it plainly. Kathleen wondered what the point of this was. It looked like an ad for some kind of ice cream, with streaks of raspberry running lavishly over the main confection. Then she gasped, clenched her mouth and tried not to be sick.

'That's little Isobel. She was sitting alone in the back of the car and took the force of the blast underneath her. That's why the legs are splayed and the clothing is torn. I'm afraid you can't quite make out her facial features.'

'Huh, huh, huh ...' Kathleen's convulsive gasping was out of her control.

Terry leapt to try to console her but she pushed him away. 'Get off me!' He turned to McKeague, who was sitting calmly with another photograph in his hand.

McKeague said, 'Of course, if you don't wish the interview to continue here, we can go to the station.'

Terry had to contain the impulse to reach for him and fling him from the house. McKeague dropped the next photograph onto the carpet.

'We think that most of this is Mrs Elizabeth Lavery. She and her husband were both wearing seat belts and it is remarkable how effective these can be in preserving the integrity of a body that has been torn by an under-car bomb. Here ...' – he dropped another picture – 'is Patrick Lavery's right leg. A colleague of mine had to fetch it out of a ditch. He says he will never forget that. A leg on its own is always heavier than you'd expect it to be.'

Kathleen was weeping and shrieking as if she was being jabbed at with a sharp knife. She had both hands in front of her face, trying to make it all go away, but it was futile, for what she was trying to banish was the past and the future, and none of it was under her control.

Four

Kathleen's phone beeped on the seat beside her. She checked the text without slowing down, one hand on the wheel. 'Are you OK?' Terry never abbreviated.

She was not OK but she felt calmer now that she had a project in hand.

That morning she had told him that she would leave if he didn't confess to the bombing. She had spent the night awake in their bed with her back to him, resenting his ability to sleep. She supposed he'd learned that too from the IRA, switching off the emotions. The only rest she got was after the whirling in her brain had settled into a resolve. She'd told him as soon as she was aware that he was awake beside her.

'What you're asking for is daft,' he'd said. 'I have done my time – in my head. Do you think I have not agonised over this for years? I suffered long and hard.' She doubted that.

He had been grilled by the nutting squad for days that had felt like years, and then he had had to go to England and work for shit pay just to stay out of the way. He had worked a year in a gay bar in Lancaster and lived in a shared house down by the river. And all of it was so that the whiff of the Magheraloy bomb would not contaminate the fragrance of Dominic McGrath while he was secretly negotiating peace terms with the government.

Kathleen had gone to the Linenhall Library that morning, to read newspaper cuttings about the bomb and the Laverys. A smiling young man with curly hair and the first wisps of a beard had carried the huge bound volumes of broadsheet papers from the time and laid them out on the big oak desk in front of her. She had to stand to be able to view them and it surprised her to see how normal Belfast had been in other ways at a time when the IRA was bombing shops and paramilitaries were shooting civilians and police officers, men and women. None of it had pushed the ads for girdles off their corner spots on front pages. The curly haired young man might as lightly have assumed she was looking for pictures of a wedding or a book review as for a murder.

None of the pictures in the papers of the time were as gory as the ones that Inspector McKeague had dropped on her floor, but there was reportage and commentary on the atrocity, the familiar condemnation of the 'animals', 'barbarians' and 'terrorists'. Some said they were the 'scum of the earth'. Clergy and politicians had vented their moral outrage; that was part of their job.

She wondered what she had been doing on the day. She worked out that she would still have been doing her GCSEs. She was surprised to find that all the local papers had given extensive front-page coverage to the bomb and had inside features on the family. She couldn't remember any of that. None of the reports speculated that the bomb had been intended for the Chief Constable and his family.

She read that Patrick Lavery had been a property developer and he had gone to County Meath, that last morning of his life, to look at a piece of land he might buy. He had chosen to make a day out of it with his wife and daughter. There was a photograph of the couple in *The Irish News*, in formal dress at a GAA dinner dance. There was another picture of the twins, Isobel and Seamus, playing on swings in the garden at home. They were only five years old, by the look of it, when the picture was taken, a few years before the bomb. There was no picture at all of Isobel as she was in the last days before she died. Perhaps the family didn't have one.

Kathleen wondered why wee Seamus had not been in the car that day, what small domestic consideration – a cold or a tantrum – had determined that his twin sister Isobel would die and he would live.

She searched online to find where Seamus Lavery was now. Google turned up several men of the name, one a priest, one a pool hall manager and one a councillor. The one Kathleen thought was most likely to be the son of Patrick and Elizabeth was a hurley player and ran a computer repair shop in Swatragh, a small town in the Sperrins.

But what could she say to him? 'My husband killed your parents and your sister and I want you to know that I'm very sorry'?

***

Terry went to see his friend Nools at her home near Templepatrick. A lot of police and security people lived out there, just ten minutes up the motorway from Belfast. The little estate was shaped like a tree, with cul-de-sacs curling off a main stem. He parked away from her home and walked there. But people were sure to notice him, weren't they?

'The only thing that ever brings you to my door is trouble,' she said, in a tone which suggested she had given up wishing it was different.

He followed her into the living room.

'I've been tidying up. We'd the book group last night.'

'Kathleen said she couldn't finish it.'

She walked through to the kitchen and he browsed her shelves as he waited. He looked for books a prison officer like her husband, George, might read. Solzhenitsyn?

Nools came back with tea and biscuits on a tray. 'Well?'

'A cop came. He raked up all this stuff about an awful bomb he wants to pin on me. Kathleen couldn't take it.'

'Now why would he want to pin a bomb on you – blame you for something you'd nothing to do with?'

'I don't do confession anymore, Nools. Not even to you.'

'I suppose till now Kathleen thought it was all Robin Hood. She should have married a prison officer and seen him come home at nights with the roared abuse and smell of shit still in his head, and leaping out of bed in the early hours to grab his gun and shoot at shadows,' she said.

'The guy handling the case is old, burnt-out and cynical. I'm guessing he's been handed a file by someone who's tired of looking at it and getting nowhere,' Terry said.

'What do you want me to do?'

'Aren't you in those circles? Don't you still have protection officers hovering round you?'

'If it's the Cold Case crowd then they have it because the A team don't see any hope of closing it themselves. They've off-loaded it. I shouldn't worry.'

'Or they've come up with something that warrants another look at it?'

'DNA? I think if it was that, they would have you in now and not be sending one of the ould fellas out to talk to you.'

***

She drove down the narrow country road to the town and looked for the cemetery. She walked along the aisles of shiny black marble headstones, learning the most common names of the town, noting those who had died young and those who had lived long. This calmed her. The Lavery family plot was a wide triple grave with a large stone angel over it but with no indication on it of how the three people below that angel had died. Kathleen wondered if it was an embarrassment in a Catholic town to have people belonging to you killed by the IRA. There were too many republican families around for anyone, even a victim, to feel free to risk offending them. She looked at other graves, some of small children, most of older people. Usually people died at the proper time – three score years and ten, indeed much later still – but there were children 'taken suddenly' and young men who had smashed cars on country roads. 'Murdered by cowards' was the tribute on one grim untended grave. Kathleen felt the need to mark her pity for the Laverys but she had not thought to bring flowers. She said a prayer.

***

Basil McKeague raised another spoonful of gloop to his wife's lips, but she pursed them against it. 'Do you want me to read to you, then?'

She nodded.

'From the Holy Bible?'

She sighed.

He lifted the black book from the table by her bed, where it usually sat beside the box of tissues and the bottle of lemon barley water. He opened it at random, allowing the Lord himself to pick the text for the day.

'And in every province, whithersoever the king's commandment and his decree came, there was great mourning among the Jews, and fasting, and weeping, and wailing; and many lay in sackcloth and ashes. So Esther's maids and her chamberlains came and told it her. Then was the queen exceedingly grieved; and she sent raiment to clothe Mordecai, and to take away his sackcloth from him: but he received it not.'

His wife said, 'What's that all about then?' and when she saw him compose himself for a considered answer, she said, 'Never mind. Read on if it pleases you.'

'Do you get no comfort from it?'

'I get no comfort from anything. Tell me about your work.'

'I met a sinner yesterday, one of the worst of sinners,' he replied.

'An adulterer?'

'A killer – one who has slaughtered the innocent.'

'And will you be able to put him in jail or is this another one that will get away?'

'He will have to confess; it's the only way.'

'Then you'll be waiting till Hell freezes.'
'But he'll be there long before that happens.'

***

It was an old grey stone church and in the porch were notices about pilgrimages to Lourdes and Medjugorje, some notices in Polish too. Once through the door she was in the hush of a different atmosphere. The aisle between the old dark wood pews led to a white marble altar overseen by a large realistic crucifix. As she walked towards it she examined the face of Jesus for an expression that would match his predicament. He had eyes that met hers wherever she stood. The blood on his brow and leaking from his side seemed almost ornate. She looked away. At the side of the church was a statue of the Virgin Mary, in her familiar blue robe. She was supposed to be the resort of all troubled mothers, but Kathleen was not a mother. She lit a candle at the foot of the statue and wondered if she would hear reassurance if she stared long enough. Then, without thinking, she held her hand over the candle flame to hurt herself as much as she could bear. She couldn't bear much, so she drew her hand higher then lowered her palm slowly again into the sharper heat. It took an act of will just to endure a second or two of pain, but it was enough to wring the tears from her eyes again and that was what she needed.

'Can I help you?'

She had not heard the priest approach and was embarrassed that he had found her like this.

'I'm sorry.'

'Don't be sorry, child. Come into the sacristy and let me find some ointment for that. You'd be surprised how often we need it for the wee altar servers.'

'No. I'll go.'

'Don't be silly. Come on now.'

Calmed by his relaxed manner, she followed him. In front of the altar, he genuflected and she did the same. She felt almost mischievous, even a little honoured, to be walking past the altar to the door in the wall panelling.

She had never been in a room like this before. It was dark and musty with the smells of burnt incense and men's clothes. This was a male space. A private space. Was she wise to be here? Not every priest was a holy man. Some – well, she'd take the eye out of his head if he tried.

'There's a toilet through there and a sink and a mirror.'

At first she was puzzled and wondered if this was some proof of the trivial thinking of men who had so little contact with others. Then she realised that he was telling her where she could tidy up. She went through to the little bathroom and saw that her face was streaked with mascara. And her hand hurt. 'What a mess I am!'

She found tissues and cream in her handbag and mopped the mascara stains off and then removed all her make-up and washed herself and brushed her hair. It wasn't the face she had planned to meet the day with, but it was the one she had now and it would have to do.

'You don't have to speak to me,' the priest said when she came out. 'But this is the house of God and most problems are a little lighter when shared with Him.'

She said, 'I should talk to someone.'

'Well in your own time, dear.' She was surprised by the solicitous manner of the man, and she looked more closely at him. She saw that he was probably a little younger than she was. His hair was greying at the sides but he had a trim build. His black suit seemed polished where most worn.

'I have found out things about my husband that have surprised me.'

'That is a more common experience than you might imagine.'

'He killed a little girl.'

'Dear God,' said the priest. 'Are you saying it was deliberate, or was it an accident?'

'It was an accident in that it was the wrong little girl, but he would have been happy enough with himself if he had killed the right one.'

Just saying it distressed her. The priest simply waited.

'He was in the IRA.'

'Ah.' The priest sighed as if it was clear now and easier for him to countenance. 'Well, a lot of good men did bad things, you know. And the blame can't all be put on them.'

'Don't you think that if a man kills a child, he ought to suffer for doing that?'

'Well, ultimately justice is with the Lord, you know. My dear, I have seen many good men crumple under the burden of what war wrought out of them. It may be that your husband needs you more than you know.'

'He has to be sorry for what he did. He has to be made to be sorry for what he did.'

'Come on, child. You know the country we grew up in and no one man needs to bear the blame for the war that was imposed on the Irish people.'

She paused. She had thought she was opening up to a man who understood the human heart and now he was talking like a politician.

'Fuck you,' she said, and then got up and walked out into the clean air.

***

If Terry was still in the office, she would be able to drive home and pick up the keys to the Damascus Street house and pack a case to get herself started. Of course, if he was guessing her moves, then he would go straight home himself and wait for her. Well, she had many strong feelings about him, but fear wasn't one of them.

As it turned out, he wasn't there when she arrived. She packed two cases, mostly with underclothes and clean bed sheets, toiletries and casual clothes, and took the keys for the house. On her way out, she saw Inspector McKeague's business card sitting on the coffee table where he had put it the night before. She picked it up and put it in her purse, not knowing if she would ever need it.

Then she drove towards town, as far as the university, and turned into the Holy Land area and Damascus Street.

***

Damascus Street, behind the university, is one of a grid of little streets called the Holy Land. There is Jerusalem Street and Carmel Street. Once these houses had been tiny homes rented by families from the city council. Women in aprons and headscarves had mopped the doorsteps and children had played hopscotch on the pavement. At least, that is how Kathleen imagined it had been. Now much of the area had been bought up by property developers like herself and converted, with the help of generous grants, into temporary homes for students. Walking through it was like discovering a town in which everyone was eighteen years old.

She turned the key in the frail flaky door, let herself into the musty house and scooped up the mail on the mat. Mostly it was bills for overdue parking tickets, bank statements and other letters with 'final warning' stamped in red across the front. There were copies of the republican paper *An Phoblacht*, *New Internationalist* and leaflets advertising pizza delivery, taxi companies, cleaning services and protest parades in memory of victims or support for prisoners. There were cards announcing prayer rallies and gospel meetings. Junk. She tried to remember when she had last been in the house. All this in two weeks!

Deeper inside the house were smells of decay, at best a piece of chicken someone had left in a bin, at worst a mouse that had died under the floorboards. The carpet in the living room was a cheap mustard colour. Terry had said, 'Don't spend money catering to your own taste; this place isn't for you.'

A large Irish tricolour was draped above the double bed in the main bedroom. She whipped it from the wall, bundled it up and threw it into a corner. The bed itself had an uncovered duvet over a bare mattress that still had sweat stains on it. At least, she hoped they were sweat stains. How much could she do now to transform this place? Her brother worked in a furniture shop in town and she called him.

'Bill, I've a house that needs a makeover.'

'Today?'

'I'd like to make one bedroom nice. Then for the living room, two armchairs and a sofa, smallish but tasteful. Let's see, slate blue or something.'

Then she ordered a skip. They said it mightn't come until tomorrow. There was a soft rhythmic thud from the house next door. She would have to do something about that too. But first ... She knocked on her neighbour's door. A youth with long ginger hair came out, and, slowly, a dark-haired girl settled behind him.

Kathleen said, 'I have some furniture in here I need rid of. I'll give you fifty quid just to lift it out.'

'Whoopy doo,' said the lad and shouted, 'Cathal!'

'Wha?' his friend Cathal shouted from upstairs.

She heard him from the window above her rather than echoing through the house.

'Beer money!'

Cathal and Ginger followed Kathleen into her house and surveyed the furniture. 'What do you want us to do?'

'Move it to a dump somewhere. Keep it if you want it.'

The boys shrugged and started heaving the furniture out into the street. They set down a three-piece suite on the footpath and sat on it, enjoying the incongruity of living-room comfort in the open air.

The girl said, 'This stuff's better than our own. Take our own stuff out and let's put this in. What're the mattresses like?'

'One smells like somebody died in it,' said Cathal.

In an hour, half the furniture from Kathleen's house was in the street along with half the furniture from the house next door. Other students, thinking this signalled a party, joined in. Some came rolling armchairs on frail castors over mottled tarmac. Kathleen's first impulse was to feel responsible and plead with them to behave, but then she decided that she had more important things to think about. And there was a furniture van coming up the street, the delivery from her brother.

'Delivery for Brankin,' said the driver. Kathleen wished she had cleaned the place better first. Shifting the other furniture had unsettled dust and scraps everywhere. She needed time to get the carpets up too, but if she let the driver put this new furniture down on the street, it would be absorbed by these crazy students into their spontaneous party.

Two men brought in the furniture and set it down roughly where she wanted it.

'There's a couple of rugs as well, madam,' said the driver.

Bill had picked them out for her. Well, she thought, they would cover the shitty carpet for now. The men spread one of them out on the living-room floor, half of it flopping against the new sofa. It was yellow and red in a mix of squares and triangles and had very deep pile. 'Perfect.'

'Anything else, madam?'

Kathleen tipped the men a tenner and they left.

The kids outside now had a music system on the street and were playing rebel songs. One of them was dancing with the tricolour she had wiped the bathroom floor with. Were they waving it in her face? They were waving it in somebody's face.

In an hour this shambles would be a home. Well, she had made temporary homes before out of dingy flats and rooms in shared houses. Terry had done it too.

He rang that evening.

'What are you doing?'

'I'm moving into Damascus Street.'

'Fuck's sake, Kathleen.'

'Let me do this, Terry. I need space right now. I'll see you tomorrow. Did you get something to eat?'

'I'm fine.'

***

At first, dreamily, Kathleen persuaded herself that the alarming sound of breaking glass had come from the party below her window and that she could go back to sleep, but then she registered that there was now only silence outside and that the damage was closer, in fact, inside the room. Clawing her way back from preoccupations that she couldn't recall, she resented the feeling that she was missing something. But the smell of petrol was not from some revved-up car. It was a vapour close enough to be irksome, like filth in her nose and gullet. She knew by the feel of heat on her face that she was in trouble even before she saw flames crackling through the curtains. She had to wake herself up and get out of there. And she was naked. She whipped the duvet from the bed and tried to fold herself into it, but tripped over. She scolded herself, bundled up the duvet and ran out of the room, hoping, as she scuttled down the stairs, she'd be able to cover herself before she reached the street.

She stopped at her front door. Downstairs still looked normal. She took seconds to wrap the duvet round herself, and then the door came crashing through and a man tumbled over her. His skin was on her skin. His hand pressed into her in the dark as he lifted himself up. He was wearing boxer shorts and trainers, and stepped on her while getting off her.

He'd rallied himself. 'Get out, Missus. Get out!'

It was Ginger, one of the boys from next door. He fumbled the duvet over her as she tried to stand but she snatched it from him and ran into the street.

'She's alright,' Ginger was shouting. 'I got her out.'

Kathleen tried to calm herself and see what was happening. She was barefoot on tarmac. The red paint on her toenails looked absurd now. Cathal and the girl approached her timidly, staring at this wild frantic woman and then at the flames at her window.

'Did one of you bastards do this?' she yelled at them.

The girl called the emergency services on her mobile, and Cathal and Ginger ran into the house to beat out the flames, so the fire was dead before the first tender arrived.

'You'll want a pair of clean knickers, won't you, Missus?' said the girl, caustically.

'I'm sorry,' said Kathleen, still unable to rally any gratitude.

The girl brought her into their house. It was such a mess she wondered if there had been a calamity here too, but the students didn't seem to notice that stacks of books on the stairs had tumbled over into heaps and that the carpet was actually sticky under foot.

The girl gave Kathleen a shirt, a jumper and a pair of jeans. She closed the living room door to keep out the boys while she put them on. The jeans were too tight to fasten at the waist. The girl said her name was Aoife. She was from Strabane.

She said, 'What would you want to come and stay in a place like this for?'

Kathleen laughed.

'Not that this sort of thing happens every night.'

'I should hope not,' said Kathleen.

There was now a fire tender in the street and firemen standing around discussing whether to hose the house. A policewoman came into the kitchen. She was hardly much older than the students and Kathleen wondered who'd thought of giving her a pistol and sending her into company like this, where she could be jostled and have it taken from her, but the students were wary and deferred to her.

Kathleen had to settle her thoughts and focus. Aoife was giving her a cup of tea. There wasn't much to tell. She had been asleep and was awakened by breaking glass. She couldn't remember whether she had heard the glass first or smelt the petrol first. Someone had firebombed her house. She was only just beginning to realise that. Kathleen sat quietly for a full minute, just rubbing her brow and wondering how to cope.

Cathal came in. 'Everything up there stinks, but here's your phone.'

There was a new text message. It was from Terry. It read, 'I love you.'

'Have you any thoughts on who might have done this?' the policewoman asked.

Kathleen tried to pay a little more attention to her now that her concentration was returning. 'No. Have you?'

'There have been a few car burnings around here,' she said. 'There's a feud on between students who are wrecking the area and those long-time residents who want them out. It could be something to do with that.'

'Thanks very much,' said Cathal sarcastically.

Aoife scowled at him.

'Do you own a lot of these properties?' asked the policewoman.

Kathleen didn't respond and walked away from them all and into the bathroom. There was a scum ring round the bath and dozens of shiny bottles of sprays and things she hardly understood herself. There were piss stains on the lino round the loo. She sat on the edge of the bath and phoned Terry.

He answered groggily. It was four in the morning.

'Someone petrol-bombed the house.' She voiced the words with contempt.

***

For a moment Terry was back at war. This was one of those exhilarating half panics, an occasion for leaping into action, grabbing a gun or jumping from a window. But there was no need. There were times in the past when he had been laughed at by comrades for cocking a pistol at the sound of a cat, once for risking his life by attempting a shot at the back of an army vehicle when the gun had not been loaded, and luckily the soldiers hadn't seen him.

He had only to drive to Damascus Street, pick up Kathleen and bring her home. Yet his senses were keen and his heart frantic. It was past dawn now and the sky was light – the perfect time to drive. He could ignore traffic lights that flipped through their settings automatically, without regard to the clear roads around them. There were a few spacers around the university, staggering drunkenly or drugged out of their heads. They might be clients in a few years, or applicants for jobs with his firm.

As he turned into University Square, his phone rang again and he punched the button on his steering to answer it, thinking the call would be from Kathleen again.

'Yes?'

'Mr Brankin, it's Sally Leeson. Your tenant in Stranmillis Avenue.'

'What is it, Sally? Don't you know what time it is?'

'Mr Brankin, our house is on fire.' She was crying now. 'I think it was a petrol bomb.'

Oh fuck! For a moment he was tempted to turn around and rush to Stranmillis Avenue. One attack could have been a mistake, something intended for a neighbour or a previous tenant. Two meant targeting, and he started sorting his thoughts around who might be responsible for this: someone with the wherewithal, someone who saw him as a problem and resorted easily to this kind of solution. In Belfast, that could be a lot of people.

'Sally, call the police. Do it now! I'll get back to you.'

Then, thinking this was all too dramatic and abrupt for a young woman he hardly knew, he said, 'I have another house burning in Damascus Street. I have to deal with that first.'

He smelled the smoke and petrol in Damascus Street before he saw the black scorch marks around the window. There were lights on in the houses on either side, and in several other houses in the street, so he had to phone Kathleen to find out where she was.

'Did you bring me any clothes?'

Fuck, he thought, of course he should have brought her some clothes.

He found her looking like a kid in the woolly jumper and jeans, and he smiled without being able to help it. There were real kids standing around watching them and he was annoyed by a sense that they expected something from him.

'Come on, Kathleen. Let's go.'

'Terry, you have to thank these people for helping me.'

'Yes, thank you everybody. Now, we have to go. The Stranmillis house has been attacked too.'

Kathleen got into the passenger seat of his car, leaving her own car on the street, and the house, for now, open to the winds and any burglar. Terry ripped out of the street towards home. He went up the Lisburn Road at 80mph.

'Aren't you going to ask how I am?' she asked.

A fire engine overtook them, its siren screeching. Then another. As they turned into the estate, they saw a huge rope of smoke twist over the rooftops and fray. He knew what it was before he was in the street, because he'd worked out how much damage could be inflicted on him in one night. He stopped the car behind a fire tender and they stared at the flames curling out of their own downstairs living-room window. Her favourite furnishings were burning. His computer and Joe McWilliams paintings were burning. The kitchen was burning. Thick stinking smoke wrung a stench out of all the things they loved.

And his mobile phone was ringing again.

'Yes?' he barked.

'Mr Terry Brankin. This is the police at Donegall Pass. I believe you are the landlord of two adjacent properties on Dunluce Avenue.'

'I suppose they are both on fire too?' he said.

***

Standing in the street in their separate rages, Terry and Kathleen made mental audits of all they had left in the world. Terry had an office in Bedford Street, for now, or hoped he had. Perhaps the fire bombers would have stayed away from security cameras there. He had a car and he had the casual clothes he was standing in. He had his wallet and credit cards in his pocket. Thank fuck for that, he thought. He also had a little cottage in Donegal, near Ardara, with basic kitchenware and bedding. In the garden of the cottage he had buried a police issue Ruger .357 pistol. He also had thirty rounds of ammunition and he supposed that they were still there and that he might soon need them.

Kathleen had a car, parked two miles away in the Holy Land, and that was about it. She had the key to a house. Her key had opened it for the last time. She had no clothes of her own, no credit cards or money. But she had a mobile phone.

'What time is it?' she asked.

'Who cares what fucking time it is?'

'I'm wondering if I could get into a hotel in this state.'

Terry phoned the night porter at the Wellington Park Hotel and told him the problem.

'Maybe you should stay here and talk to the police,' said Kathleen.

He made another call.

'Jack, sorry to wake you up. All my houses, including the one I live in, have been petrol-bombed tonight. Yes, that's what I said. You've done all the work on them before, so can you get round them now and see what can be saved and then seal them up? Yes, I know what time it is.'

Kathleen said, 'What insurance company do we use?'

He ignored her and dialled another number.

'This is Terry Brankin of Sallagh Crescent, Belfast 7. I have five properties insured with you and all are currently on fire. Thank you.'

He said, 'Kathleen, take the car and go up to the Welly Park. They have a room for you.'

She didn't move.

He turned to her and tried to speak softly through his anger. 'Go on, love. It's best if you let me handle this – whatever *this* is.'

Kathleen knew what she looked like walking into the hotel lobby but she was past caring. She had no plan yet for how she would get clothes in the morning, but she hadn't the energy to think about that either. The night porter gave her a key and asked if he could help her in any other way.

'Would you have a toothbrush, maybe?' she asked.

He opened a drawer and took out a little plastic toiletries bag. 'You'll find most of the essentials there.'

At a glance she saw a toothbrush, toothpaste, skin lotion, a nail file, condoms and Alka-Seltzer. She thanked him and went to the lift.

The room was an enormous bridal suite, more like three rooms than one. The sumptuous bed seemed almost a sarcastic comment on the state she was in. She undressed and buried herself in the comforting darkness. With the drapes closed, it could have been the darkest hour of night and not the advancing daylight of early morning. So she expected she might sleep. She'd give it a try.

Five

Terry Brankin sat on the kerb watching firemen fight the blaze and waiting for the police. He looked at the house he had lived in for seven years, watched it burn and felt as if he had never really got to know it. He was thinking of the day he and Kathleen had first viewed it and discussed whether they could afford it. He remembered the legal delays and the day he got the key, the way they had walked around from room to room and spent their first night on a mattress on bare floorboards, feeling rich and poor at the same time.

They had planned how to decorate and furnish it and had worked slowly on it, Kathleen having to organise the other houses too, making them fit for tenants and cleaning up after them. The moment they had anticipated, at which they would feel contented and secure, their work on the house done, had never really come, and now it was a crackling shell. He remembered climbing onto the roof himself to put cowls on the chimney pots, arguing with Kathleen about the colour of the frontage and watching her spend whole days managing the window boxes. He had said she was daft to spend thousands on kitchen furnishings that were just cupboards out of a flat-pack store. And he knew that in the sixty years the house had stood before he had taken ownership of it, others had loved and died in it, strangers had accumulated memories that would be sharpening in their minds now if they knew it was burning down.

The next to arrive were a couple of constables, who asked him if he would like to come down to the station and make a statement, there being nothing that they could do here until the fire service was finished hosing down the flames. He sat in the back of their car and endured their small talk.

'An awful thing to happen, Mr Brankin.'

He was trying to work out who might have burnt his houses, and already he was suspecting the police themselves. Inspector Basil McKeague of the Cold Case team knew that he had killed the Lavery family and got away with it. He might be happy that someone should torch nearly everything Terry owned. Maybe George Caulfield, Nools's husband, had seen him leave the house and found an old-fashioned explanation for their meeting up. George had never liked him. There were loyalist paramilitaries who fancied they had defended Ulster against the IRA. Some among them might have done it. Even Benny Curtis. Who knew how complicated and perverse were the workings of that nasty mind? Benny might say it was nothing personal. But why not just shoot him on his doorstep? Well, because that would be breaking a ceasefire, while burning his house down could be passed off as vandalism. Or maybe somebody below Benny in the hierarchy of his mob was aggrieved that Terry wasn't doing enough to keep men out of jail. There were also the other republican groups, at least four of them, all of which occasionally shot someone or burnt a house or shop, to remind everyone they still functioned. But what gripe would they have with Terry Brankin? None that he could think of. Maybe they thought he was a tout.

It could have been somebody who knew the Laverys. That's a possibility, he thought. But there were other attacks that Terry had been involved in that nobody was currently talking about. The Cold Case team might get round to some of them too. It might be one of those cases the arsonists were avenging. And there were the hoods he had shot in the legs, maybe a dozen of them, any one of whom might have taken a notion to avenge himself. It's funny how little of that there is in Belfast. And there were the rattled neighbours of noisy students who had burnt the odd car in protest, or daubed a house with paint, though never one of his own. All these thoughts he turned over in his head as the inane young peelers in the front of the car prattled on about how it was almost like the Troubles coming back, a bad night like this.

Who else? 'Come on,' he urged his brain. 'Think! Who else might have done this?'

It was Ig who had called to tell him that the Cold Case crowd were digging into him, so Ig had known first and had had time to think through the implications. He'd had time to plan. He would have been able to put a team together; he had men at his disposal for what he called 'operations'. But why? What advantage would Ig get over the Cold Case detectives by burning his houses?

Well, suppose he confessed to McKeague and let him build a case. What would happen then? Ig wouldn't have too much to worry about, would he? He hadn't been there. He had come in only afterwards to debrief Terry and make sure he wasn't going to embarrass Dom McGrath. That was it! If Terry confessed to the Magheraloy bomb and told the whole story, that story would have to include the information that it was Dom McGrath who had ordered the operation. McGrath was now a respectable politician at the head of a party in partnership government, running Northern Ireland. But why didn't they just come and talk to him? Probably because he was outside the movement now and wasn't to be trusted.

At the police station, he was kept waiting in the reception area with one truculent drunk and a maudlin woman with one shoe on, but after the constables had reported the fire to a senior officer, he was invited through to a more comfortable room and offered a cup of tea. As a solicitor handling occasional criminal cases and legal claims against the police, he had been in the station before and most of the staff knew him to see. And, having seen senior officers being civil to him, they did the same.

In came Sergeant Jamie Spick. Terry had met him many times over the years when he'd been in the station to sit with clients or vet identity parade line-ups, and he was always civil. 'Och Terry, this is a bad one. What are we looking at here?'

'Five of my houses burnt down, including the one I live in.'

'And the missus?' said Spick.

'I've sent her up to the Welly Park. They'll look after her.'

'Well look, you keep your spirits up and give me a call for anything at all that you need.'

He was at least playing it friendly, making it easy for him.

'Now let me fill you in on what's going to happen here. I mean, you know it all yourself but it's as well to focus. In here, they're going to be asking two things: is this an insurance stitch-up or is it violence against the person? Of course you didn't burn your own houses down, but the peeler mind works that way, ticks that box. OK? The insurance company is going to be asking if this is civil disorder, in which case, it's the government that pays out, or if it is arson of the old-fashioned kind, in which case, they pay. But you know all that.

'One other thing,' said Spick. 'After you've done the paperwork, there's an Inspector McKeague wants a word with you. I don't know what that's about. I thought they'd kicked him upstairs.'

Spick left him then with a warm firm handshake, and for an hour Terry took questions from a sergeant writing up his statement. At the end of it, he signed, confident that he had told the story correctly and that he had nothing more to add.

'You'll be heartened to know that no one was injured in any of the fires, by the way,' said the sergeant. 'Funny how often a firebomb lands in a bedroom and everybody gets out alive. Pure fluke though.'

'Of course.' Terry had not even been wondering about casualties.

'Now, do you mind holding on for Inspector McKeague? He's on his way specifically to see you.'

'I'm sorry. Tell him I am much too busy.'

It was only when he was out on the street that Terry remembered he had nowhere to go. His car was up at the Wellington Park and Kathleen had the keys and, with any luck, was asleep. She presumably had the keys to her own car too and that was in

Damascus Street. He could go to his office and at least have a computer and a desk on which to make plans. He would have to talk to the bank and make sure there was a steady flow of cash to Kathleen. Right now, she didn't even have a credit card, unless it was in the house in Damascus Street. It wasn't far, so he decided to walk round there and see what state it was in. There were more people and cars on the streets now. Office workers and university staff drove in to town early from the suburbs to try to claim a parking space.

The Holy Land was quiet but there was a strong stench of soot and petrol from the house. The front door opened on a nudge. The acrid fumes were almost stifling on the ground floor. He saw what had broken the downstairs window. A petrol bomb had come through into the front living room but had not exploded. This told him how thorough the attack was. If this one had gone off, Kathleen would not have got out alive. In the old days, he had made petrol bombs with milk bottles, but everybody got their milk in cartons now. That left beer bottles, which were too small, or whiskey bottles, which, if they were the large size, would carry their own weight through double glazing but often not break when they landed. The neck was narrow and long, so the fuse cloth often burnt out too. That's what had happened to this one. But he could tell that, otherwise, it was a well-made bomb. There was sugar and detergent in the mix – the working man's napalm. It didn't mean the bomber was a seasoned terrorist; he could have learnt that from a TV documentary, or from some old reminiscing rioter. But it didn't mean the arsonist wasn't a pro. You could get so good at murder and sabotage that your own skill singled you out so you disguised your style by being amateurish.

Kathleen's overcoat was still draped over an armchair and her handbag was on the floor beside it. Her car keys were in the bag. Her red leather purse with her credit cards was there too. Well, wasn't it great, he thought, that she had such nice honest neighbours? The coat stank of petrol and would have to be cleaned. Terry went upstairs. The main bedroom, where Kathleen had slept, was badly scorched. The flames had reached all the walls, and the mattress and sheets too. Apart from the fumes and stench, the bathroom was all right. So were the other two bedrooms. He stripped for a shower. He needed one.

Under the steaming water he didn't hear the door open and a man with heavy feet ascend the stairs. The man opened the bathroom door and was as surprised to see Terry as Terry was to see him.

'Jack! An early start. Good on you, man.'

The recovery had begun.

***

Kathleen had not slept well. She got snatches of sleep for half an hour at a time and then would snap awake. Her nerves jangled. The shock and adrenalin alone would have made her restless without the fear and anxiety tormenting her. What if the arsonist had followed her to the hotel? He might have been on the street when the fire had started and seen her run out of the house. Maybe the man who had burnt her out of two houses in one night was sleeping soundly now, as content as if he had killed her, perhaps assuming he had.

She got up, went into the bathroom, looked around it and walked out again. She crossed the large room, sat in a deep armchair and picked up the hotel's guidelines, which detailed where she could get a masseuse or a dentist and the times of church services. She opened the drawer by her bed and took out the Gideons Bible. Her eye lighted on a familiar passage: 'Inasmuch as ye have done it unto one of the least of these My brethren, ye have done it unto Me.' Clothe the naked and feed the hungry and comfort the outcast. Yes to all three, she said to herself. As for the prisoner? Yes, she would visit Terry and try to love him if he went to jail. She would feel better about him having two grim years in a cell to think about what he had done and to say sorry, if only to himself or to God. She believed in God. That's what it came down to. There has to be a God, she thought, if things like this are to be resolved, for it is not right to just put them out of your mind and move on.

But she had more practical things to think about. It was now eight o'clock. She was in that dreadful limbo between not having slept properly and not being tired enough to reverse the habit of being up and doing things at this hour. Her mobile rang.

'Hello, Kathleen Brankin.'

'Mrs Brankin, it's Gilly McDonald. I need somewhere to live. Our house was burnt out last night and you've to get me somewhere else to live. I've nowhere.'

'Gilly, give me your number and I'll get back to you.'

Gilly was frantic. 'You could have killed us last night.'

'*I* could have killed you? How do you work that out?'

'That's what everyone is saying; this was for the insurance. What else would it be when every house you own was burnt out in one night. It's on the news.'

'I doubt that the news is saying we burnt our own houses.'

'Well, that's what it sounds like.'

'Gilly, I have nowhere to go today yet either. Give me your number.'

'I bet you're not sleeping on a sofa out in Andytown, are you?'

'No.' She felt ashamed that she was in a nice suite in the Welly Park and then angry that she should be justifying that.

'Gilly, we did not burn the houses for the insurance, whatever anyone is saying. The best I can offer you now is to give you money. Go to the estate agent and get another flat and we'll pay the deposit.'

'If I come up and see you now, will you give me £500?'

'Gilly, I don't even have clothes to wear today. I don't have my chequebook or anything.'

'Aye, that's all right, Mrs Brankin. You just worry about yourself. Well, I'll see you in court and I hope the pair of youse go to jail for this.'

There was another call coming through. It was Terry, so she took it.

'Hi.'

'I'm over in Damascus Street. Your things are OK, though your clothes smell of petrol and smoke. Your bag is here with your cards. I can run them up to you now.'

When she finished that call, the phone rang yet again. 'Mrs Brankin? My name is Sam. I'm a producer on the *Nevan Toland Show*. We were wondering if you would take a call from Nevan about the fires last night.'

She could not help but be curious. 'What about the fires last night?'

'Well, it's a terrible thing that so many of your properties were burnt down. Have you lost everything?'

'I don't know the scale of the damage yet. Our home was well ablaze this morning. I doubt that there is much left of it.'

'Would you be happy to talk to Nevan about it?'

'I don't know what's to be gained. Some people apparently are already saying that we did all this ourselves for the insurance money.'

'Well, *we're* not saying that. Nevan would never say a thing like that. No, our concern is just for the tragedy of a family that has lost everything, and your tenants, who were nearly killed but now have nowhere to live.'

'It is appalling.'

'I take it the houses were properly insured, though.'

'Well, of course.'

'Well, sure, why not take a call from Nevan at nine o'clock and just let him lead you through a conversation like this.'

'I don't think so. I'm beginning to see that this could be twisted in some people's minds to make us look bad. I think it's better just to leave it.'

'We'll have others on the programme talking about this. You can see the danger, can't you? If your tenants make allegations against you, and we have to say that you declined to take part ...'

'I'm not declining to talk to the tenants. I'm just declining to do it on radio.'

'Why, Mrs Brankin? Do you have something to hide?'

'Screw you,' she said and hung up.

A text had come in from Nools during that call: 'You okay? Call if you need anything.'

Kathleen called reception to find out what time they served breakfast to. She ran a bath and sank into it and then there was a knock at the door.

'It's me, love.'

If only she could have just half an hour to relax and not think about her problems. She climbed out, dripping, wrapped herself in a towel and opened the door for Terry. He was energised with purpose and plans and seemed to bring urgency into the room with him. She got back into the bath. He paced fretfully about the room talking to her, only glancing in momentarily to see how she was reacting to him.

'I'm nearly on top of this. Jack will have Damascus Street sorted out today. I'll stay there for a couple of days anyway. You can stay here for a few days if you prefer, and by then we'll have one of the flats in Dunluce Avenue ready. I had a quick look in and a clean-up and a new window will do for one of them. I need to get on to the insurance company but this looks paramilitary so it'll be compensation from the state. If the police play ball.'

'What could the police do?'

'They could say I brought this on us through paramilitary activity of my own. Look, the worst is that we would have to sell the site and get somewhere smaller. We wouldn't be able to rebuild.'

'And we wouldn't get compensation for the lost furniture and everything?'

'No.'

'Well that's fair.'

'Jesus, the things you come out with,' he said.

Terry stood at the bathroom door and watched the way she was soaping her body as if it was no concern of his, her sullen face turned away from him. He shuddered to think she could have been killed. It would have been a horrible death.

She said, 'Turn on the radio.'

He looked puzzled.

'They'll be talking about us on the Toland show.' She could see that he was trying to grasp the implications of this news as he walked to the bedside and picked up the remote control. He found the station. The discussion had started.

'This was a busy night for you in the Fire and Rescue Service?'

'Well, the first call out was at 3.15 to a house in Damascus Street. This is a residential property and in the area popularly known as the Holy Land. We despatched two appliances but by the time we arrived there was significant scorch and smoke damage and I think it is important to say that incidents like this illustrate the need for a working smoke alarm, which we would urge people to have in their homes and to check every week.'

'The house had been petrol-bombed,' said Nevan, trying to bring the man to the point.

'At this stage we have not ascertained the precise cause of the fire.'

'Of course you have,' said Nevan. 'It was a petrol bomb, wasn't it?'

'Well, it is up to the police to issue an official statement, but we can say that first indications are that the fire was exacerbated by an accelerant. That makes it suspicious.'

'I'll say it was suspicious. The poor man who owned it had four other houses burnt down last night. Tell me about the others.'

'The largest fire was at a house in Sallagh Crescent. This fire was at an advanced stage when we got there and there was nothing we could do but control the flames and let it burn out. The premises were totally destroyed. Fortunately, though it was a private residence, there was no one at home.'

'Is that unusual?'

'No. Sometimes people leave electrical appliances switched on and plugs in the socket, so this is an appropriate time perhaps to remind people of the necessary precautions. Always unplug all appliances when you go to bed or leave the house—'

'Yes, yes, yes, of course. But you're not telling me that this was caused by the pilot light on the TV, are you?'

'It would be premature to declare the precise cause of the fire.'

'Really. Why's that?'

'Because a police investigation is underway.'

Toland was getting exasperated. 'OK, well, let's just confirm the basic facts and move on. Five houses were petrol-bombed last night and all belong to the solicitor Terry Brankin, isn't that right?'

'I am sure the police would be better able to confirm details like that when their initial investigations are complete. Our role was to bring the fires under control and report our assessments of the likely causes to the police. We have done that.'

'Good. Now we are getting somewhere. And did you tell the police that all these houses had been firebombed.'

'We alerted them to the fact that traces of accelerant had been found in all the houses.'

'Thank you, Fire Officer Tomasin McCourtney. Now, we have a call coming in from a young woman who lived in one of the burnt-out houses. Tell us your name, love.'

'Don't love me, Nevan. I'm not one of your big fans. Gilly McDonald.'

'And what was your experience, Gilly?'

'I was living in the house in Dunluce Avenue that was petrol-bombed last night.'

'And you are sure that it was a petrol bomb.'

'Of course it was a bloody petrol bomb. I saw it come through the front windy at me.'

'Well take us through this whole thing, Gilly.'

'I was in the front room watching a DVD at about four in the morning and I might have been dozing off, but then there was a mighty smash through the bay window. Now the big curtains did stop it but there was a stink of petrol and suddenly there were flames leppin' up all over the place. I screamed my head off and ran out the front door.'

'Were there others in the house at the time?'

'There was lads upstairs. They got out the bathroom windy into the yard. I'm telling you, we could all have been killed and all for that fuck—'

That was the last of her voice they heard. Nevan or his producer had closed the fader.

Nevan seemed a bit unsure what to say next. 'Well, we don't tolerate foul language on the airwaves and we always cut it off, and I know people say that's the ordinary way that people talk in this town, but that's beside the point. The rules are the rules. Furthermore, this programme has no insights at all into the identity of the person Gilly was alluding to, nor does it support her in any allegation that might be implied, intentionally or otherwise, by the terms she used.'

Terry reckoned Toland had just about covered himself legally against a defamation action, but the point had been made. Gilly McDonald had blamed someone, and it would be easy for many listeners to conclude that it was him.

'We've another caller. Good morning.'

'Good morning, Nevan. I used to rent a house from Terry Brankin myself and I don't believe he would do a thing like that at all, for any amount of insurance money.'

Nevan roared at him, 'Right, if you can't come onto this programme without swearing and slandering people, don't come on at all. And you might think you are doing someone a favour by saying they didn't do something that someone else said they did do, but if you name someone in connection with an allegation, whether to try and get them off the hook or hang them on it even higher, let me tell you – it is still actionable, because you are perpetuating the original defamation.'

Nevan's producers would be crapping themselves now.

He spoke slowly. 'So listen clearly – we on this programme wish to dissociate ourselves entirely from any speculation attributing those fires to any specific individual. We have no information about Terry Brankin other than that he is a respected solicitor and property developer. We should point out that one of those who was nearly killed last night was his own wife. Now let's move on.'

Nevan altered his tone from the hectoring of his audience to the more upbeat inflections of reportage. 'An audit office report this morning says that the police have still not got sufficient computer power to catch speeding motorists. If you think you have been caught by a speed camera but not been summonsed, phone us and tell us about it. You needn't give your name. OK, caller on line two.'

The man had a thick country accent. He said, 'I often drive down the M2 at a hundred miles an hour and was never caught and I think it's no surprise that Terry Brankin would kill—'

Nevan slammed the fader in time to shut off the end of the sentence. 'I don't know what's come over you lot, this morning,' he said.

Kathleen watched Terry getting more and more agitated. She knew what usually happened when he was like this: he acted rashly for the exultant sense of being momentarily in control. He was thumbing his mobile.

'Hey, Finian. Who's producing Toland now? Have you got a mobile number for him. Great.' Terry scribbled down the number and then dialled it.

'It's Terry Brankin here. I think you know now that the only way to avoid an action for defamation is to give me an immediate on-air right of reply.'

There was a pause and then he picked up the remote and turned down the radio. That's what the voice on the other end had told him to do.

'Well it might be a good morning for you, Nevan. It's far from it for me. Look, I have one thing to say: I know who attacked my houses last night and I have a message for him. I am coming. Don't you dare cut me off! Fuck!' For a moment Terry Brankin seemed to consider throwing his mobile at the wall.

Six

Ig Murray's first feeling every morning was a profound sense of injustice. Sleep wasn't easy for him, but it was plain wrong that he should have to come out of it when he was just getting the hang of it, that his head should feel like a bag of rocks, that his nose should be blocked and his joints stiff. There was no way that waking up was ever going to be a joy for him. If the hangover didn't get him, then his worries did. Not that he would have put it as plainly as that himself if asked. It wasn't Ig's way to think about life and its meaning or to dwell on the past. He just wanted to get through another day and meet his responsibilities to his master, and he knew that a wee drink would always help.

He rolled over on to his stomach and dropped an arm to rummage about under the bed for a bottle. The fact that the first one he found was lying on its side wasn't a good sign. Busy times – lots to do. He would need a slug right away if he was to function at all. But he'd probably have to go into the kitchen to find one. He faced a whole stretch from the bed, across the floor of the cluttered room, to the door, out onto the landing and a jaded walk down the stairs – all without the aid of a brain stabiliser, a stomach settler, a drink. 'Shit,' he said as he geared himself up.

Ig was trying to piece together some images from the night before. He recalled that he had been in the club with some of the lads; not much different there. Some old 'Ra men from back then had made it into a wider circle but most hadn't. And who else understood you, your humour and your silences, but guys who had lived the same life, fought the same fight? Not that Ig Murray, or many of the others in the club, had done much of what you could really call fighting. There'd been a few hard nuttings – some never owned up to – but if there had even been twenty down the years, it didn't amount to a full-time job. Then there was going after wee thieving hoods into back alleys and shooting them in the legs; he had done a lot of that and had got clever. His hallmark was doing both legs with the one bullet. Ha! He'd liked that, the bewildered look on the victims' faces thinking you were leaving them one leg to stand on until they tried it out.

There was a lot less of that stuff now that the party was in government. The big man – McGrath – didn't mind the odd bit of mischief, but he had two conditions: that he knew about it and that he was well away from it when it happened. The rule was: no surprises. And in a spirit of considered planning, the big worry of the week was the Cold Case enquiry into the Magheraloy bomb. It would have been so much easier if Terry Brankin had stayed in the 'Ra. Some chance of that after he had met that bird from Ballintoy. If Brankin was still a 'Ra man, he'd be living nearby and drinking in the same club, and Ig would be able to get the drift of his thinking just by watching him, without having to probe and plan. Now the 'Ra had got to the stage of discussing a wee visit to Terry Brankin. Ig was sorry about that. Terry had paid his dues.

But that was the way it was. Ig served the movement and that made conscience simple for him. He had never shot a man for a selfish reason; he did not even think he could. When Eileen left him, he had raged with jealousy. She and her new man had moved away because the other guy knew Ig's form and was scared of him. But it would hardly have crossed Ig's mind to whack him – thump him maybe but not shoot him. Yet if the movement had lined up a hundred strangers – even a hundred of his neighbours – against the wall of a barn, and told him to nut them all, one by one, Ig could have done that and gone home for a shower and a nice wee dinner afterwards and felt OK about it. Well, that's what he told himself; that's even what he told some of the lads when they discussed these things. Right now, however, Ig needed a drink and he doubted he could get downstairs without one.

What was the decision on Terry? He couldn't even remember. Delegate to the hoods for a start, but keep them in check. Then take it a day at a time. That meant they would give him a bit of latitude, and move on him if he took it. It gave him a chance. Well, that was only fair. But if it appeared that Terry was going into the dock to take questions about Magheraloy – questions that might extend to whether or not the party leader had helped out there – then Terry would have to be stopped, even taken down. To Ig it was as simple as that.

Ig saw himself as a soldier and he prided himself on discipline, even in his drinking. He would always need a gulp of whiskey in the morning, which meant that he would always have to leave a drop untouched at night. It wasn't easy. The temptation was always to finish the bottle. Ig was confident that there was about a teacup full of Paddy in a bottle under the sink because he trusted himself. And there it was. He drank it neat and straight back, and in a few moments everything came right. His head was clearer and his body more at ease between its warring parts. Now he could function, and it was as well, for someone was at the door. On the way to answer it, he found a text message on his mobile on the kitchen table. He blinked at it: 'Terry Brankin has just told Toland he'll nut the fucker that burnt his house.' Old Provies texted in full sentences; some were even particular about punctuation. That's what a Christian Brothers education does for you.

That message helped Ig feel slightly ahead in the game when he recognised the caller through the peephole as Terry Brankin himself. He was in his business suit but with no tie on. Ig wasn't sure what was coming but there was no point in puffing himself up for a fight since Brankin was bigger, faster, angrier and probably sober. So he opened the door with a smile.

'Don't fuckin' a chara me,' said Terry before Ig had a chance to speak. 'I want a word with you.'

'Sure, a chara. Tar isteach. Cupán tae?'

'Just your undivided attention while I tell you plainly that I know it was you fuckers who burnt all my houses last night and that is no way to get me on your side.'

'No, Terry. Don't say that. Slow down.'

'Magheraloy! Fucking Magheraloy! You think I haven't worked out who needs his name kept out of it?'

'Terry, sit down, sit down.' Ig wanted him calm so that he would remember what he had to say to him. But Terry was charging on.

'So, I have a message for you, Ig, and for that fucker who only learnt to polish his shoes last week: leave me and mine alone.'

Ig would grant Terry Brankin this much; he was a scary man. And Ig had seen them all. There were guys who could kill and guys who wished they could kill. There were guys so scary they often didn't have to kill; Brankin had been one of those. Ig also knew that whatever he or Terry did to the other now would count for little against them at the Pearly Gates, not compared to what they had done before.

'Got that off your chest then? Sit down and listen to me, Terry.'

Terry stood where he was, awkwardly in the doorway of the kitchen.

'OK,' said Ig. 'The first rule is you don't threaten the 'Ra. That alone could get you dropped down a hole – you know that. So don't do it. Now, all the 'Ra wants is to be sure that you are not going to take some silly middle-aged flight of conscience and start talking to the peelers about Magheraloy. That's all.'

Terry was more enraged by Ig's poise than he would have been by a punch in the face, but he was unnerved by it too. 'Did you have to burn my fucking house down?'

'I don't know who burnt your house down.'

'Of course not.'

'But let's see if we can get things under control now, because this isn't helping.'

Terry had to consider for a moment whether he would let Ig dictate the pace now. 'You want a deal?'

'Just tell me what the Cold Case people want,' said Ig.

'They want me to go down for Magheraloy. Maybe they think there's a chance I'll confess and take the two years.'

'And are you thinking of doing that?'

'Fuck off.'

'Well, some guys find it tempting. It clears the slate. And you never felt easy about that. We had you under our notice before.'

'The only slate I want cleared is the one that you fuckers have in your heads that reads – Nut Terry Brankin. You tell McGrath that if there's another fucking cheep out of him, I'll take him down. Leave things as they are and he's OK. But you're right. In some ways it would make life a lot easier to clear this lot up, so that I could look my wife in the face again.' He was shouting now. 'But McGrath is safe from me *only* if I am safe from him. Tell him that.'

Ig spoke coldly and flatly. 'So your wife wants you to take your medicine.'

Terry exploded. 'Don't you fucking touch my wife!'

'And don't you tell the 'Ra what to do, is all I'm saying, Terry. I don't think we have sorted this out.'

'We have,' said Terry. 'I am not going to make any statement to the peelers about Magheraloy and you are going to leave me and my wife alone. OK?'

'That's what I need to hear, Terry. That's all. If I can take that as gospel, we have no problems.'

'Except that you burnt my fucking house down, you wee bastard.' And Terry, beyond all possibility of containing the reflex, lunged his knee into Ig's groin and took relish in the sight of his face slackening as he slumped to the floor. 'I'll let myself out.'

***

After breakfast, Kathleen phoned Nools. 'My head's away,' she said.

'I'm not surprised,' said Nools.

'I haven't a stitch to wear. I have to get organised.'

'Well, let me help. We're about the same size.'

'I'd at least be able to go out the door if I had a skirt and top, tights and a pair of shoes.'

'I'll come over now.'

'Thanks, Nools.'

There was a knock on the hotel door. She had nothing on but a bathrobe when she opened it. 'You?' This was a shock.

'Can I come in for a minute?' said McKeague. 'You're hardly dressed for a meeting downstairs.'

She turned from the door, he followed her in and let it swing closed behind him.

'I don't know what we have to talk about here.'

'No? Let me tell you something. I am an old burnt-out peeler who took early retirement on a decent package, like a lot of others who didn't like police reform. But I got this chance to come back and work on the Cold Case reviews. Beats gardening.'

'I'm sure it's more than that.'

'Yes, it's a way to wrap up some of the old loose ends. A second chance to catch some killers. But I don't seriously expect to be banging up a lot of them.'

He sat on the bed, oblivious to it being a mess, and set down his briefcase. She was standing. Reluctantly, she turned a chair from the desk to face him and sat down. He laid out his vision for her as if he assumed she had nothing else to do but listen.

'This is a political job. We keep two constituencies happy. One is made up of the hard old unionists who want justice. We tell them we are still trying to catch the bad guys. And they hope, of course, that we'll get big names locked up. It could happen. You never know. We don't promise. But the other constituency we serve wouldn't like to see political damage. So one bunch think we are the Untouchables and the others think we are the guardians of the peace. The truth is I'm the sweep; I gather up the old dirt and someone else decides what goes out the door and what goes under the carpet.'

'If you are so cynical, why do you stay in the job?'

'Do you know what a lot of the families of the dead say? They say: don't bother charging the killers. Leave them to suffer their consciences, if they have them. Don't insult us by sending them down for only two years. You see, they don't want them to go to jail, Mrs Brankin; they want them to go to Hell.'

'So why bother? Why come here?'

'Because people like you fascinate me. You can love a man who did a thing like that. You can make it all right in your own head. How do you do that?'

She said, 'He is not the man he was.'

Basil only knew one way for a man to free himself from being dogged by past sins and it wasn't by getting forgiven by his wife.

'Be aware that this is complicated. I'm not sure my bosses really want me to catch anybody. If your husband keeps his nerve and you support him, there is no reason why he shouldn't brave this out and survive.'

'But you do want to charge him, don't you?'

'Oh, yes, and to bring down a whole parcel of gangsters with him.'

'And who do you think burnt our houses last night?'

'I don't know,' said McKeague. 'I would happily go along with the theory that it was yourselves. I've no doubt we'll be looking into ledgers to see if you – or your husband – needed the insurance money.'

'It wasn't us.'

'Well, there's a lot of things that Terry didn't tell you. Maybe this is just another one of them.'

She judged that he was not just toying with her, that he really did think this a possibility. 'He wouldn't have burnt down our own home and he would not have thrown a petrol bomb at a house I was sleeping in.'

'Ah, well, plans get made and wires get crossed and all sorts of things happen, as you know. Who's he saying did it?'

'He's not telling me, whatever he thinks. Perhaps some of your crowd are behind it. You've good reason if you can't charge Terry and you know that even your own higher-ups don't want you to. So it's another way of punishing him.'

'No, the police don't do things like that, whatever you think.'

'Oh, they'd clean hands through it all, had they?'

'No, but now stability is everything. That's what the peace processors want, and what they want, they get.'

'So you'd like to have been able to do it, would you?'

'There were guys in Special Branch who would have looked the other way or nudged a thug, but I'm not like that. Those guys will face their judgement too. I'm a believer, Mrs Brankin. I believe in a God who will consign your husband and his likes to Hell, where they belong. For me that's enough. The rest is the job – looking busy, ticking the boxes.'

'Why do you hate the peace process when it has brought the Troubles to an end?'

McKeague inhaled deeply, as if he was thinking it would be too much trouble to explain. Then he decided to try. It would involve a history lesson.

'Have you ever,' he said, 'tried to comprehend the mind of a man like Dominic McGrath? That's a man who had peelers shot in the head, just to send a wee message to government negotiators when things weren't going well. To him, we are pawns. Do you remember at the start of the talks, there'd suddenly be these huge bombs in London and everyone would be asking what that was all about? Dominic would have been round the table in some hotel in Dundalk with the Army Council, and they'd be discussing the need to test that the Brits were for real. And Dominic would say, "OK, blow up a skyscraper in London, and then if the Brits are still on your doorstep with a note from the prime minister offering talks, you'll know two things: you'll know they are in this for the long haul and you'll know they accept that the price is high." Isn't that a laugh? He was bombing London to prove to his men that the Brits were serious and would show it by taking it on the chin, and the Brits were going along with it because they trusted he would con the Army Council into negotiating on terms they'd never have accepted before. Isn't he one smart bastard?'

'Do you think he had our houses burnt, to warn Terry?'

McKeague always paused before an answer, as if he had to make several calculations first.

'Well, what's the logic? On the one hand, he might be thinking that Terry needs a good shot across his bows, at the least. But you have to see this as a serious attempt to kill both of you, if it wasn't yourselves that did it. How many petrol-bombed houses do you see on the news that are burnt to the ground? Very few, because most of the bombs are thrown by wee brats who wouldn't know how to knock over a chicken coup. That house you lived in is rubble and ashes now. So maybe McGrath thought he was better off rid of you, and it wouldn't do to send somebody to shoot you, since that would show he still has guns and he isn't supposed to have guns. Yes, maybe that accounts for it. But he also knows the rules of the big game, by which terrorism is turned into politics, and the big rule is that he's covered. Or that's how it has been up to now.'

'So he's a suspect?'

'Some of his gophers might be suspects. Not him. Never him.'

***

The strength in Nools was that she was sussed. Kathleen had seen that in her at the book group, if they were discussing a crime thriller or anything about terrorism or the police. She came out with the most confident plain statements about the psychology of cops and criminals, usually not making much of a distinction between them. She had an edge. She would know what to do if she were in Kathleen's position. Then again, she would never have got into that position in the first place.

Nools swept in with a couple of carrier bags, as if she was moving surreptitiously, on a mission. She was clearly going to take charge. They kissed cheeks and stood back and looked at each other. Nools was wearing a black leather jacket over a knee-length skirt and boots. 'Shall we get you dressed?'

'Well, let's have a look.'

Nools laid out the different pieces she had brought on the bed: cotton and silk tops, a chunky mustard-coloured woollen sweater.

'Oh, God, it's like having to be somebody else for a day,' Kathleen said.

'Treat that as part of the fun,' said Nools.

Dressed and self-conscious, Kathleen kept turning uneasily to the mirror, reminding herself that she had nothing else and that it was better to go shopping looking like a lesbian with money than like a tramp in a student's cast-offs.

'I'm grateful. I'm sorry; I'm such a fussy bitch.'

'You wouldn't have been much use to Terry's old mates in the IRA.'

'I heard some of them were quite glamorous, the ones who dressed up to woo soldiers to parties to be shot?'

'That was part of it for some. What about the others who had to carry guns stuffed down surgical stockings and wear big tweed skirts to cover the bulge?'

'God, the things people did.'

'A hit man didn't carry his own gun with him but met a handover near the scene. And some of them went into prison visits with balls of Semtex up them, which at least must have been more comfortable than gun parts.'

'And you know all this because George talked about it?'

'No, I read it in books. George doesn't talk much. He comes home drunk and then drinks some more. He has always lived in fear, all the time. Some of his mates seemed fairly relaxed through the worst of it and just accepted the risks of the job. Others fretted constantly and were impossible to live with.'

'It was hard on you too.'

'Any time George and I went for a holiday in Donegal we always had to tell the people we met that he was in the civil service. We could never tell anyone he was a screw. We couldn't hang his shirts out on the line or they'd be a giveaway. A nuisance really. Meeting nice people in hotel bars and chatting the night away with them, lying to them.'

'Terry didn't deceive me, really.'

'You preferred to imagine that the past was over and done with. You had a man who could put it out of his mind; he's a stronger man than George in that way. He came through all that and still was able to live a professional and home life without constantly thinking about it. That's strength. Maybe if you had known all the things he did, you wouldn't have wanted anything to do with him, but you'd have missed out on knowing a man who copes better than most.'

Seven

Dominic McGrath had aches and pains and some of them were physical. Two and a half decades before, he had taken three bullets through his body in an attack on his constituency office. He knew people who had taken seven or eight bullets and survived and, by a natural injustice, others had taken the ricochet of a single round that had not even been intended for them, and had died in an instant. McGrath had been lucky, but he didn't feel lucky. His scars itched and he still carried a sense of having been comprehensively invaded.

His other aches were people. He was tired after more than twenty years of peace-processing – a particularly arduous destiny for a man with a creative imagination. Much of politics was saying the same drab things over and over again. You get into a deadlock – deadlock might indeed be the place you want to be in for a while – but you still have to show a willingness to talk. And how he had talked – to British and Irish prime ministers and US presidents as they probed him for signs of commitment and real intention. He had recited for them again the historic grievances of the Irish people. He was sick of it.

Now there was some prospect of politics settling down, and he no longer had to manage the embarrassment of untimely acts of barbarism by his own men – some of them carving up a lad in a bar, for instance, or robbing a bank and making off with tens of millions, when one million would have been a good day's work and would have brought no political damage. Now that McGrath should be cruising through life and enjoying the fruits of his statesmanlike achievements, he was bored.

He was thinking of putting in a Freedom of Information request to the BBC for sight of his obituary. It would be a bold move. He had heard that the obituary was already in the can, or in some folder in their network, to be updated from time to time. He wanted to know what it said, but he was afraid that if he forced them to release it to him they might just go ahead and broadcast it, or release it to other media too. He was afraid they had stories that they had not broadcast before and would not risk broadcasting while he was alive, in case he sued them. But then again, McGrath would never be able to persuade a jury that he hadn't been a suburban warlord, that he had no blood on his hands. Maybe he was best leaving well enough alone. But what was it all for, he wondered, if he was going to go down in history as a psychopath? McGrath was confident that he was not a psychopath. In fact, he didn't relish killing people at all – that's why he had always got others to do it for him.

He had been at the head of a political party and its military wing for decades. In some ways he was the most successful politician in the western democratic world, for he had held his position longer than any other. But there was a taint on that achievement that rankled with him. It was emerging now that several of his closest colleagues had not been working for him at all but had been spying for the British. His personal security people had included spies; his private office staff had included spies. This was fundamentally humiliating, and it created a practical problem for him: he had to stay in control of his organisation just to stop others from speculating that he might, all along, have been a tool – or at least a patsy – of the British himself. While he was at the top, he could deal with dissenters, but when a new leader took over there would be no way to manage what was said about him and what his legacy might be.

The phone on his desk rang. 'Yes?'

'Are we putting out a statement about the firebombs?' It was Aidan, his new young press officer.

'What should we say? Now that we don't burn people out of their houses any more, we don't think anyone else should either?'

'I'm assuming that we don't.'

'Don't be a smart alec. There'll be a standard response on file: not the way to solve problems in the new dispensation, micro groups with no real mandate trying to bring us back to the dark days – something like that. Hoke it out and I'll sign it. Anything else?'

'Terry Brankin wants to talk to you.'

'Really? It was his houses.'

'Didn't know. What'll I say to him?'

'Keep him well away from me.'

Eight

It was before a peace strategy was even being discussed. The IRA was calling him back from exile. The card just said, '*Tar abhaile*': 'Come home'. Terry wasn't sure. He had a shift to work at the Farmer's but he could leave now. He had not accumulated much in his year, never having planned to stay on, but now that the choice was before him, he considered it.

He liked the bar and the area. Lancaster was nominally a city but it was really only a town on a hill. Walking up that hill was the only thing that kept him fit now. He liked that the boys he worked with knew nothing about Ireland. In the beginning it had annoyed him that they weren't even curious. It never seemed to have occurred to Scotch Jimmy or to Billy that Terry might ever have killed anybody, handled a gun or seen his own death looming and narrowly pass him by.

What they cared about was that he could pour drinks at speed, grip two beer-bottle necks together, wrench off their tops – and count the total as he turned to the till, having already spotted who next to serve.

The card had ushered him home, but this place now felt like home – almost. It wasn't so far away that someone like Ig might not walk in someday and ask what he was doing, seek a little advice on where to store some gear for a whack at the courthouse. There were occasional trials up there that would interest the 'Ra.

'*Tar abhaile*' sounded like an order. It certainly wasn't an opener for a conversation.

McGrath had assured Terry that he wouldn't be under IRA orders when he was away, but exile was over now. He hadn't much choice. Ignoring this would not spare him the need to explain himself one day to hard men with guns in their hands who would insist on clear answers. Perhaps he'd go and see McGrath, tell him he was out now and come back to Lancaster. He'd just phone the bar, tell Jimmy his mother was ill and he'd to go home – *abhaile* – for a few days. He'd keep the room. There was nothing in it that he owned but a few books, LPs, his clothes and toiletries.

Looking round, he realised that he had missed a chance to settle himself here. Instead, he'd always just been waiting for this day. So here he was, a 'Ra man again. Time to start thinking like one.

Was there anything here that might later be used by the police? Hardly. Just the card. He crouched by the little grate, struck a match and set it alight. What would anyone learn about him from the room? That he usually slept alone, had read most of Dostoevsky, preferred *Playboy* to *Penthouse*, drank Irish whiskeys and smoked, and that he was untidy, like a man who had not learnt in prison how to fold a blanket – not yet.

Terry closed the door on that life, took only the clothes that were clean, a toothbrush and a book he hadn't finished yet: *The Idiot*. He didn't go up the town but round by the old dock to the footbridge. There, high above the river and looking towards the town and taking it all in, he felt he was mentally photographing the hill, the castle, the wooded park and the folly. Then he turned towards Morecambe.

The spring sun added a little warmth to the day. This was the same time of year he had first come here and it was a good time. The place was coming out of hibernation. It was the wrong time to be leaving. But Belfast would be bright and sunny too. Still, he should have connected with more people, been less like a stranger. The start of a second year was when the place started to look familiar. He thought he might miss it and regret not having been more open.

Working at the Farmer's, he could have had a different lover every night, but they all learnt quickly that he was a boring heterosexual and, beyond bemoaning what a waste that was, befriended him as Terry Pat and looked elsewhere. A philosophy lecturer called Lynne Doniger had provided him with a break from his abstemious life. That was early in his stay. She had come into the Farmer's with a group of other academics. She had sat at the bar and chatted with him after extracting herself from a heated conversation among some of the men. And she went home with him for vigorous sex, in much the same spirit in which she might have played with him on a seesaw in the park, until she came with a whimper. He was glad of it. So was she.

'Fair blows the wax out of your ears,' she'd said.

A week later she was in the Farmer's with a fat girl in dungarees and the pair of them drank pints of Boddingtons. She'd smiled sheepishly when Terry picked up their empties and said hello. He was tactful enough not to embarrass her.

A woman called Nuala turned up as a reminder that he wasn't so far from home. She was working at the Playhouse theatre and had been coming to the bar with some of the actors.

'Are you from Belfast?' she said sharply when he served her, then, 'Oops, I wasn't supposed to ask that, was I?' She had read him better than any of the English had done.

'It's okay,' he said. 'You too, obviously.'

'Falls Road, up to here,' she said. 'Will you go back yourself?'

'Maybe.'

They met the next day, which he had off, drank cider by the canal and then went back to his room where she studied his shelves and wondered why a man who read Dostoevsky worked in a bar and had no friends.

'I was in the IRA.'

'Really? Are you supposed to tell me that?'

'You'd rather not know?'

'Actually, if I'd taken you for a Provo, I wouldn't have come near you.'

'What did they do to you?'

'They are the whole problem over there.'

'You grew up on the Falls, yet you really think that?'

'And so do a lot of other people who grew up on the Falls. Do you think we all happily left the yard door open for your mates to skip through? No way. I'd have slammed it in your face.'

Then she said she had to be at the Playhouse. She let him walk her there, though they didn't say much on the way. At the front door of the theatre she said, 'I'm sorry, I shouldn't judge.'

Little did she know he had done enough self-judging to last a lifetime. He didn't tell her about that summer night when there was no moon and still a tint of blue in the northern sky at midnight. He had walked alone on the beach at Heysham, ascended the barrows, the hill with the old stone graves of monks, and sat on one of those graves by the broken wall of the old church. There, he had faced the horror of what he had done. There he had wept and howled, spoken aloud to the darkness and told his secret: 'I have killed. I have torn a child to shreds. I have burnt and lacerated her mother and her father, blasted them to bits and scattered them like the scraps of meat you would throw to dogs. That I have done. And I belong in Hell.' There he had emptied himself until he was asleep on the cold ground among the dead and buried.

He had awoken shivering with the dawn, the light metallic and pure but weak. He had waded naked into the cold sea and contemplated going under forever, but the water awakened and refreshed him and then, with its icy sharpness, drove him back to the land and to life. Dying wasn't so easy, no easier than living. He had dressed, walked the miles back to his room – cold, hungry and humble – and lain for hours on his bed without a thought forming and slept the whole day.

When he arrived for his shift at the pub the following day, there was a letter waiting for him behind the counter. It was from Nuala.

Terry,
I don't want to quarrel about this, but I do want you to understand. Then we needn't talk about it again. I grew up

in Devonshire Street, off Albert Street, in the lower Falls. My brother and father were often picked on by soldiers on the street as likely republican suspects. My father was a Holy Joe. He was in the Legion of Mary and went to Mass and communion every day. He was a pioneer and wore the pin and a Fáinne on his lapel. So he was a teetotal, Irish-speaking Catholic whose religion meant more to him than politics, and he would never grant to anyone the right to kill soldiers for Ireland.

But we looked the part to ignorant Brits. Those raiding our house about once or twice a year, probably just because we were on a rota, saw pictures on the living room wall of the Sacred Heart, John F. Kennedy and Patrick Pearse. They saw matchstick Celtic crosses made by prisoners and heard my father speaking to us in Irish, usually just telling us to behave, and all their briefings prepared them to see us as mad rebels.

Actually, as you know, the IRA in our area at the beginning was practically communist. Once the army took Daddy and my brother away, kicked the shit out of them and held them for days. I will never forgive them for that. But – and you can call this perverse if you like – I also blamed the IRA for bringing the Brits into the area in the first place, for pursuing a pointless unwinnable war by stupid means. I could tell you the names of all the big Provos in our area and they are men you probably know. I never liked any of them and they never liked us. As far as I could see, they were a mix of mad fanatics and powermongers, and I grew up knowing that it was best to keep out of their way.

Nuala

Terry phoned her at the theatre.

'Did you get my letter?'

'Yes. Thank you.'

'For what?'

'For taking the time to explain,' he said. 'I'm not going to argue. How's your da now?'

'He's at home with his rosary beads. My mother is dead.'

'And your brother?'

'Canada.'

Nuala invited him over to her flat for a meal that night. He brought six cans of stout, a half bottle of vodka and a three pack of Durex. She lived in a studio apartment that belonged to the Playhouse and she opened the door with a smile. She was wearing a cotton frock. She didn't kiss him, not even on the cheek, but she thanked him for the drinks and took them away to the fridge.

She had made the place homely. There were framed theatre posters and family photographs on the walls. He paused for a moment to admire the print of a snowy Mount Errigal under a crisp and cloudless winter sky. She had a table set with wine glasses. He wasn't keen on her making such a fuss. They were going to eat and who knows what? This seemed a bit ritualistic to his mind.

'I hope you like fish,' she said, coming back in from the kitchen.

'I like smokies,' he said, 'and willicks.'

She laughed, thinking he was joking, and poured him a glass of white wine. He never saw his stout again. She put on a soft jazz LP. He was okay with the soup but saw things on his plate during the main course that he had never seen before.

'Did you eat like this on the Falls?'

'No. Did you work in a gay bar in Belfast?'

He had annoyed her. He was suddenly afraid that he would keep on doing that if he wasn't careful. So he tried to pick the bones out of his teeth discreetly, not letting her see how uncomfortable he was.

'I'm sorry,' she said. 'I thought I was doing something nice for you.'

'It is nice.'

'You'd have preferred sausage and mash.'

'I'm a bit basic,' he said.

He drank the wine too quickly and the bottle was nearly empty before she was ready for her second glass.

'What did you think was going to happen tonight?' she asked.

'I don't know. I sort of hoped we were getting on and might take it a bit further.'

'Well, that's what I was hoping for too, but that's not where it's going, is it?'

For dessert she gave him a meringue with ice cream in a bowl and left him to eat it on the sofa while she washed the dishes and reconsidered. He watched her through the door, trying to judge from her back if she was hurt or angry. He got up and went into the kitchen. He stood behind her and rested his hands on her hips.

'Talking isn't going to get us there. It just keeps going wrong,' he said.

'It was just a bad idea.'

***

'*Tar abhaile*' echoed in his head with every footstep. Terry walked into Morecambe instead of taking the country road through Heysham and didn't consider that he was pointlessly prolonging the journey. From the promenade, the hills of the Lake District were visible through the haze. The tide was out so far that he wondered if he could walk across the whole bay. Further south he saw the big concrete box of the nuclear power station. Could energy so destructive be so easily contained?

The police at the ferry terminal searched his rucksack but seemed more focused on finding drugs than guns or explosives. And by evening he was in a lounge seat with a plate of dry, barely edible fish and chips in front of him and a pint of lager.

Belfast the following morning was bleak and cold. The dockland was the worst possible introduction to the city. Terry walked down the gangway where two police detectives screened those coming through. They'd be expecting him.

'This way, sir.'

A tall balding man, who was probably only thirty, escorted Terry to a small interview room. He asked him to set his rucksack on the table between them and open it.

'You don't think I'd bring gear in that way, do you?'

'Just open the bag, Terry.'

The detective reached into the rucksack and took out every item of clothing as if preparing to hang them on a line. He snorted when he picked up the book.

'*The Idiot*, eh? Any good?'

Terry didn't reply. He just stood back and let the man pack the bag again, offering no help.

'On a visit?'

'Homesick.'

'We'll be keeping an eye on you.'

'Suit yourselves.'

The detective gave him a look of cold contempt. He was angry that he had to go through this routine with suspects in the certainty of losing the game every time.

Terry walked through the city as it opened for work – a good time for surreptitious warfare, setting up a hit, leaving a bomb or an incendiary. The contrast between security in England and here disturbed him. He had got used to the freedom to move around unwatched, to never being questioned or searched, but he also started to feel relief at being back in familiar surroundings.

He had no plan, though he walked towards Castle Street and the bus up the Falls. Maybe he would see Nuala. She had returned to Belfast three months earlier to see her father buried, and to sell the house, he presumed. She had written to him twice. Her father had had a heart attack; a natural death but she blamed the Troubles for shortening his life. And she blamed the Troubles on the IRA and on Terry. Arguing wouldn't help. He'd decided to leave her to work that out for herself.

He got on the number 12 bus as far as the Andersonstown Road and called at Thomas Clarke House. He pressed a button on the security grill at the door and looked up into the camera to let them have a proper view of him. Inside, the first person he met was Ig.

'Are you right yourself, Terry? Good to have you back.'

He wasn't sure he was back.

Ig took him through to the kitchen, made strong tea for them and sat him down. 'You have a wee flat now in Twinbrook. There is the key and the address. You will be with Civil Administration. OK?'

'What the fuck is Civil Administration?'

'A new department. Mostly responding to crime in the area. You'll get a list of local hoods to keep an eye on. I'll be with you or at hand anyway. If someone doesn't take a clear warning to buck up his act, we do his knees. Knees and elbows, at worst. Someone doesn't get the message after that, we give him the full whack.'

'That must make us popular.'

'Power is always popular.'

'So you don't need me for the bigger stuff?'

'We'll see.'

'And tools?'

'You won't need much. A wee Ruger and some rounds. You can keep it with you, but it's your responsibility not to lose it. OK?'

Nine

From just over Ballintoy, where Kathleen grew up, the view to the north seems infinite. On a clear day, the sun will light the cliff faces of distant Scottish islands and make you wonder if people there are looking south, themselves asking if you are as bored as they are. Kathleen understood that this was beautiful. Obviously. She saw the tourists come in their big buses and stop in the lay-by and gaze through mounted telescopes at Islay, 'the place the whisky comes from', though plenty of whiskey came from down the road in Bushmills too.

'If you do go away, it's that view that will pull you back,' her mother had said, 'and you'll ache to see it again, for there is none like it in the whole wide world.'

But Kathleen, at that age, was more interested in seeing the bookshops and bars of Belfast. She wanted a student flat, decorated to her own taste, and with a Laura Ashley duvet – a place she could bring friends, a place where she could make love to a man she hadn't met yet between fresh satin sheets.

'Your father, if he was alive, would never let you go,' her mother had said. 'To have the good fortune to live in a spot that has hardly been touched by the Troubles and you want to go to where you could be blown up for just walking in the street or have soldiers frisking you – frisking you! It makes no sense.'

On her last night living there, Kathleen waited till the sun's edge touched the water, melted into it and disappeared before she turned and walked back up to the house to finish her packing and sit awhile with her mother. Nothing would reassure the poor woman. She would be lonely and she would be worried, but

Kathleen was going to university and it just wouldn't be right to pass on that prospect, to give up her life.

'It's only fifty miles down the road, Mammy. I can get a bus home nearly every weekend and any time you need me.'

Her mother was sitting watching the television news and it was bad. Some men had kicked their way into a house on the Donegall Road and shot dead another man trying to run from them out the back.

'Dear God, bless us and save us. How far's that from the flat you're staying in?'

'Mammy, that sort of thing never happens in Camden Street.'

'That's no more than a mile from where you'll be.'

'And yet on the other side of the world. Those guys knew him. They had some sort of a reason for it. They didn't just shoot him because they didn't like his shirt.'

'But what about that wee girl that went to a party and ended up raped and her throat cut down an alley. That was only because she was a Catholic. That's all it was.'

'Well, I'll stick to my friends and not go to parties and I'm sure I'll be all right. Mammy, I can spend the whole of my life in this house to stay safe from the bad world. Or I can get my degree and earn a living.'

'And you'll go even further away for that, to London maybe, and lose your faith altogether.'

'Maybe so.' She relished the thought, but it seemed beyond dreaming about yet.

The house in Camden Street belonged to Packie O'Connor, a landowner from near Ballycastle who had property in Belfast. He rented the house out to student nurses and had a wee self-contained flat at the top that would suit Kathleen well.

'Actually,' he'd said when he gave her the key, 'if you'd any wit you'd buy a wee house there yourself. Get a couple of girls in to pay you enough rent to cover the mortgage and you'll be living for free, and then when you've finished your degree, just sell the house again. You're daft if you don't.'

Kathleen loved university. She sat enraptured in crowded lecture theatres, surrounded by restless and bored students, while a bearded man, who looked as if he hadn't slept, explained how Seamus Heaney had fulfilled his artistic responsibility. She hardly distinguished between her enthralment with ideas and her yearning to be just as wise and insightful as he was.

She heard a cynical remark from a boy behind her: 'I came here to get off the fucking bog, not to praise it.'

And where, at the end, the others would scramble out past her, handling their books as if they were of no more concern to them than the seats they flapped up brusquely behind them, she would wait and see if she could have a moment with this wonderful literary man to let him see that she was of his kind.

He groaned softly as he saw her homing in on him.

'Do you think it matters that Heaney is a Catholic?' she said. 'Would he have written the same poetry if he'd been raised an atheist or a Protestant?'

'One of the great imponderables,' replied the bearded lecturer, turning away from her.

Kathleen went to plays in the Lyric Theatre and the Old Museum. She saw Brian Friel's *Translations* and Beckett's short plays which she could make no sense of. She went to subtitled French films in the Queen's Film Theatre. But there was little life in the city at night. There were two Italian restaurants that she had to queue to get into.

Belfast offered a basic cultural life but in her head she contrasted it with Ballintoy, not with London or Dublin, and she was happy. She furnished her room to look and feel like the cosy refuge of a lover of books. She had a work desk with nice pens and crisp notepads. A Bobbie Hanvey photograph of Heaney sat on her mantelpiece, and she had set up a stereo system beside her bed with a stack of about a dozen CDs, a mix of classical and Andean pipes – music you could play while you were reading or writing an essay.

She discovered the nice fish shop and the best grocers for fresh vegetables, and she cooked for herself most evenings in the shared kitchen and took food to her room to eat alone, sometimes with a glass of rough wine, which she thought she should learn to appreciate. She had little awareness of the city's violence. At first it had annoyed her that there was always a helicopter hovering high over her. In time she became almost oblivious to it. The first time she heard the distinct thud of a bomb blast she lay awake fretting that somewhere outside, and not far away, dozens of people may be screaming and bleeding under rubble, but most bombs killed nobody and injured few and she got used to hearing one most nights.

She had, in effect, established a nest. It wasn't ideal but it was the best she could manage and she hoped in time she would invite a man into it, probably a literary man, maybe with a beard, someone who would appreciate books and her cooking, someone for whom she had made herself fragrant and interesting.

***

In the year that he was a Civil Administration enforcer in Twinbrook, Terry had been the law there. He kneecapped about thirty boys and everybody he met every day knew that that was what he did. The first of these had come to his flat on his second night there. He was a surly and skinny teenager with a spider-web tattoo on the left side of his face.

'Where do you want to do this?' he'd said.

Terry didn't know what he was talking about.

'The alley is the usual place,' said the boy.

Terry fetched his pistol from a hiding place on the other side of his yard fence while the boy waited and then he followed him to the corner of the street.

'Do it here,' the boy instructed.

Terry raised the pistol and fired one shot into the boy's thigh and he crumpled, astonished. 'You fucker!'

He fell on his back, his face clenched, his hands flailing. He needed to clutch the wound but also to bite his fist to contain the pain. The blood was flowing thickly and he turned pale.

A woman came running out of her house still drying her hands on a tea towel. 'Away with you now,' she said softly to Terry. 'The ambulance is coming.'

'You called one?'

'No, it's waiting round the corner till you're gone. Go.'

Ig had only laughed when Terry told him the story and then said it was better to get them to lie down and do them from behind.

After a year at this, McGrath asked him up to his office in Thomas Clarke House. He had seen little of him since coming back from Lancaster. The office was at the top of the stairs and had extra security, the door opposite a little toilet that no one else dared use. Terry knocked and the door mechanism buzzed, allowing him to push it open. McGrath was writing in longhand in a large notebook with a Conway Stewart fountain pen and kept writing for a moment while Terry waited.

This was not a luxurious office for the top man. There were posters on the wall depicting Pearse and Connolly and one of a young Nelson Mandela. The bookshelf had some interesting choices; McGrath had been acquainting himself with the thinking of the enemy.

'Sit down, a chara,' he said when he looked up. Terry felt like a pupil in the headmaster's office, wondering if this was going to be difficult.

'Ig tells me you are doing good work in Twinbrook.'

'Good.'

'But that's wasting your talents, Terry. Things are shifting fast now and we need people like you for political work. Can I make a suggestion?'

'Go ahead.'

'Law. Let's make a lawyer out of you.'

'Just like that.'

'Doherty and Cullen will take you in as an apprentice and you'll do a degree at Queen's.'

Terry didn't bother to ask how a place at university could be found for him without him having applied for one. If McGrath had solved that problem in his own way, then that was enough. 'You're full of surprises, Dom.'

'Are you on for it?'

'Yes. I like the idea.'

'So, you'll be off operations most of the time. As far as anyone knows, you're just a trainee solicitor and a mature student. There'll be republican groups around the university; you stay away from them. OK?'

'Yes.'

'Mick Cullen is expecting you to call into the office.' Then he put his head down and picked up his nice green pen and started writing again.

Terry didn't wonder why McGrath needed lawyers. When he had been held for questioning before, the movement had always provided his solicitor; he'd had no say in the matter. Whether that solicitor was working for Terry or for McGrath, it made little difference if he was trying to keep him out of jail and if he didn't have any secrets to keep from the IRA.

Terry went back to the house in Twinbrook to pack up. He had a similar feeling to that with which he had left Lancaster: that something was unfinished here, hardly begun. He saw again the bare walls and his rucksack in the corner, still not packed away – potential unrealised. The house had never become a home, never more than a billet.

***

Cullen turned out to be a decent spud. He had an office in Dunluce Avenue, near the university. It was a large terrace house that had been converted into offices. The stairwell was dusty and worn, a sign that no one was taking responsibility for it. The company's own space was clean, well polished and even a little salubrious. A dark-haired young woman at reception, in a white blouse and tight skirt, swivelled from her typewriter to face him and was entirely unflustered by the contrast between her demeanour and his. She was used to seeing scruffy men about the place.

'You're my new apprentice, then?' said Cullen, when Terry was shown into his office. He was a portly little man in tan tweeds. He didn't rise to shake his hand, perhaps because he was heavy and didn't lift himself more often than he needed to. There were no political posters here, just framed diplomas. No family pictures either.

'So I'm told.'

'What have you done before?'

'I was a barman in Lancaster in my last job. Before that I was on the dole.'

'And school.'

'St Mary's. Three A-levels – English, Art and Religious Studies. A diploma in Media Studies from the Poly.'

'Good. You can read and write then. That's important. I want no letters going out of here with any spelling or grammar mistakes at all, even if the people getting them wouldn't know the difference. You'll have a flat in the house next door; that's ours and we'll take rent out of your earnings. I'm assuming you'll have a student grant too. I'm sure that's being sorted. Do you want some advice?'

'Of course.'

'This is going to take four years. Enjoy those years. They'll pass quickly. Stay out of trouble. No politics in the office. And I don't want to see your photo in the paper at some picket or other. Meet new people. Get your hole. OK? There's more to life than the fucking revolution.'

'Yes,' said Terry.

Cullen gave him keys to his new flat and he went next door to inspect it.

He opened the front door with a Yale key and stepped into the dark and dusty tiled hallway. The immediate smell was from the bathroom at the top of the first flight of stairs where someone had just had a shower. There was warm vapour in the air and perfumed scent mixed with sweat.

He had the front of the house on the first floor, with a large bay window giving him a view up and down the street, which was good. The room was beautiful, better than any he had lived in before. He surveyed the sanded and polished floorboards, the nice rugs and the big double bed with clean bedding on it. Prints like those all students liked, two of Mucha's seasons and Doisneau's *Kiss by the Hôtel de Ville*, hung on the walls. They'd do. There was a telephone beside the bed. He picked it up and heard the tone; it worked. He opened the wardrobe and saw that someone's clothes were there – suits and shirts. Or were these for him? He checked the sizes and they were right. Dom had thought of everything.

He had the use of a car for clearing the flat in Twinbrook and completing the move. He drove back up the Lisburn Road and into the estate from the south. On Dunmurry Lane he was stopped at an army checkpoint. The soldiers had parked an Armoured Personnel Carrier at the side of the road and spread themselves out along the footpath, four of them squatting with their rifles aimed at traffic moving through, one of them checking drivers. The soldier waiting for Terry to hand over his licence was standing with his rifle cradled in his arms to leave his hands free.

'Where are you going?'

'Twinbrook.'

'Get out of the car,' said the soldier.

Two others joined him and they searched behind and under the seats, opened the glove compartments, thumped the panelling of the doors with their fists to decide whether anything was concealed there and opened the boot and took out the flooring and the spare tyre and tools packed below it.

The lead soldier then ordered Terry to stand against the car with his hands on the roof and directed one of his men to search him. The soldier frisking him was being observed by an officer, so he wasn't going to be dilatory about it. He clenched each arm and leg and worked his way along them, back to the shoulders, up to the crotch. Then they turned him round again and told him to empty his pockets. Terry did everything he was asked to do but made no eye contact with the soldiers and said nothing apart from giving minimal answers to their questions. At the same time, he was making mental notes about them – the regiment, Royal Artillery, the build of the men and their hair colouring – on the off-chance he would see them in civvies.

'What's your line of work, Mr Brankin?'

'I'm a law student,' he said, feeling so unsure of that new reality that he would probably have registered as lying to anyone trained in looking for the indicators.

'Yes, and I'm Prince Charles. On your way, then.'

They let him repack his car, offering no help.

He hadn't much to remove from Twinbrook, just clothes and some books, his stereo and a few CDs, kitchen things and the gun. Right enough, what was he going to do about the gun? He couldn't chance driving it across town and meeting another checkpoint. Ig had never asked him about it and he wondered if he had forgotten or had decided it was his own to look after. He decided he would keep it and say nothing until someone asked for it, but he still wasn't sure how to move it. In the end, he decided to take it in the car and trust to luck. On his way back to Dunluce Avenue, he drove further west through Lisburn and back into town along the motorway. He kept the gun on the seat beside him so that he could throw it out the window if he saw a patrol ahead.

An hour later, he was sitting on his new bed admiring the arrangement of CDs beside his stereo, the books on his shelves and the wardrobe and the little drawer for ties and cufflinks that housed the gun, but which could not be its permanent home. He went downstairs to see the kitchen. It was used by everyone in the house and he saw small box-like cupboards or lockers arranged on one wall, each with a name on it: Shirley, Tom, Wilson and New

Guy; that would be his own. He opened it and it was bare. He checked the bathroom and saw the array of toiletries belonging to the other residents. The shower was over the bath and the enamel was faded and chipped. But it was all clean.

Then he walked over towards Queen's University to familiarise himself with the area. Dunluce Avenue backed onto the perimeter of the City Hospital, so many of the houses there were broken up into flats for nurses. Across the main Lisburn Road was Methodist College, a private school for middle-class Protestants. No one who was in the IRA had ever been a pupil there. These were kids who would go on to be academics, lawyers and property developers. The fascination of the place for himself and his schoolmates when he was a boy was that the school was mixed. The Catholic schools were sexually segregated.

He walked up a private street alongside the school and out onto University Road. He knew this area from having passed through it many times. He'd frequented some of the bars and had even planted a bomb in one of them. That had been a right carry-on. He'd calculated that the timer on the bomb allowed only six minutes for people to get to safety, and, not wanting to leave the customers and the dozy barman in any doubt about their need to save themselves, he had picked a glass from the bar and smashed it into a wall mirror to get attention.

'There's a fucking bomb for you. Three minutes is all you're getting, now fuck off out of here.'

It had worked. No one was hurt. He had been pleased with himself.

The main university building looked palatial, built at a time when education was a privilege for the wealthy. Behind it, the new buildings of the library and a block of lecture theatres and offices were in the prefabricated style of the new secondary schools in the suburbs: lots of glass and panelling slotted into a concrete frame.

Terry had hoped to go to university when he was younger, but rioting and then volunteering for the IRA left little time for study.

Inwardly, he bridled at the sight of this place, the feeling it created in him that he might not be good enough for it. He walked down University Square to see where the School of Law was. It didn't look like much, another house turned into offices. Then he realised that he didn't know what to do next. He had no friends around here and no work yet. Dom had effectively exiled him again.

Later that evening, Terry went into the kitchen to make a light meal and found it so complicated and awkward to work around other people's food and pots and uncleaned dishes that he resolved to buy a microwave oven for his room.

'I blame the taigs,' said a man's voice at the door.

'Sorry?' said Terry.

'It's the way they are brought up. Hello, my name's Wilson McCrea. Are you the new—?'

'I'm the new taig,' said Terry.

'Good ho,' said Wilson. 'You might be a messy lot but you do brighten the place up a bit.'

In Terry's world, sectarian assumptions like these led on quickly to head-butting, but Wilson obviously understood the rules differently.

'Terry Brankin,' said Terry. 'Don't call me a taig again or I'll break your arm.'

'Done. House rule is that you don't buy a drink on your first night. Are you OK with that?'

'I've study to catch up on.'

'Balls. We're all going round to the Welly Park. Bring Durex.'

Shirley and Tom arrived then. She was taller than Terry and thin and wore tight jeans and a little black leather jacket. Tom was tubby and balding.

'The new guy,' said Wilson, introducing him.

Terry reckoned that Wilson was gay and that Shirley wasn't with Tom. There were no sexual connections between these three.

'He's a taig,' said Wilson.

'I don't know how he gets away with that,' said Tom, who didn't like it either.

'He gets away with it,' said Shirley, 'because he really doesn't give a shit what you are.'

The lounge bar of the Welly Park was packed, so they stood, jostled by the crowd around them, shouting to be heard.

'This is the best knocking shop in town,' said Wilson.

Most of the customers, as far as Terry could make out, were young professionals rather than students. This wasn't like the pubs he knew. There were no serious discussions in corners about politics and strategy. No one seemed to be looking round to work out who the hard men were that had to be treated with respect. These weren't people who checked under their cars for bombs in the mornings or expected to be given a hard time at a checkpoint. They were managing to enjoy themselves. And yet, if he made that observation to Wilson and the others, they would think he was the odd one. If a bomb went off more than two streets away, no one in the bar would hear it.

He asked Wilson, 'Is this where people party while Belfast burns?'

'Is Belfast burning? I hadn't noticed. I thought the army had it all under control.'

Tom said, 'I'm from Cavendish Street. What I discovered when I moved here is that people in this part of town have no idea how obsessed the west is with the Troubles and the west has no idea that people over here couldn't care less.'

Terry wondered to himself if a bomb in this pub would wake them up. But he had felt the same in Lancaster at first – that people needed a good shake – and then he had settled in.

Shirley changed the subject. 'You're doing law?'

'Just started. Haven't even been to my first lecture yet. You?'

'I'm a radiographer. I can X-ray you if you've got gallstones or something stuck up your bum.'

'Do a lot of people get things stuck up their bums?'

'You'd be surprised. But that's the lighter side of it. We do cancer as well. But we had a guy in last week who said he had slipped getting out of the bath and landed on a torch battery that just happened to be on the floor. The worst part for him now is that the whole town knows about it.'

'I'll take care, then,' said Terry. 'I heard of a few accidents like that when I worked in a gay bar in Lancaster, people improvising for want of butt plugs.'

'Oh,' said Wilson. 'I was so afraid we were going to talk about British imperialism again. Butt plugs! Excellent.'

Terry saw half-familiar faces around the bar, people who might be who they looked like, boys he had been to school with, one of the Twinbrook hoods though dressed better, and therefore perhaps not him at all. The boundaries between his life in the west of the city and here might not be as firm as they appeared.

Ten

The work in the solicitor's office developed a routine. Terry had a small office and access to a library room containing most of the legal texts he would have to refer to. The business managed compensation claims against government departments, often from people who had tripped on a step or slipped on ice. He handled claims against the RUC for harassment, wrongful arrest and imprisonment. Many of these came from IRA members who had long expected to be harassed or arrested and thought it a novelty to be getting paid for the trouble.

Towards the end of his first week, the young man he had seen in the Welly Park came into the office. He was now sure it was him by the slouch, the limp, the shaved head and the spider-web tattoo. He had been one of Terry's first punishment shootings. The bullet had gone in at the front above the knee and broken the femur and torn some muscle but it would all mend.

'Remember me, Mr Brankin?' said the hood. The young man was laughing nervously, like a lazy pupil trying to stay on the right side of his teacher.

Terry checked the name – Brendan Doris. He didn't remember ever having known it.

'Is it you that's handling my claim? That's a laugh.'

Terry sat him down, went through the file and found that the police were not contesting the case and were expected to settle on a payment of £30,000.

'I suppose you lot are taking that anyway?'

Terry didn't know what to say. The hood expected him to be in charge and to make a decision.

'When my brother got done, he had to give the 'Ra half of it.'

'You'll hear in good time.'

The boy got up to leave.

'By the way,' said Terry. 'You're barred from the Welly Park.'

'Sure thing, Mr Brankin.'

Then he went to Cullen and explained the problem to him. 'He's asking what portion of the compensation payment the IRA expects to get.'

'That's between him and the IRA, Terry. Nothing to do with us.'

Cullen returned his attention to the papers in front of him, apparently exasperated at having to deal with a stupid question.

Terry attended lectures with nearly a hundred other students in the Peter Froggat Centre and took notes on the law of contract, tort, defamation and libel. One day, outside the university bookshop, he met Nuala. After locking her bicycle to a lamp post, she walked towards the shop and he ran to catch up.

'Hi.'

She turned to him, distracted at first, then astonished. 'Terry?'

They had too much and too little to say to each other.

'Shall we go for a walk?' he asked.

She laughed. 'Yes, OK.'

They crossed to the Botanic Gardens where students mingled in groups. On bright sunny days, hundreds of them would be lounging on the grass but today, though bright, was chilly.

'OK,' she said. 'You start.'

'I live in Dunluce Avenue. I have a room in a shared house. I'm studying law and I have an apprenticeship with Cullen and Doherty, though I've never met Doherty.'

'So you're still a Provo?'

'How do you work that out?'

'Do you know what the police think of Cullen? They think he is the IRA's counter-intelligence man. When they arrest someone and try to turn him, he turns up, says he's the prisoner's solicitor and the prisoner has to go along with it or he really will look like a tout.'

'You seem to know how it works better than I do. Sounds plausible though.'

'I can't see you. I can't be seen anywhere near you. I can't take any risks here.'

'Going out with a peeler?' It was a joke but it touched a nerve.

She didn't correct him. 'You see? How dangerous could that be, you even thinking that?'

And she turned and walked back towards the gate. He walked back the same way, a little distance behind her, leaving her alone. Suddenly, two men approached and stopped him. They were tall and wore loose woollen jackets, trying to look like university lecturers are supposed to look yet leave enough room for an underarm holster.

'Just let her go, Terry,' one of them said.

They blocked his path and held him until she was back at her bicycle, unlocking it and riding away.

'We'll be keeping an eye on you.'

He assumed they were Special Branch.

Had he simply stumbled on the knowledge that a woman called Nuala McCartan, who meant nothing to him, was going out with a likely target, he would have passed that news back and let Ig track her and plot how to get close enough for a hit. He wondered now how many other IRA men kept secrets from the movement to protect friends or friends of friends.

***

The criminology lecturer announced one day that a local journalist would be coming in the following week to talk about the working of informal justice systems in republican areas. She said, 'Our concern is to ask whether informal systems such as those run by the paramilitaries have a quasi-legitimate role, for all that they are illegal. Might they evolve into structures which could complement the state systems? So think about questions you may want to put to him. OK?'

The students around Terry all nodded their heads or muttered half-hearted assent as they stuffed their books back in their bags and, with a clattering of seats flapping up, shuffled out of the hall. This would be interesting, thought Terry.

The journalist was Finian Hardwick. He was a big lumbering man who looked like he could lift the back of a small car off the road to help mend a puncture, but he lacked the aggression that Terry expected to see in men who were built to be dangerous. He looked like he could fell anyone with a punch but wouldn't even dream of doing it.

Eileen, the lecturer, introduced him briefly. 'Finian is the author of a series of articles in *The Irish Times* about the punishment systems run by paramilitaries in Protestant and Catholic communities. He is a frequent guest on Radio Ulster current affairs programmes and ... what else, Finian?'

'And he is single and lives with a cat called Smirk.'

Hardwick stepped up to the podium at the front of the hall and scanned the sluggish faces of the students, many of whom had worked out that this would be an easy lecture to coast through, even doze through.

'The key question we have to ask about paramilitary punishment is whether the rationale provided for it by the paramilitaries themselves is a sufficient explanation.' He said he was going to argue that it wasn't.

'The IRA says, for instance, that they have to kneecap joyriders and drug dealers because the communities it is based in do not respect or co-operate with the police. There are certainly problems in the relationship with the police, but I've seen that the people with strongest connections to the police are the families of the young delinquents themselves. Many told me they frequently called the police to report their sons, perhaps motivated by a desire to get them caught and imprisoned before the IRA caught up with them. So the IRA's closer attention to these men becomes an incentive for the families to work *with* the police, against the declared intention of the IRA. And everyone I have spoken to who was kneecapped had actually been in prison already, in the young offenders centre mostly. The IRA has to wait sometimes for people to be released before they can shoot them – yet this on the rationale that no one else is doing anything about them.'

At the end of his talk, Hardwick stood with a studied slouch at the podium and the lecturer invited questions. Terry had a few in mind but resolved to stay silent rather than risk exposing himself as someone who knew about the inner workings of the IRA.

'Yes, Sinead.'

A girl with a Tyrone accent asked, 'Have you ever been afraid that you might get shot yourself for probing so deeply into the IRA?'

Hardwick raised himself up and, part flattered part humble, said, 'Actually one of the safest jobs in Belfast is journalism. The IRA don't attack journalists. They could probably get you beaten up and then deny they had had anything to do with it, but their policy is to leave us alone. There have been a few exceptions when somebody at a high level has got particularly annoyed or when they bombed newspaper offices in the early 1970s, but generally they have worked out that a bad press wouldn't be good for them.'

'Yet,' said the young lecturer, 'bad press is something they expect and wear quite stoically, isn't it?'

'For sure.'

There being few other questions, the lecturer thanked Hardwick and gave him a bottle of wine and a thank you card. When Terry left, Hardwick was unlocking his bicycle at the side of the building. He went over to him.

'Do you know,' said Terry, 'if the North Koreans set up offices in Andytown and didn't bother anyone, apart from shooting their own dissidents and South Koreans – if there were any up there – then sooner or later someone would call on them and say, "Could you do something about my noisy neighbours, or about my violent husband?"'

'Do you think?'

'When people need access to power, they go to the people who have it, and in parts of Belfast those people are the IRA.'

They walked back across Botanic Gardens together, at first discussing this theory, then Hardwick probing Terry about how theoretical his knowledge was.

'Do you think a journalist could get to talk to the people who actually do the kneecapping?'

'Well, there have been hundreds of kneecappings, so there are either a lot of people who have done a few or a small few who have shot a lot of kids,' Terry replied.

'Which do you think it is?'

'Where I used to live, it was commonly believed that there were only two guys doing most of it.'

'And they get good at it?'

'It's part of the common lore that a surgeon went into Thomas Clarke House and showed them where not to shoot, unless they wanted someone to bleed to death, which usually they didn't, unless maybe a paedophile.'

'And you believe that?'

'You're a journalist. It doesn't have to be true; it just has to be plausible. I'm sure if you run that story, no one will deny it.'

That week, the *Sunday News* led with a story that a Belfast surgeon had shown IRA kneecapping teams how to avoid the main artery in the leg:

'Police sources confirm that since the training session there have been fewer botched kneecappings and no deaths from punishment shootings. But Alice Molloy of the action group Stop said she was appalled at the behaviour of the anonymous surgeon. "He has effectively shown them how to kill and how not to kill, how to be better at their work of maiming young men," said Ms Molloy. The *Sunday News* also understands that the IRA is prepared to aim straight for the artery in some extreme cases, like paedophiles. These will be "deniable executions".'

By chance, Terry saw Hardwick outside the Bookshop at Queen's the next day and greeted him with a smile. 'So that's how it's done – you pick up an idea in conversation and turn it into a scoop.'

Hardwick said, 'It is basically true, though, isn't it?'

'I don't know,' said Terry, taunting him.

'Well, I have other sources and they back it up.'

'Well and good then,' said Terry.

'Tell me,' said Hardwick. 'Do you think the IRA will be rattled by that story?'

'Rattled? Why?'

'Well, it gives away something of how they work.'

'Finian,' said Terry, 'they will love it.'

'But why?'

'Because it makes them look responsible – they want to shoot people without killing them. It makes them look well integrated into society, since a surgeon comes to them and trains them. It's in line with the new image: the IRA as decent people trying to do the decent thing in difficult times.'

'Oh.'

'You thought you were taking a risk and sticking your neck out? No, they will be very pleased with you.'

'Do you have a card? Could I call you from time to time?'

Eleven

A month into his new life as a law student, Terry still hadn't found a proper hiding place for the Ruger. At the weekend, the house was usually quiet with Shirley and Tom often going to their family homes, Shirley's in Tyrone, Tom's in Cavendish Street. So he explored the backyard. People only ever went out there to put things in the bin. It hadn't been brushed or scrubbed for years. There was slimy moss on the concrete and a couple of used condoms, either slung over the wall or from a window above. There was a rusty old bicycle with flat cracked tires, a little pile of breeze blocks and the ruins of an old toilet shed. The toilet bowl itself had no seat and was blackened by God knows what, though there was scummy water in it, and when he tested the cistern with the long side chain, it failed to engage. The lever inside had broken from its fitting.

The most important consideration was that the gun should not be found, and everyone who had seen *The Godfather* would look in the cistern. The second consideration was that, if it was found, it could not be proven to be his. He had scrubbed it well. He found a loose brick in the shed wall and there was enough room for the gun and some rounds behind it. If the police raided and found it, they would know it was his, but they wouldn't be able to prove it. They'd have its forensic history from kneecappings he had done, but they'd need more than that.

He soon learnt that they were keen to find the gun. He woke early one morning when it was still dark outside and they were already in his room, one of them shining a torchlight into his face. He'd have heard them if they had smashed in the door. One in black fatigues, with a sub-machine gun crouched in his arm like a baby, had his back to him as he lifted items off the mantlepiece one by one and inspected them – a coffee mug that hadn't been washed, an ashtray he never used now and a half empty bottle of aftershave.

'Just don't move yet,' he said, without looking round.

If this had been loyalists they would have shot him and been gone by now, so he knew he was safe. This was a mobile support group, the guys who could act fast, who would be well able to chase him or shoot him in the back if he ran, but he wasn't going to run. If they had come to arrest him, he'd be out in their vehicle now and halfway down the street. This, it seemed, was a social call.

Some of them searched his drawers and test-tapped the floorboards for a loose one.

'Right, now get out of the bed, but slowly.'

Terry was naked. He picked up a shirt and put it on.

'Where's the wee Ruger?'

'I don't know what you are talking about,' he said.

'Terry, we know everything. We know every gun and bullet you guys had in Twinbrook. And there's a Ruger gone walkies.'

The one at the mantlepiece turned around and walked towards him with the opened bottle of aftershave he had been sniffing still in his hand. His face was mostly covered by fireproofing. His breath smelt of stale tobacco, his clothing of some toxic fabric softener, or something.

'We're the Branch, Terry. And we know everything. Stay away from Nools Caulfield or we'll just plant a gun on you and do you for that one.'

Caulfield? So Nuala was married. And to a cop or someone in security.

The Branch man handed him a form on a clipboard and asked him to sign it, confirming that the search had caused no damage. Terry signed it. If he hadn't, they'd have stayed to discuss it further. The cop then upended the aftershave and it glugged onto the bed. He then tossed the bottle over his shoulder into the grate, where it didn't break.

When they'd gone, Tom and Shirley came into his room, Tom in his striped pyjamas, Shirley in a tartan dressing gown and slippers.

'Are you OK?' said Tom.

'Aye. They turned the place over a bit. Sorry to bring this on you.'

'Fuck, it's not your fault,' said Shirley. 'It's jobsworths in the RUC. It was probably a fucking training exercise.'

He remembered as the shock subsided that he was standing talking to her with nothing on but a shirt. This neither perturbed her nor roused her curiosity.

'I'm going to make a cup of tea. I'll not get back to sleep now,' she said. 'Anybody want one?'

***

Terry was walking home from the university library one evening a couple of weeks after the police raid. A woman crossing University Road, and reaching the footpath about the same time as him, stumbled and screamed.

A moment before, he had run an eye over her and thought her quite lovely, entertained a quick notion that he should have a girlfriend and a life. Now she was sitting on the kerb, tousled and distressed. Terry was alert, glancing quickly round him, tracing the threat, weighing his options. He had no weapon. He didn't even know what had happened. He saw no one coming towards him or running away. But something had felled her and his immediate instinctive fear was that it was something intended for himself. That would have fitted the pattern of his life.

'Are you okay?' Terry asked, crouching beside her.

'I've broken my heel,' she said.

He thought it was almost bad taste for her to react with panic to such a small accident in a city like Belfast. In his own republican circles no one made a fuss over anything. They managed their lives as if even calamities were incidental.

She held a red shoe in one hand. The heel skewed, a little semicircle of nail points bared.

'Let me see.' He took it from her and tried to work the heel back into place. The inside of the shoe had been worn smooth by her bare foot; it smelt faintly of sweat and old leather.

'My God, this is awful,' she said.

Terry was amused. He could have gone with an impulse to sneer at her but he allowed himself to be gentler and asked, 'Have you far to go?'

'Now? Just down Camden Street,' she said. 'But the problem is I have to take my tights off.'

Right enough, he thought. She'd ruin them if she walked without the shoes.

There was a second-hand bookshop and café just a hundred yards away. He'd sometimes gone in to browse.

'There's a toilet in Bookfinders,' he told her. 'You could go in there and take them off.'

He helped her up. She put weight on his arm. She was bigger than him when she was standing. She had shoulder-length coppery hair that she shook and arranged with her hands. She was smiling.

'I feel such an eejit.'

Her face close to his was bright and warm. She had full make-up on. He could see the powder of foundation on small hairs on her cheek and her lipstick was faded.

'I'll walk with you, in case you fall again.'

She kept hold of his arm and walked slowly and tentatively over the tarmac. Bookfinders was an old terrace house full of musty books, most on shelves, some stacked in piles on the floor. The backroom was a little café where the smell of coffee took charge, and the woman who ran the place was as solicitous towards Kathleen as she would have been had she broken her leg. Terry had seen some of the wee hoods he had shot in Twinbrook make less fuss over a bullet wound.

'What size are you, love?' said the woman when Kathleen came back down barelegged. Presumably her tights were now in her handbag or pocket.

'Five and a half.'

Her own were sixes and she offered to let Kathleen walk home in them and bring them back before four o'clock. Terry thought that was a good idea but Kathleen whispered, so close to his ear that she was almost kissing it, that she would rather go home on a pogo stick than in shoes like those. She sat at a table and rubbed her feet. Terry sat with her and ordered coffee for them.

The woman in the shop said, 'Shall I call you a taxi? How far have you to go?'

Terry didn't fancy explaining to a taxi driver that they only wanted to go round the corner. There were traffic lights right outside and nowhere to park, anyway. Walking to the taxi would be nearly as awkward as walking to the flat.

'I think you're just going to have to take the hit,' he said.

He walked slowly beside her, carrying her bags as she picked her steps carefully in bare feet over tarmac. She felt her soles and heels yield abrasions to the grit and rough surfaces, but the worst was when she cut her big toe on a piece of glass. They stopped and she sat on a wall to examine the damage. Terry rubbed the soles of her feet to loosen small fragments of stone and examined the little slice the glass had made.

'That's some toe,' he said. 'You could hurt someone with that.'

She laughed. 'Oh God, this is terrible.'

'Is it far?'

'Really not. Just down there on the other side.'

'I could give you a piggyback.'

'You might have to, to get me across that street.'

'I don't know why you didn't take your woman's shoes.'

'They're like the shoes I wore to school.'

He decided that she was one of the most stupid and impractical people he had ever met, that her vanity outstripped her survival instincts. She was no soldier.

'You think I'm a fool, don't you?'

'Well, you made a foolish decision and now you are paying for it.'

They didn't say anything to each other after that until they reached the house.

She opened the front door then turned to him and said, 'I'm sorry. I've put you to a lot of trouble.'

She looked hurt and wary of him now.

'Not at all. It was a laugh. A story to tell another day.'

'I thought you were annoyed with me.'

He was a little contemptuous of her but not angry.

'We got you home, didn't we?'

'Do you want to come in for a bit?' She wasn't thinking of anything other than extending the conversation so that it might end on more clearly amicable terms.

'OK.'

Inside, he studied her bookshelves and music collection while she was in the bathroom washing and treating her feet. She was obviously into poetry and modern novels. There were no politics or history books. There was a copy of *The Joy of Sex* which piqued his interest. But the general impression was of a woman whose interests did not overlap with his own.

She returned in thick woolly socks, jeans and a jumper. 'I think I am restored to normal now,' she said. 'Would you like a cup of tea?'

'Look, I'm fine and you're alright now, so I'll just head off.'

'Have you work to do?'

'Not a lot. The usual. An essay to write.'

'There's a book launch at Queen's at 6 p.m. Would you fancy coming to that?' She picked up a card from the coffee table and handed it to him. The book was poetry, three new writers being introduced in a series called *Trio*.

'That's really not my thing,' he said.

They settled for going to the pictures to see a re-run of *A Room With a View* at the Queen's Film Theatre.

A friendly routine was established between them of going to a film or out for a meal. And they got to know each other. He would hire a car some weekends and drive them up the coast or into Donegal, and while amicability was softening into laughter, easy touching and kisses at the end of the night, it was a month before she tucked her fingers under his belt and drew him closer.

'You don't really know me,' he said.

'Tell me, then.'

'I'm a volunteer. Not that kind. I'm in the IRA. They are paying for my studies.'

'Why are they doing that?'

'Because they want a lawyer on their side.'

'So you are not actually a bomber?'

'No, but I am a full member.'

'Shit. Why didn't you tell me this?'

'Well, the rule is you don't.'

'So, if we had a relationship, they would come first?'

'Or I would leave.'

'Do you want to leave?'

'I didn't expect this choice to come at me so fast.'

'Well,' she said, 'it's yours to make.'

***

The professor was young, about forty, and he sat behind an oak desk overburdened with books. He smoked a pipe. 'What's the problem?' he asked.

Terry composed himself then said it. 'I am in the IRA.'

'OK. You'll know that one of your people shot a lecturer here a couple of years ago.'

'Yes. That wasn't me.'

'And what do you want?'

'I want to leave the IRA and continue with the course here.'

'A laudable decision. Where's the difficulty?'

'The IRA is paying for my course. They set me up with an apprenticeship and they provide me with a flat.'

'How comprehensive of them.' The professor then added, 'Your fees are paid till the end of the year. We could help you get another apprenticeship with little difficulty. As for accommodation …'

'That's OK. I'm moving in with my girlfriend.'

'And far be it from me to concern myself with paramilitary affairs, but aren't you putting yourself in some danger by extracting yourself?'

'I don't think so.'

Twelve

Kathleen waved as Nools got into the taxi at the Wellington Park gate. It felt good to be outside in the fresh air. Although she was grateful to Nools for having come with clothes, she needed to buy some of her own. It was time to get practical. The first thing she needed was a handbag, so she went straight to Debenhams. She was delighted to see they still had the Jasper Conran hobo bag in grainy black leather that she had bought a few months back but had gone up in flames at home last night. On another level, she tried on one pair of cords to confirm that she was even fatter than the last time and then bought three pairs in different colours. The jumpers were fairly standard. They came in smoky grey or a shade of toffee for those who weren't feeling flash, or in stark primary colours for a girl brave enough to want attention. She didn't, so that was two dependable jumpers on her arm. Now she felt she was getting her life under control. Bras and knickers next. In Marks & Spencer, on the escalator coming up from the food hall, she saw a tall lean man she recognised as one of the IRA prisoners who had gone on hunger strike for political status back in the 1980s. She entertained a gratuitously nasty thought about him: I wonder how many broccoli quiches you have to eat to make up for what he went through?

Then she went into Pretty Woman, thinking she might be of a mind to buy some nice tops. There she discovered she was still as fat and weary as she had been in Debenhams. She would need to plan full outfits and she just didn't have the creative energy. She had to keep reminding herself of the base line: she had nothing. She visualised what had been lost in the fires – dozens of full outfits. Some of them were twenty years old but too precious to discard.

It wasn't a few clothes that she had to buy, it was a life. So she sat with a latte and made a list that started with practical shoes and a coat and expanded to include make-up, shampoo, jewellery, a toothbrush, a wee radio, her essential oils, cotton buds, Nurofen and her favourite toilet paper – everything. She felt disconsolate and helpless. Then she started again and wrote down the most urgent items, knowing well that she would overlook some things, but that she had no choice but to start. Pyjamas, tights, soap, socks and shoes, tops and blouses, two jackets and Nurofen. That would be her target list for today. Then she would go back to the hotel and sleep – properly this time.

***

Once into open countryside, Terry began to relax. It was a beautiful day for a trip to Donegal whatever the reason for going. But the energy was draining out of him. At a lay-by on the Sperrins, he stopped to stretch his legs and think. He sat on a stile and surveyed the humpbacked granite mountains around him. Once they had been peaks like the Himalayas but the polar ice had come down and polished them smooth. That's what he had been told at school anyway. Presumably the ice would come again some day and finish the job.

Back to mind came memories of past trips along this road, almost all of them holidays. He was going farther north-west towards the mountainous fringe of the Atlantic, where his problems had always seemed smaller. It had never felt to him that his war had been for this land. He had never felt remotely conflicted about it. He had no sense of entitlement to it or any sense either that the British had taken it. What would they do with it, cart it back to London? The war had always been about life in the city, the behaviour of soldiers on the streets, the people who wielded power.

He had known some of the country IRA men who could read the fields and hills the way he could read the streets, knowing which part of the land was Protestant, which valley had been stolen from which family 400 years before. All of that had seemed irrelevant to him. Anyone who was killing policemen to restore rights lost in the seventeenth century was just too ambitious altogether.

Further on he went into a garage shop and checked what was on offer. He didn't like the look of the cooked pasties, chubby chips or runny confections, so he took a bar of chocolate. Back in the car, he turned on the radio news and heard that the police were looking for him.

'Following last night's horrific house fires, all of them at properties owned by Belfast solicitor Terry Brankin, police say they hope to speak to Mr Brankin, who apparently has disappeared.'

He sensed mischief behind this. The police could have phoned him if they had more questions. He cursed them and decided to take the scenic route! Instead of carrying on into Derry, he turned into the hills at Claudy and drove the meandering road through the valley towns of Donemana and Artigarvan. From the hill over Artigarvan he had a clear view to the far north and could see Errigal and Muckish, small on the blue horizon.

He crossed the border on the Camel's Hump, the bridge between Strabane and Lifford. There was no checkpoint on it now but he had seen it, and circumvented it, when it was one of the most heavily guarded frontier posts in Europe. He had driven guns and explosives from dumps in Donegal into Derry, along unmapped little roads and across the river at night. No power on earth could have stopped the IRA smuggling across such a frayed border.

There were reminders all around him now of a changed country: the huge supermarket with a carpark near the size of a football field, and it full. But it wasn't so long since he had been a skulking guerrilla here. This area had been drab then; the statistics still said it was poor. He had acquired skills in these streets and fields: physical skills like averting danger, using weapons and priming bombs; psychological skills like reading other people's moves, coping with the emotional backwash of his own bloody actions, keeping himself sane and keeping others sane.

He stopped again in Letterkenny and bought fish and chips to bring back to the car. There would be fewer people who would know him here or have heard the news beyond reach of the radio station's signal, but there might be some of his old republican comrades around town. Some had bought holiday homes in the area and just preferred to stay away from Belfast, where they had offended too many people over the years to be sure they were safe.

From Letterkenny he drove west to Glenties along a much more meandering road that clung to the side of the valley and avoided the floor of it. Beyond Glenties he turned south towards Inver and across a high moor. This would have been great battlefield terrain, he thought, if we had ever had that kind of war, for a man could lie down in the heather with his rifle and no one would see him; he'd even be warm. But no one worth shooting ever came here.

He saw the roof of his cottage first and it looked bleak and dead, but at least the slates he had put on it still held. It was close to a little fishing river in which he had plodded occasionally and had long intended to learn to catch trout in some imagined future when he and Kathleen would be free to pass weeks at a time here. It chilled him to consider that it was the only home they now had, and it was a dump.

The cottage itself was a single-storey long cabin, probably built in the nineteenth century, with a stone floor and an open fireplace. There was a half-attic where there was a double bed, but no dividing wall. One day he might get out of that bed drunk and fall down onto the dining table, or crack his head on the floor. The smoke from the fire used to fill the whole space when the wind blew down the chimney. He had liked this cottage because he felt it connected him with his peasant forebears, though it did nothing of the kind. It wasn't fit to stay in yet. He expected to find no fresh food in the cupboard. He should have stopped in Glenties and bought food and drink in the Spar shop. He'd have to go in to Frosses now, because although he was exhausted, and would soon fall asleep if he went in and lay down, it would be horrible to wake up in the dark and have nothing for comfort, nothing to eat and only the spluttering peaty water in the tap to drink. But he would have to face people who knew him.

In the Irish countryside, strangers tilt the head at each other as they pass on the road. Drivers meeting on country lanes greet each other with just a light lift of the index finger off the steering wheel. He had been noticed often enough in the neighbourhood now and word would have gone round that he was back. Should he expect a visit from the Gardaí? Well, he would be able to gauge how seriously the police really believed he'd burnt his houses by the level of interest they took in him now. Let them come.

In the Spar he bought tea, bread, cheese, potatoes, a cabbage, half a dozen eggs, butter, a dozen cans of Guinness and a couple of bales of peat briquettes. Back in the house, he found clean bedding in the trunk, sniffed it and decided that it was as good as dry. In half an hour he was asleep. He didn't care when he'd wake up.

***

Terry awoke to soft daylight and birdsong. He lay still for a while and wondered what time it was and found he couldn't even be sure of the day. Still, he was well rested and even felt for a moment like a man who had a home and a wife, but then consciousness sharpened and disabused him. And he remembered that he had battles to fight.

Without washing or eating anything, he went to the front door of the cottage. He judged by the angle of the sun that it was just about an hour after dawn. He had the whole countryside to himself. Cattle stirred far off. Perhaps some had mistaken him for the one who would come and feed them. There was a near-metallic chill in the breeze. From the doorstep he could see the line of the sea in the distance, between low round hills, one with a tower on it – a folly. At the back of the cottage the hill rose steeply and roughly. He had often relied for water on a spring at the foot of that hill, having bought the cottage in the days before water was sold bottled in the shop.

He stretched and breathed deeply and contemplated the gravity of what he would do next. There was a small meadow below him, where he had once considered growing vegetables. He had given up the idea and his whole attachment to this place when his workload increased. He took a small trowel from a lean-to that he used as a store. It had probably been built onto the side of the cottage to house a goat. In the meadow, the grass was high and brittle, and the dead yellow growth of previous years was tangled in it so that it was spongy underfoot. Anyone suspecting that there was something secretly buried there would look for a marker, like a rock or a tree stump. His private joke was the measurements in paces from a flat stone: nineteen in the direction of the oak tree then sixteen to the left. When he stood on the spot there was nothing to indicate that the ground had ever been broken through. He would have to trust his calculations.

Down on his knees on damp earth, he pulled at the thick grass to clear a patch of soil. Clumps came away in his hands by the roots, but this was too difficult. It was fifteen years since he was last on this spot. To get started, he had to plunge the trowel in like a sword. He tore away more bunches of grass in his fists and scraped the ground to make more room for his digging, then hacked at the soil and tangled grass until he turned fresh, wet, heavy clay. If he was in the right place, he would not have to dig deeply. If he was in the wrong place, just a few inches of penetration would confirm that, and he would go back to the stone and pace the directions again.

He was off by just inches and knew it when he scraped the corner of the tin. That meant that he had to rip away more of the grass around it and dig further to the right. There could be no cheating with a job like this. He had to get the whole tin out and therefore had to take away all the soil that covered it and much that pressed around it. He had imagined this would take five minutes; it took forty. Still, the morning was clear and there was no sound of traffic nearby.

It was an old Huntley & Palmers biscuit tin. The rust on the rim of the lid had formed a seal. He had filled the tin with motor oil but it had somehow mostly drained away, though the inside and the rag were still moist with it. The rag was tied with string and he cursed himself for having been so pointlessly thorough. No one who had got this far would have allowed their curiosity to be deterred by his knots, no matter how good they were. Finally he had the gun uncovered and in his hand, drenched and blackened with dirty oil. There was the little bag of bullets too, looking fine. Just holding it and feeling the weight of it reminded him that he knew well how to use it. Muscles have memories. Once cleaned, the wee Ruger would work perfectly. He flipped open the chamber and loaded one round into it.

Now was the time to test it. One shot. Who would hear?

He pointed at the ground about ten yards ahead of him and, with outstretched arms to take the jolt, he squeezed the trigger. It felt good, like an awakening.

***

A shot fired in a city street always misses more people than it hits. Most don't notice how lightly chance has spared them. There may be hundreds in a city like Belfast who were once nearly killed and don't know it. They heard the loud clean pop and before they turned to look around, the bullet had finished its journey, through a window, into brickwork or timber, or through flesh and bone into one or even two people. You don't hear the one that gets you. Some of those in whom bullets finish up have been waiting for them, maybe for years; they will have known the danger. Some of them, perhaps, have been shot before, or have shot others. That's the economy of violence.

Kathleen did not know for sure, at first, whether she had heard a gunshot, a firework or a car backfiring. In the same moment, someone tugged her sleeve and jolted one of her shopping bags from her hand. She swung to defend herself but no one was there. She was crossing the Malone Road in front of the hotel, where no one had tugged at her, no one had jolted anything out of her hand and where the traffic flowed on past. Shoppers walked the footpath unperturbed, some a little bewildered by the sharp bang, but already putting it out of their minds and wondering if she was drunk, that woman, scrambling to pick her bags up off the road.

A girl on a red bicycle, her hair lifted a little by the breeze she made, turned momentarily to look, as if these events were merely interesting. Kathleen got herself to the other footpath and examined her shopping. There was a large tear in the bag that had been ripped from her. Inside it she saw her purchases apparently intact. She did not notice that a grey Nissan Micra in the hotel car park now had a perfectly round hole punched into a side door. Nor would anyone else notice it until the car's owner checked out of the hotel the next morning.

Kathleen still hadn't understood what had happened. She was tired when she got to her room and lay down and slept through the night, bewildered and worried but mostly now just exhausted. Next morning, before even having a shower, she could admire her nice handbag, still intact. She unpacked the carrier bag and set each item out on the crumpled bed. The woollen jumpers were nice. She had chosen well. First she saw a tear in one of the blouses and then discovered that nearly all the new clothes of lighter fabrics were torn and the packet of Nurofen looked as if it had been crushed by a hammer. She checked the woollens again and found holes in them too.

'Jesus, no!'

There was worse. When she hung up the new coat she had worn out of the shop, she found two small holes in the sleeve. The bullet had passed within millimetres of her skin.

***

'I need you here. Where are you?' Kathleen said.

Terry wondered what had changed.

She needed protection.

'Someone shot at me.'

'Are you sure?'

'Yes, I'm sure.'

'But you're OK?'

'How could I be OK?'

'The bullet missed?'

'It ripped up all my new clothes and even the coat I was wearing.'

He asked for every detail and she knew he was reading meanings that she couldn't conceive of. That annoyed her.

'I hope you don't think this is some fucking adventure that will be great crack for you.'

Terry knew others who had been missed as neatly. One took the bullet straight through the trunk of his body and with no organs damaged needed no medication but valium. One had had his hair parted without the bullet breaking skin.

'Have you told the police?'

'No. And everyone just assumed it was a car backfiring. That's what I thought myself at first.'

'Fuck, have they never heard a car backfiring before?'

'Maybe they have never heard a gunshot before.'

He'd have to attend to her mood while thinking this through.

'When did this happen?'

'Yesterday afternoon.'

'And you've waited till now to tell me?'

'I'm still wondering if I should have bothered. Someone shot at me!'

The words sounded ridiculous, like they shouldn't be believed. She'd not believe them herself if someone else was speaking them. 'You seem to think that that is merely interesting.'

Well, it was. It required a lot of thinking about but there was no point in exploring the implications with her. Terry suggested that she book out of the hotel. She should then drive to the cottage and stay there.

'Just relax for a few days here and let me sort out what I can in Belfast. Please, love.'

He reasoned that the Provos would be coaxed out of attacking Kathleen if they could see there was no point, that the damage was done. He realised that he was going to have to confess to the Magheraloy killing and serve his sentence. Giving himself up would be the best way to outflank them. Otherwise this would just go on and on.

Yet there was much that made this shooting unlike any planned IRA attack. Single shots weren't their style. There was always a support team and usually another gun in case one jammed. But the IRA was broken because, more often than not, one of those on the support team would be an informer. Actually, Terry thought, if I was going to shoot somebody, I would do it alone, and maybe Ig too has copped on that that makes more sense. But Ig wouldn't have missed.

***

Kathleen did not know what she wanted to do. She was raging that she had nothing of her own but a handbag, her car and a few clothes. At least there was still money, but at the rate at which things were being stripped from her, she feared she would soon be a bag lady on the street.

Ha, she laughed to herself. At least there wasn't much to pack.

She went through the bag of clothes that had taken the bullet and found a few pieces that were not marked or torn. She put on one of the woollen jumpers and assured herself no one would notice the holes in it.

'I hope you enjoyed your stay,' said the receptionist.

***

She stopped at the big new supermarket in Strabane and walked the aisles with her trolley, first thinking about food for the next few days then noticing that she could get clothes here and toiletries, even a new laptop. She filled one trolley and took it to the car and then went back and filled it again and piled bags and boxes into the rear seat.

It was late afternoon and raining lightly when she turned up the stony lane. The sight of that evening sunlight reflected on the whitewashed old frontage had heartened her a hundred times before, when they had come here only for pleasure, and even now a reflex anticipation of ease and comfort relaxed her fears. She could smell the turf smoke from the fire; turf from their own share of the bog on the hill.

Terry came out to the half door and smiled at her as she drew the car over the rough path alongside his own. She got out of the car, and he held her tightly. He was going to have to protect her. He helped her unload the groceries and bags and boxes, wondering where everything would go but knowing better than to comment.

'I've a dinner on and there's hot water for a bath,' he said.

The bathroom in the cottage was a gauche flat-roof extension with mould on the inner walls. There were a few things of her own that she kept for visits – her oils, shampoo and her own towels, which were a bit musty from the cupboard. She was reminded that some semblance of home still existed for her. Unpacked, her purchases filled the little cupboards; bottles lined the edge of the bath and others stood precariously on the toilet cistern, like a model of Manhattan. The taps chugged at first then ran vigorously. She didn't mind the water being peaty; it was good for her skin. When she was settled, he came in, handed her a gin and tonic and left without saying anything.

The dinner was smoked haddock and potatoes boiled in their skins. The sauce was butter. The vegetable was broad beans. There was a choice of Gewürztraminer or Guinness.

'I had no idea how much I needed this,' she said, when she settled on the sofa before the fire after they had eaten. 'Can we just leave the conversation about how we cope until the morning?'

'Of course,' he said.

In half an hour she was asleep, and he nudged her and coaxed her to the bedroom. As he laid her down she opened her eyes for a moment and said, 'I'm sorry, I'm fit for nothing.'

He kissed her on the brow then drew the duvet up over her. He went back, sat by the fire and looked into the flames. There was someone who would have killed this woman. He could accept his own death more readily than he could accept hers. If he had to, he would kill to protect her. And he could, now that he had the gun.

Thirteen

Summer always takes Belfast by surprise. The narrow streets around the university where Terry and Kathleen lived were not a natural space for carnival. During winter, the house fronts were in shadow for most of the day. They were transformed when the sun was high and strong. Terry came back from lectures one day to find Kathleen sitting on a chair in the doorstep to savour the heat on her arms and legs, her cotton dress turned up above her knees, her feet bare.

He had gone out that morning with a jumper on under his jacket as if he hadn't noticed the arrival of a new season.

'Go and take that off. Put on a T-shirt or something. Oh and bring me a wee cider; there's a bottle in the fridge.'

'I've an essay to write.'

'Everyone on this street has an essay to write. Look around and tell me if you think they are bothered.'

He had seen the bare-chested boys playing with a frisbee and his first thought had been to pity their innocence. She saw them differently.

The news that morning said that a young policeman called Thompson had been shot dead getting out of a car on Ulsterville Avenue. He had been driving his pregnant wife to the antenatal clinic. She hadn't got out of the car and they hadn't shot her, but she had seen her husband crouch first, as if a child's thrown ball had hit him on the shoulder. Then she had seen him go down.

'That was awful,' said Kathleen, when they had heard the news on the radio over breakfast.

'Out of order,' said Terry, who only meant that he would have done it differently, though he wasn't even sure of that.

'Life goes on, love,' he'd said. And here now was the evidence of that: the summer sun was making the streets glow, and though the pregnant Mrs Thompson was no doubt suffering the worst day of her life, young men played like children on the street, the cider was nicely chilled and Terry was now in a T-shirt and shorts.

She said, 'We have a new lecturer for Modern Irish Poetry, a nice fella. Tom Donnelly.'

'I know him. Is he lecturing?'

'Well, he's a post grad. Still doing his PhD on James Simmons. How do you know him? Don't tell me he was in the IRA too.'

'We shared a house in Dunluce. Used to go drinking with others in the Welly Park and the Four in Hand. Nice fella.'

'We could have a barbecue and invite him over,' she said.

'If you had a barbecue here you'd have half the street turning up.'

'Then let's invite him to dinner. Has he a girlfriend?'

'Not that I know of. Shirley was one of the others in the house. We could ask them both. Then there's Wilson, but he's a bit hard to take.'

'What's wrong with him?'

'He's a Prod and a fruit.'

'Terry! Do people still talk like that?'

'He does.'

Terry walked over to Dunluce Avenue that afternoon. A young woman he guessed was German opened the door to him. She went back to the living room and said to someone there, 'Are you Tom?'

Wilson then came out to the door and roared, 'Terry boy. So they haven't caught up with you yet?'

Wilson was dressed in cycling shorts and a bright yellow, tight-fitting shirt. 'Don't come too close, I'm stinking. Just been humping drumlins and haven't had a shower yet.'

'Well you know I'm over in Camden Street with Kathleen, my girlfriend. We're having a wee dinner party and wondering if you and Tom and Shirley would like to come over.'

'I don't think the others are in, but I'll come and I'll make sure they come with me.'

'Great,' said Terry, and left him the details.

On the day of the party it amazed and slightly annoyed him how much work Kathleen was putting into preparing it.

'For fuck's sake, these are people I shared a seedy old house with. They probably think if the place is spotless they aren't really welcome. They're the kind who put their feet up on a chair. They don't know what coasters are for, and if you give them a starter they'll think you are being pretentious.'

That wounded her. 'It shows respect. If they don't know what that is, the loss is theirs.'

She bought crystal glasses to replace the goblets she had brought home in her handbag over several weeks from the Four in Hand. She had a set of embroidered napkins that had only been used once, when he moved in, and she told him what wine to buy and not to be coming back with wine in a box or anything South African.

'As if.'

He prolonged his shopping to be out of her way while she hoovered and scrubbed and timed the roast in the oven.

'Jesus,' he thought. 'They don't have these problems in Long Kesh.'

When he came back she had spread out a tablecloth he had never seen before and set five places, with napkins and two wine glasses of different sizes at each. Perfumed candles were flickering in the sitting room.

'What if one of them is asthmatic?'

'Then we'll blow them out.'

Terry noted that she had carefully placed a book on the coffee table, to look as if she had just been reading it. It was a copy of *The Selected James Simmons*.

The doorbell rang.

'Action stations!'

'I'll get it,' he said.

He ran down the two flights of stairs and opened the door to Tom and Wilson. Tom had a bottle of wine. Wilson had wine and flowers.

'Shirley's at home this weekend,' said Tom.

'With a month's accumulation of knickers for the wash,' Wilson added, with a smirk.

Upstairs, Terry introduced them to Kathleen.

'Mwah,' said Wilson, kissing her cheek and sending a frisson of delight through her.

'I know you already, don't I?' Tom said.

'I'm one of your bothersome undergrads.'

'Well, thanks for the invitation.'

Terry took the wine and poured the drinks and led them to the living room. Tom and Wilson sat side by side on the sofa. Tom picked up the poetry book and put it back down again.

'I hope you haven't had more police raids since I left,' Terry said.

'Funny that,' said Wilson. 'They just don't seem to have the same interest in the rest of us. Should we feel slighted?'

'I knew a guy at school whose brother was in the 'Ra and he was getting stopped all the time,' said Tom.

'We haven't been raided here either,' said Terry, to make the point that the police weren't still hounding him and didn't regard him as dangerous any more.

'How's the course coming along?' said Tom, throwing away his own hopes of not spending the night talking about university.

'It's good. I'll be a lawyer and will make a living.'

Then Kathleen called them to the table.

'You don't say Grace now, do you?' said Wilson. 'I mean, one can get these things so wrong.'

'We're taigs but we're not Catholics,' said Terry, and Kathleen slapped him playfully with the tea towel.

Terry filled up the glasses again and Kathleen served the first course, which was prawn cocktail. Tom and Wilson talked about how different life was now in the house in Dunluce Avenue.

'Her name is Eva, the German girl,' said Wilson. 'She leaves notes in the bathroom. Like, "Please flush also after urination".'

'I didn't see that one,' said Tom. 'She leaves them in the kitchen too. And she puts Post-it stickers on her milk and butter in the fridge. She's horrific.'

'Sounds to me,' said Kathleen, 'as if she's domesticated. Maybe just what you boys need.'

'Listen,' said Wilson, 'I have been wiping my own bottom unaided since I was three years old. The last thing I need is to be overseen by Frau Himmler in my own home.'

'Her name isn't really Himmler, is it?' said Terry.

'No, of course not.'

'And she brings men back and howls like a stricken beast in her bedroom,' said Wilson.

'I've yet to hear that,' said Tom.

'Are you sure it wasn't the man who was howling?' said Kathleen.

Wilson said, 'I've been with a lot of men at the critical moment, and I have yet to hear anything like that.'

The second course was roast beef with roasted potatoes, carrots and cabbage, and Kathleen was pleased to see that both her guests finished everything and accepted her dessert of apple tart and ice cream.

The conversation had ranged from the housemates in Dunluce to the growing number of gay clubs in Belfast.

'I worked in a gay bar in Lancaster for a time,' said Terry.

'I'd forgotten about that. Bet that was fun,' said Wilson.

'Oh aye. You'd have been right at home in the Farmer's Arms.'

'I've never shagged a farmer,' he said. 'How could he ever be clean, working with all that silage? I mean, what is silage anyway?'

By the time they were settled on the sofa and into the third and fourth bottle of wine, Tom was ready to talk poetry with Kathleen.

'I like Simmons because he is unpretentious. He doesn't go for all that stuff about curlews and Odysseus. What the fuck has that to do with me?' he said.

Kathleen said, 'I don't know. Sometimes I think he is just bawdy for the sake of it.'

'Yet, you listen to that song about the Claudy bomb. He knows how to really stun you: "And Christ little Kathryn Eakin is dead". That line, you know, it's like it's just sunk in with you that they have killed a child. Amazing. Like you're with the neighbours when they've been told. I don't think Heaney or Longley would have been as colloquial or even as immediate as that. It's like he's acknowledging that things are so bad, all you can do is swear. "Christ!" Like these other guys would have worked to hone the most succinct summation of horror and dazzled us with the apposite word, and he has got it straight from the gut. A child is dead; it's the only thing that matters. "Christ!" The curse that is a prayer. I just have to find a way of describing that in 20,000 words and I'll have a dissertation.'

Then Terry said, 'Are we ready for a wee nip?' and he produced the whiskey.

'For me, Heaney is the daddy of them all,' Kathleen said.

'That's because he is so personally nice. Heaney could sit on stage and read you an Enid Blyton story and you'd go oooh and aaah and find depth in it you'd never known was there. He sells more poetry than anyone else, but people buy it to remind themselves of his rustic charm.'

'That's not fair.'

'No, you're right. But that personality thing is in there too. He gets a thousand people coming to the Whitla Hall to see him read. You're not telling me they are all poetry lovers, when no other poet sells more than a few hundred copies of a book. We don't have a thousand poetry lovers in the whole country.'

Wilson said, 'Answer me this, though. Who was it that wrote "The Good Ship Venus"?'

'You know, I left that one off my reading list this year,' said Tom.

***

Terry woke the following morning with a horrific hangover, feeling as if he had been punched in the head. Kathleen was beside him breathing softly and he nuzzled into her for comfort.

'What time did they go?' he asked her.

'Don't you remember?'

'No.'

'You were competing to see who could remember most verses of "The Good Ship Venus",' said Kathleen with a giggle.

'Oh God.'

'Tom's nice, isn't he? Wilson's just appalling. I doubt my mother has any sense that people like him even exist.'

He got up and walked through to the living room and then the kitchen, where he saw that the glasses had been tidied away and all the dishes washed. He doubted he had played much part in that. He turned on the news and heard that a man's body had been found on the Hightown Road; the unionists were meeting the Secretary of State to complain about something and a factory was closing. 'Nothing changes,' he muttered. He put on the kettle and brought Kathleen tea in bed. Then he realised he was exhausted and got back in beside her.

'Have you any lectures today?' he asked.

'Yes. In fact, we have Tom.'

He was asleep again when she left.

A little while later he was aware of her sitting on the side of the bed. She was dressed and made up.

'Not gone yet?'

'I've been and come back. Tom didn't show up.'

'He's probably sleeping off a hangover.'

'I feel guilty about that. I knew he was working today and yet kept topping up his glass.'

'He's a big boy.'

'But it's bad. He's taking lectures for his supervisor and he needs to be on the right side of him.'

Terry tried to end the conversation and get over the awful feeling of being half drunk. 'I'm sure they expect this sort of thing to happen.'

'Should I phone him and check he's OK?'

He was on his way to the bathroom and didn't hear her. It was now past two o'clock in the afternoon. He wondered if a bath would be better than a shower for taking the edge off his nerves. He felt too sensitive for a shower. When he had settled she came in and sat on the rim, looking worried.

'They've found a body up the mountain. Hightown Road.'

'And you're thinking it's Tom. What are the odds?'

'Can you not phone him and check?'

He knew she would only worry until she knew Tom was safe.

'I need to just soak here for a while and mend.'

But when she left him he couldn't relax, so he got up and phoned the house in Dunluce Avenue.

'Tom is not here,' said Eva. 'I don't know where he is.'

He asked about Wilson.

'I will see.'

He heard her knocking on a door and calling, 'Wilson, there is a call.'

But there was no answer to that either.

'It still doesn't mean anything,' he said to Kathleen. 'Maybe they went somewhere after they left us. Maybe they have been home and gone out again. Maybe they are sleeping it off in their rooms and just not answering.'

He wished she wasn't listening to the radio news throughout the day and making herself more anxious. Yet again, he heard the earnest voice of the newscaster: 'Police are still trying to identify the body of a man, thought to be in his thirties, found at the side of the Hightown Road in North Belfast this morning. They say he is about 5 foot 6 and has thinning brown hair. A post-mortem is to be held this evening but police say early indications are that the man was beaten and shot in the head.'

'Oh, Jesus,' said Kathleen. 'I know it's him. I just know it.'

'Up the Hightown Road? That's miles away.'

The evening paper didn't tell them much, just that some

speculation suggested that the man was killed in a dispute between loyalists.

The six o'clock television news had the name and a picture: 'The man found shot dead at the side of the Hightown Road this morning has been identified as Martin Thomas Donnelly, a student at Queen's University Belfast.' The picture showed a younger man in a graduation gown.

'It's not him,' said Kathleen. 'Thank God.'

'Kathleen,' said Terry, 'it *is* him.'

'He's Martin. He's a student not a lecturer.'

'Lots of people have two Christian names. It is him, love.'

She sat in stunned silence as the presenter came back to the story: 'Police are asking anyone who knows the last movements of Mr Donnelly to get in touch with them.'

'We'll have to go and see them.'

Terry stood up and put on his coat. 'I'm going to see Wilson. Don't call the police yet. The little we can tell them won't be much use.'

Terry walked over to Dunluce Avenue and Eva answered the door again.

'Tom definitely isn't in yet.' She hadn't heard the news. 'Wilson I think is in but not well. He's not answering.'

He brushed past her into the hall and sprinted up the stairs to Wilson's room.

'Wilson, we need to talk.'

He opened the door and saw Wilson sitting inert in an armchair, looking up at him, sluggish and stunned. Terry walked into the room and sat on the edge of the bed and faced him. 'What happened?'

'I can't believe it,' said Wilson. There was none of his playful gay affectation now, just a sombre and dull voice.

'Do you know any of what happened?'

'Two guys stopped us when we left your house. They had been watching. Loyalists. They had guns. They took us into the alley at the end of your street. They worked out that I was a Prod. They asked me how I knew you. I said we lived in the same house once. Then a car came and they put Tom in the car and told me to fuck off. I came back here. When I heard the news this morning, I knew it was Tom.'

'And you didn't go to the police?'

'No.'

'Why not?'

'I don't want the hassle.'

'What hassle? You know these guys?'

'I would know them again. I'd end up being a witness. That can get you killed.'

Terry wasn't sure whether to believe him. 'You've seen these guys in the area. You know them.'

'I don't know their names. There is one that I've seen on the street. A skinhead with a snake tattoo on his right arm.'

'What's his fucking name?'

'Tatlock. He's a wee creep that went to the same school as me. We called him Dinko, and there he was standing in front of me with a gun pointing at me and pretending he didn't know me.'

'You're going to have to talk to the police. Kathleen will tell them we had you over. Just say that you don't know who the guys were, that they were wearing masks. Leave it at that. I'll do Tatlock,' Terry said.

'You'll do what?

'I'll pass his name up the line. He'll get done.'

'Oh fuck. I don't want to be part of this.'

'You're not. Just go to the police. Tell them everything. Just keep yourself covered by saying you have no idea who they were and that you wouldn't be able to identify them. If you get called to view an identity parade, just pick the wrong guy.'

Terry left, knowing that he could have done some good for Wilson by sitting with him a while and helping him to absorb the shock and grief and had chosen not to bother.

Kathleen was sullen and quiet when he went back to her. 'Did you find him?'

'Yes. They were picked up off the street near here by loyalists who let him go and took Tom away in a car.'

'Oh God. It could have been any of us.'

'We better talk to the police. I'll go down to Donegall Pass and make a statement.'

'Are you sure? Would that be enough?' she asked.

'If they want to talk to you separately they will say so.'

'I can't take it in,' she said.

At the police station, Terry pressed a bell on the door of the security cage. A policeman stood in a reinforced brick sangar to the side of the door, studied him from behind the armoured glass but said nothing and made no sign. A buzzer signalled that the gate was ready to open. He went through and faced another armoured door. He heard a click and then he pushed that and was through into the reception area. A couple of people sat on a bench waiting to be seen. He went to the counter and spoke to a middle-aged balding policeman in a white shirt with his jacket off. It surprised him that people were so relaxed in here when the architecture outside was designed in readiness for snipers and mortar attacks.

'I'm Terry Brankin.'

'I know who you are,' said the policeman.

'I was with Tom Donnelly last night before he was killed. Do you want me to make a statement?'

'You didn't kill him, did you?'

'No.'

'What do you want to say in your statement?'

'That he and another friend were having dinner with me and my girlfriend and that he left us about 1.00 a.m.'

'OK. Sit and wait there and I'll get someone to talk to you.'

He sat on the bench beside two skinny fretful people, a man and a woman. And he waited. He studied the wall, watched his breathing and took care not to get restless or impatient, knowing that they would have little inclination to make this easy for him.

After about twenty minutes, a trim young man in a grey suit came down the hall and said, 'Mr Brankin. So sorry to keep you waiting. Will you come this way?' He led him to a bleak little interview room. 'I'm Detective Sergeant Derek Marriot. I believe you have a statement to make about the killing of Martin Donnelly.'

'Yes, we called him Tom.'

'And how did you know him?'

'We lived in the same shared house in Dunluce Avenue. Then my girlfriend knows him through Queen's.'

'So, what have you to tell us?'

'Not much, but you asked for people who could account for his movements to call you. Tom had dinner with us last night and left at about 1.00 a.m.'

'Who else was there?'

'Another friend called Wilson McCrea, who also lives in the Dunluce house.'

'Very well. You didn't see Mr Donnelly or hear from him after he left you?'

'No.'

'And you didn't hear any commotion on the street outside?'

'No.'

'Had you all drunk a lot last night?'

'Yes.'

'Including Mr Donnelly?'

'Yes.'

'OK. Let's get something written down. It won't take long.'

After he had completed the statement, Marriot said, 'I suspect they were watching you and would have been very happy if you had come out with the others last night.'

'Knowing that, will you be keeping a close eye on the house?'

'These are busy times. I suggest you do what you can within the law to look after your own security.'

***

Kathleen moved fretfully about the flat as if looking for distraction. Terry found he couldn't comfort her.

'OK, I'll be frank,' she said. 'I can't help feeling that this is our fault. Your fault. It's you they wanted to kill.'

'That's right,' he said. 'This is what they do. They go out looking for IRA men, generally don't find them, and then shoot someone else instead, so long as it's a Catholic. If they hadn't been trying to get me, they would have had some other name on a target list and most likely have ended up shooting some other Tom, someone like him.'

'This country is fucking crazy.' She wouldn't sit down. 'If you are out of the IRA, they shouldn't be looking for you.'

'I doubt it matters much to them.'

'What did you tell the police?'

'Just that Tom and Wilson were here last night, got pissed and left about 1.00 a.m.'

'What did Wilson say?'

'He knew one of them.'

'So he can report that?'

'He'll not do that. He'd be afraid of getting killed. People don't, Kathleen. You can't expect them to.'

'So he gets away with it?'

'Yeah. Unless you want me to shoot him.'

'Fuck, are you serious?'

'It's how things are done in this town.'

'Promise me something. You are finished with all this. You are not going to do that.'

'I promise.'

***

This was hard for Kathleen. She went to Gardner's on Botanic Avenue the next morning and bought most of the papers to read their various accounts of Tom's murder. *The Irish News* and *News Letter* both led with it. The English and Dublin papers gave less space to it.

'Catholic Student Assassinated' – Was it right, she wondered, to emphasise his religion when, as far as she was aware, he had no strong beliefs?

'You don't have to believe anything to be a Catholic in this country,' said Terry. 'It's just a way of saying Irish. Though we don't say Irish because we don't want to suggest that the Protestants aren't Irish too, though ask them what they are and they say they're British.'

'Oh God.' Just bothering to rouse the breath to rationalise any of this annoyed her.

They walked to Cavendish Street. It would have felt strange to go to a wake on their bicycles and there was no direct bus.

'Can't we just walk up Donegall Road?' She had a map that showed her it was the most direct route to the Falls Road.

'No,' he said, 'we can't. It wouldn't be safe.'

'We don't have marks on our foreheads, Terry. They can't just tell to look at us.'

'There will be someone looking out for strangers,' he said, though he joked quietly to himself that those who kill in the night were probably still in bed.

So he led her down Great Victoria Street and up the Grosvenor Road while she fretted about the awfulness of not being free to walk where you wanted in the town you lived in. He had never seen her so gloomy, so unresponsive to his stabs at conversation, his attempts at affection, then concern. The street showed no signs of harbouring grief. Two boys played a game with a plastic football. Standing on opposite kerbs, they tossed it in turn to the other side, attempting to bounce it back to themselves off the concrete edging of the footpath.

A group of men stood round the door. Terry led her through them into the narrow hallway, where more people stood, talking softly. There was a barometer shaped like a porthole on one wall and a little glass-topped hall table with a white telephone. Strangers nodded to them, indicating the way to the living room. There, a dozen more people stood awkwardly positioned but relaxed with each other, talking casually as if they were in the pub. The coffin sat on a collapsible plinth by the window that looked out onto the street. The veil curtains were closed. The coffin was closed and decked with Mass cards. Kathleen handed their card to a woman who stood up and faced her.

'I'm sorry for your trouble,' said Kathleen, knowing how these things are done.

'We were with him that night,' said Terry. 'Or rather, he was with us.'

The woman nodded, too stunned to work out whether this was something she had to take in or respond to. Her eyes bulged sore from weeping. Kathleen and Terry simply stood silently in front of her, and then a man touched his shoulder and said, 'Sure come through to the kitchen for a cup of tea.'

Terry was inclined to retreat. Kathleen knew they had to have the tea.

'You were with him, you say?'

'We'd had a wee party.'

'Them gits that took him would have taken any taig they got. That's the way of them,' said the man, not having grasped that they would rather have had Terry. Kathleen could have corrected him, but knew not to. She was living with secrets now too.

***

For days after Tom Donnelly's funeral, Kathleen remained sullen and fretful. Whenever Terry would go into the living room, he would find her sitting with her head lowered and she would hardly acknowledge him.

She had no idea how to comprehend this. She knew, because she read the papers and listened to the radio news, that things like this happened in Belfast, but she had never expected the killing to come so close. She was confronting her naivety, and she had no one to talk to about it. She certainly couldn't call her mum and say, 'We had my teacher over for drinks. He was shot dead when he left us. He was pretty pissed by that stage, so I don't know if he understood what was happening.' Kathleen knew she needed to find a way to get the measure of what had happened, to find the language to explain it.

She needed that detachment from it before she could speak, and she couldn't find it. And she sensed that Terry was more on top of this than she could ever be. And that worried her. Where did he get that from? What had changed him into someone who was not flustered by murder? It made her fear that he was like the people who had done it.

'You've seen this stuff before?'

'Haven't we all?'

'No. I haven't. The other students in my lecture group are going to be just as bewildered as I am. They haven't been at war and they don't have any sense that anyone is at war with them.'

'But Kathleen, they see the soldiers on the streets. They hear bombs in the night.'

'But it has nothing to do with them. It has nothing to do with me, until now. But you are different. None of this fazes you.'

He didn't want to argue with her. 'People I was close to have been killed before. I was in the IRA. I told you that.'

'Did you kill anybody?'

'Well, I was part of the whole thing. If they killed 500 people in the time I was there, then I am part of all of that; I share the blame if we were wrong to do it, and I'm out now.'

'But do you know what it takes to stop a man in the street and drive him to a country road and shoot him in the head? Have you that in you?'

He was sitting beside her on the sofa now. 'I was interrogated by the IRA security team. These are the guys who leave bodies on the border with their hands tied behind their backs and tape over their eyes. They would have done that to me if they hadn't believed or liked my answers. On the night before they finished with me, they left rosary beads beside my head and a wee note, "Say hello to Jesus", just to freak me out. I spent the whole night convinced they were going to do me in the morning.'

She took his hand in hers. 'I have been so stupid,' she said. 'I thought I could have a normal life here.'

'You can. Go out tomorrow and see all the people who didn't know Tom Donnelly, who only heard it on the news, and some of them will say how shocking it is and they will ask what this place is coming to. And they'll watch the funeral on the news, and then they'll be over it. This place is normal. Everything about it is normal except for the bombs and the murders, and they don't really bother most people very much.'

That night he held her close for an hour before she fell asleep and turned away from him. In the morning, he would have to tell her they had to move out, to a flat or house a little further away from the trawling gunmen.

He woke up before her and went out to buy croissants and milk. When he came back, Kathleen was in the kitchen talking to Nools.

'Hi. Do you two know each other?'

Kathleen said, 'Nools just called to see you.' There was a hint of suspicion in her voice.

Terry approached her and kissed her lightly on the cheek and she smiled. He said, 'She was a Catholic when I knew her; now she's a Protestant.'

'That's not true.'

'No?'

As he put the croissants into the oven and filled the kettle, he said, 'Nools and I met in Lancaster. She was working at the theatre and I was a barman in the Farmer's Arms.'

'Lovely,' said Kathleen, meaninglessly.

'But I was in the IRA and her heart was in Special Branch.' This was his way of signalling to Kathleen that they had not been intimate, but it failed; acrimony suggested they had tried and failed and might try again.

'Nools heard about the killing.'

She said, 'I thought you two might be thinking of moving, since it was rather close. I have a wee house in Stranmillis that needs a dependable tenant.'

Terry knew they would have to take it but didn't want to alarm Kathleen.

Nools said, 'It's only a mile away but it might as well be on the other side of the world as far as those goons are concerned. Here, someone takes a notion with a skinful of drink to shoot a Catholic and you're walking distance from the pub.'

'Can we go over and see it this afternoon?' said Terry.

'Great.'

'And will you stay for breakfast?' said Kathleen, being nice just to cover her worry.

'No thanks. I'd better head on. Maybe we could get together when everything is more settled?'

'Yes, Nools. That would be nice. Thank you.'

Terry walked her to the front door. 'Is this just your idea, or is someone working moves here?'

'No, it's for real. We bought a wee house to rent out and we've just done it up. It's what everyone with spare cash in this town is doing.' At the door, she turned to him. 'Those guys were looking for you. They were going to come into the house and shoot you and they'd have shot Kathleen too. That was their brief. They chickened out and settled for an easy target, I presume. But you need to get her out of here.'

'I know. Just help me do it without scaring her.'

When he went back upstairs Kathleen was full of questions.

'So were you lovers or weren't you? I'm not jealous but I need you to be straight with me.'

'We weren't. We thought about it and sniffed around each other, but there was nothing there.'

'That seems a bit unlikely.'

'It's the truth. We were never together for long before we'd be arguing.'

'Then why does she want to do this for us?'

'Take her at face value. It suits her to get a tenant for her house. And she knows more than we do about the dangers of living here because she's married to somebody who has protection around him, and her. Let's go and see the house.'

And yet, sensible and all as that seemed, Kathleen just knew in her heart that there was more to it. 'She will have a key to our front door. She will be able to walk into our bedroom any time she likes, whether we are there or not.'

'There are laws governing those things; they apply to her too.'

'But we can't pay her the rent she'd expect for a house in Stranmillis. Why would she give up the chance to get more for it?'

'Let's go and see it and hear what she's asking for.'

***

The house was a three-bedroom, detached redbrick with pebble-dash frontage, probably built in the 1950s. What had been a small garden at the front was now paved. Nools pointed out the alarm system and the discreet camera over the door. The front door was heavy, and immediately inside they were confronted by a large metal grill at the foot of the stairs.

'George's big plan was to make this secure against attack and then to rent it to the police for staff who are vulnerable, and there are a lot of them. It didn't work out and no one else will buy it like this.' She took them into the living room.

'Double glazing?' asked Kathleen.

'Look closer,' said Nools. 'There are seven layers of glass in that. It was done by the same firm that did Dom McGrath's house. It is sniper proof. And you would need more than a sledgehammer to get through that front door.'

'This gives me the creeps,' said Kathleen.

'Don't think about it,' said Nools. 'You'll be safe here. I've seen some houses with even stronger defences, steel shutters on the windows. You couldn't live with that. But you won't even notice the defences here after a while. And they keep the heat in.'

She showed them the kitchen and the utility room and took them upstairs to the bathroom.

'What makes you think we can afford this?' said Terry.

'It would be cheaper for you to buy it.'

'That's crazy.'

'No, it's not. In a few years you will be able to pay the full mortgage. You get it now on an endowment mortgage, then just pay the interest until you are working or resell it and move on.'

'Like they'd give that kind of mortgage to me?'

'George has friends in finance, and they're not going to lose anything. They'll just take the house off you if you default and sell it at a profit. No one loses.'

Kathleen said, 'You've got me completely bewildered.'

'I'll get a broker to call round and see you and explain the figures. You'll be amazed. Otherwise, you can rent it, maybe get other students in to share.'

The figures were simple. The house was valued at £25,000. The interest repayments were £117 a month and the endowment payments another £50, the idea being that when the endowment matured in twenty-five years it would pay off the capital on the house, but they'd have moved on by then anyway.

Kathleen showed the figures to her family's solicitor and he said everybody was doing this, that he had half a dozen houses himself now, that it was all kosher.

Nools let them move in straight away though it would take two months to finalise the contract and make them owners of an armoured house.

'One other thing,' Nools had said when she showed them how to work the heating system and the tumble dryer. 'Do you want to join our book group, Kathleen? Girls only.'

'Oh, yes,' said Kathleen, without hesitation.

'Good, the next meeting is at our house on the last Friday of the month. Salman Rushdie's *Satanic Verses*, so we can see what all the fuss is about. The Bookshop at Queen's has it.'

Fourteen

Basil McKeague's file was growing. In his first months in the job, the inspector had visited the homes of twenty or more families who had lost someone and who felt that the law had let them down. It was all familiar to him. He had sat in the little front rooms of terraced houses where toys cluttered the floor and the television stayed on, sometimes with the sound down, while he tried to explain his job and its limits to distraught thin women and fat angry men. He had met families in farmhouses with a picture of the Sacred Heart of Jesus on the wall over an old wooden table while sullen men with their caps on listened and did not respond. He had met wealthy professionals and property developers in mansions they hadn't families to fill them with and told them that the investigation into the murder of Denis or the explosion that killed Maggie or the stray bullet that had crippled an aunt was the end of the story and that his investigations and reinvestigations had come to very little. And none of them had expected any more than that from him.

While policing Northern Ireland for decades, McKeague had met people who had lost more than one relative in high-street bombings or shootings. Some had lost relatives in attacks years apart, and others had mourned both Protestant and Catholic relations, for not every family was firmly locked into one community or the other. He had met people whose loved ones had deserved their brutal deaths, though he would never have said that to them and they would never have agreed.

Over 3,000 people had died in the Troubles, and the political ethos of the peace process that ended the killing virtually assumed that all were innocent. None had brought on the Troubles, had they? The intergovernmental agreements, leading up to the settlement, all conceded that the violence had been a legacy of bad history. So you were not supposed to pass moral judgement on someone who had taken a random civilian off the street and shot him in the head, or bombed a supermarket and killed a little boy as he went in to buy his comic. You had to factor in the history and see that Elizabeth I had had a part in this too, and so had Martin Luther and Oliver Cromwell and Winston Churchill. And when you saw it that way, you understood that the random civilian and the little boy were products of that history too; they had been born to meet the bullet and the bomb that awaited them, just as the man who had pulled the trigger or primed the bomb had no choice but to do what history demanded of him. That was the understanding at the heart of the political resolution, the theory underpinning his work.

Presidents, prelates and prime ministers had endorsed that understanding, congratulated themselves on having had the vision to realise it, but Basil McKeague thought it was nonsense. He believed that he lived in a moral universe in which you could say that some people were bad and some were good. He had known shopkeepers burnt out for not paying protection money, and he wondered how history could be blamed for that. He had sat in the homes of paramilitary killers who had been shot by their own comrades or by a rival gang – which might even have been a gang on the same side as their own, in terms of the historic war. McKeague was supposed to care as much about Dinko Tatlock as about Isobel Lavery, but he didn't. He believed that some people bring consequences upon themselves.

And he knew that the dead didn't match the story – if they did, most dead Protestants would have been killed by Catholics and most dead Catholics would have been killed by Protestants. That wasn't how it was at all. The IRA had killed more Catholics than anyone else had. The loyalists had been a poison in their own communities. So, McKeague thought, don't talk to me in the language of conflict resolution and the historical legacy of conflict. But in his job, which had been devised by those who cherished that theory of the Troubles, he believed he was able to do a little good: to stitch-up bastards like Terry Brankin and deliver some justice to those who wanted it, like Seamus Lavery – a man who missed out on growing up with his parents and sister.

He sat silently in an armchair with the file in his lap. Above him, his wife was sleeping, which meant that she would have a restless night. He knew he should check on her, but he didn't want to move. He wanted just to be still and to talk to God.

'Thy will be done,' he said. 'Thy will be done.'

Not so fucking easy, is it though? He had stopped suppressing thoughts like that. That would be what he called timid Christianity. 'Not so easy, is it, God?'

And there wasn't an answer; there never was. Expecting one would be what he called childish Christianity. The one part of God he could depend on was His perpetual silence. That's where he ultimately expected to find peace, in the silence. He had only one expectation of God and it was ultimate justice, the rectification in an afterlife of all that was wrong with the world he lived in now: his wife's immobility and her moods, the evil going free, the deaths of children. And if that world didn't exist, wasn't being made ready for him, then he wouldn't be disappointed, for he wouldn't know; he'd be dead and death would really be the end. He didn't believe that. He believed that there had to be a balance; things had to be made right. But still there were consolations in the occasional doubt, and the chief of these was that if he was wrong, he wouldn't be around to know that.

He heard Alice's bed creak, so he rose to go to her. He looked at the worn patches on the old stair carpet. Should he buy a new one? What was the point? It would only be for him to see. Alice rarely made it downstairs now, and whatever he'd pick would be wrong in her eyes. No, it was better to let it be, tattered and worn though it was.

'What sort of day did you have?' she asked.

Her room was stuffy and smelt of creams and staleness. He opened a window. Outside, no one moved. Other families were either at work or as confined as his own. He stacked pillows behind her and hoisted her into position.

'Did you catch any terrorists?'

He sat on the edge of the bed and said, 'Do you need to go to the toilet?'

'I'll manage. But I'm out of gin. I want a wee gin tonight.'

'OK, I'll get you some.'

'It's a pity you didn't think to go to the off-licence when you were out.'

She was daring him to frown so that she could crush his disapproval. And he understood that. 'Is there anything else you would like?'

'Hand me up my library book. I dropped it on the floor.'

As he stooped, she sighed. 'God forgive me, how did I come to marry such a boring man?'

He stood and handed her the book without looking at it. 'You used to like me.'

'I used to think you were a brave and heroic policeman who would stop the Troubles and gun down the hoodlums. Wasn't I pathetic? Aren't I even more pathetic now? God, what has happened to my life?'

'He's the one to ask, Alice. Leave that question with Him.'

'Oh, fuck off. Go and get me my gin.'

He kissed her on the forehead and left the bedroom. He crossed the landing and entered his own room, where he stood quietly to compose himself before going back downstairs.

Then the phone in his pocket rang. It was Terry Brankin.

'Can we talk?'

'Of course. The line is quite bad though.'

'Sorry, I'm driving. Listen, I'm not ready to make a statement. And I won't be at the end of our conversation either. But that time might be drawing closer.'

McKeague didn't like a suspect to think he was managing the exchange between them. He liked to have his man in an interrogation room with a recorder running and a scowl on his face.

'I'll help you towards that in whatever way I can.' There was little point in having a row with Brankin and warning him off.

Terry gave McKeague the address of the house in Damascus Street.

'Well, you know what happened on the road to Damascus?'

'A man changed his mind,' said Terry.

Basil was lighter on his feet going back upstairs to update his wife and tell her he'd to get back to work. Alice's mood had not improved, but at least she turned her ire towards the Brankins.

'If that fucker is too smart for you, and he is, go for his fucking wife. That'll learn him. She deserves it, standing by a devil like him. Are you man enough for that?'

***

Terry was exhausted by the time he reached Damascus Street. The drive from Donegal had felt longer than usual, and he had slept badly the night before. So he was in no mood for the raucous partying on the street.

In the year that he had been a Civil Administration enforcer in Twinbrook, he had been the law there. None of the students partying in Damascus Street were at risk of being kneecapped but, fifteen years earlier, no one their age would have been blithely rowdy if Terry Brankin walked past. Then, if they were bothering the neighbours with their noise he would simply have taken their drinks away and some of them would even have helped him pour the stuff down the drain to stay on the right side of him.

Today young people were more free. They were sitting out on their steps drinking cider, smoking and arguing, their windows open to the sound of music blasting inside. Terry felt as if he had stumbled into a teenage holiday camp. He actually had to suppress an impulse to snap his fingers and dish out orders. He half wished now that he still had his old authority or that McKeague would come in an armoured Land Rover with a few men with sten guns, the way they did in the old days. That would be enough to scatter them.

Inside the house smelt of fresh paint and polish. Jack's boys had made a good job of it. He checked to see if Jack had left any surplus paint. Bingo! There was a huge 10 litre tub of matt white still half full on the floor by the fridge. He placed his wee Ruger, wrapped up and sealed, into the brilliant white paint and pressed down the lid. That would do for now. Then he sat and waited. McKeague, he calculated, would not want to seem too eager. He was right. An hour later he walked through the front door.

'Mr Brankin, I trust you are well.'

'Thanks for coming.'

He stood in the doorframe. 'Just doing my job. Now what was it you wanted to say to me?'

Terry sat in an armchair and offered McKeague the other. McKeague hesitated.

'Fuck, if you think I am going to get a crick in my neck for you ...' said Terry.

McKeague crossed the room and sat down.

'Here's the problem as I understand it,' said Terry. 'You want to put me down for the Magheraloy bomb. You're confident that I was there but you haven't got evidence that will stand up in court. What you need, if you can get it, is a confession. And I can give you a confession, if it suits me.'

'How might it suit you?'

'It might be the way to stop the fuckers who burnt my houses from coming after me or my wife again.'

'Why would they come after her?'

'Someone fired a shot at her.'

'We've no report of that.'

'You don't know everything.'

'I don't understand why she didn't report it.'

'She called me. She didn't call you. My sense is that it was another warning to me to keep my mouth shut. But they won't go on shoring up a dam after it has broken. They have at least that much wit.'

'Yes,' said McKeague, not fully agreeing with this logic but having no motive to dispute it while things were going his way. 'So your reasoning is that it's your old mates in the Provos who burnt the houses and shot at Kathleen?'

'I suppose it would be touting to say so.'

McKeague knew that Terry was leaving something out of the story, and that he would want to make a limited confession that didn't implicate anyone else. That was to be expected. 'And there's more?'

'My houses. The police will have a lot of influence there.'

That was true. If the police report said the houses had been burnt as part of a political conspiracy, then it would be up to the state, rather than the insurance company, to pay compensation. And the state would not compensate a retired IRA man who had brought all this on himself.

'The report could say that the police suspected no paramilitary involvement in the burnings. Half the town thinks I petrol-bombed them myself. You'd have to knock that on the head too. But I am *not* going to jail unless my wife has a house to live in and I have a property and resources to come out to.'

'You're telling me you think the Provos did it and at the same time asking me to ignore that?'

'That's the deal.'

'Well, maybe you did bomb those houses,' said McKeague. 'And you can't expect me to pre-empt a live investigation.'

'I didn't fucking set fire to my own houses. Would I harm Kathleen?'

'You've done a lot of bad things in your time, Mr Brankin.' McKeague regretted the words as soon as he'd said them. There was nothing to be gained by making Terry Brankin angry, so quickly he added, 'OK. I'll get the drift of the investigation and see what way it's going, see what my options are.'

***

Then Terry cracked open a can of beer and settled himself to watch Finian's interview with Seamus Lavery. Being at home alone now, he could afford to relax his perpetual guard against the past. He could watch this programme and allow himself to feel some sympathy for the man whose parents and twin sister he had murdered. He could allow the whole experience to be chastening, purgative. He could even do that. If he chose to.

The programme opened with the familiar, orchestral brass flourish followed by thumps of percussion and then the presenter's voice: 'On this week's programme, *Bereaved by a Bomb*, we'll meet a man who lost both his parents and his twin sister to a callous IRA mistake.'

The camera focused in on Finian at the side of the road in Magheraloy.

'On a chilly March evening, a little over thirty years ago, an IRA bomb team crouched in hiding at this spot. They were waiting for a car. They had set a massive Semtex bomb at the side of the road, concealed by a bush, and they had paid down an electric cable from the detonator of the bomb to a switch trigger. It was a night of mizzle and mist, of low visibility. We don't know precisely how they located their target. Perhaps a lookout scout further down the road was able to signal to them that it was on its way. Inside the car were three people.'

Now they showed a reconstruction of a happy family in a large saloon car, the father and mother smiling and perhaps sharing a joke, the little girl in the back playing with her doll.

'This family was about to be destroyed, and for nothing. This was not the target the IRA was looking for that night.'

Then the picture and sound faded on a view of the car from behind, cruising in the mist into bright oblivion.

A man's voice said, 'I should have been in the car too. I don't know why I wasn't. Maybe I had a cold and had to stay at home with my aunt minding me. Maybe I just hadn't wanted to go. I was into my Lego and didn't like long journeys in the car. I got sick in the car. That can make all the difference in this world, between who lives and who dies, a child with a cold and ... Lego.

'I'd wanted to stay up until they got home. I probably thought it wasn't fair if Isobel got staying up later than me, but I think I fell asleep in front of the television. I woke up when I heard my aunt Mary screaming, and there were two policemen standing in the living room, and I thought they were hurting her and I was afraid. There were soldiers at the door; they didn't come into the house. There were more soldiers out on the road.

'And Auntie Mary panicked at the sight of me and she knew she was confusing me and she didn't know how to stop confusing me with her screams and her hugging me at the same time. I was frightened. I was a wee boy of ten. It was like it now fell to me to do something when she was in bits. I had this notion they had come to arrest her or even to arrest me. One of the policemen tried to talk to me. He said something like, "You're going to have to be a brave boy now."

'Then my uncle Tommy came round to the house and at first he was shouting at the soldiers outside and swearing at them. Then he was hugging Mary and hugging me, and the policeman and he were being civil to each other, even though he was shouting at the soldiers. And then he thanked the policemen and they left and it was just the three of us, and it was cold because someone had forgotten to close the front door, and then more neighbours were coming in. I don't remember anyone telling me that my mummy and daddy and my sister Isobel were ... were not coming home, but I knew that that's what this was all about, somehow I knew that.'

He said, 'I have seen the funeral on TV. Sometimes it just comes on. They'll be talking about the Troubles and then they'll just put a moment of it up without warning you, and that can be a gunk. That can spoil your whole day, for all they care. But I don't actually remember having been there. I can see that I was there, in my wee suit and with my hair combed by Auntie Mary. But I don't remember.

'And there's Auntie Mary clinging to me and crying all the time. I can remember her doing that. I can remember the smell of her perfume making me choke. But I don't really remember the funeral. What was there left of them to bury anyway? You think a ten-year-old wouldn't ask a question like that? Did they think I hadn't worked that one out for myself? They showed you the wreckage of the car on television. Well, if that was what the bomb did to a car, it wasn't hard working out what it had done to the people inside it.'

Terry watched this, keeping his emotions under control. He would allow himself the sadness of the ordinary viewer, feeling pity for a boy whose life was destroyed by war, but he had cried enough and would cry no more.

Seamus Lavery told how he had gone to live with Tommy and Mary, who were themselves republicans.

'They supported the IRA so this was all an embarrassment to them. They had pictures on the wall of Bobby Sands and Mairéad Farrell. They had ornaments that had come out of Long Kesh, a harp made of matchsticks by a prisoner, Celtic crosses, that kind of thing. And I questioned that and said, "But you don't know that the bastards who killed my mummy and daddy and my sister didn't make that." And Tommy and Mary would just be saddened by that at first, and then, when I was older, the tone changed. They said, "If you're going to live in this house, sonny, you're going to have to show more respect."'

Finian asked him a question that made Terry cringe. 'Now that we have a peace process, is there any prospect of you putting this behind you, even forgiving the killers?'

'I am sick of being asked that,' said Lavery. 'I don't know why I should be expected to forget what was done to me and what I lost. Are the people who started the trouble being asked to forget everything and put it behind them? No, they are being asked if there is anything more we can do for them to keep them sweet.'

The scene switched then to Finian sitting on a hillock overlooking the town. He turned from surveying the landscape to facing the camera.

'Seamus Lavery's uncle Tommy, who took him in as an orphaned child but would not tolerate any criticism of the IRA, has now sided with republican dissidents opposed to the peace process.'

Then there was a clip of a man in a balaclava reading a statement at a republican graveyard ceremony. He was saying: 'The Irish Sovereignty Movement will never criticise any republican who takes up arms against the British occupation of our country, against those who artificially divide it, against the sell-out merchants who led our cause into compromise and betrayal.'

Finian's voice-over said, 'We believe the speaker behind the mask is Tommy Lavery.'

And then they were back in Seamus's living room and Seamus was saying, 'Tommy has his own way and his own mind and I have nothing to say about that. He was good to me when I left school and helped me set up a wee business, and I keep my head down and get on with that. Strangely enough, things have changed, and people who wouldn't have heard you say a bad word about Dom McGrath now say that he was the worst thing that ever happened to this country.'

'But those same people, many of them,' said Finian, 'would give us more bombs and more killings and more accidents and more deaths of innocents.

'No one seems to be very good at confining themselves to killing the ones they say they want to kill.'

***

After watching the programme, a conviction settled more firmly in Terry's mind that he should own up to what he had done, to ease his own conscience, to secure his marriage and even to give some comfort to Seamus Lavery. He'd never get any thanks from him, but that was the right thing to do.

Terry had never seen McGrath travel anywhere alone. Usually he had a driver and a couple of minders. But, like everyone else, he had a mobile phone and an e-mail address. There was bound to be someone among his contacts in the legal profession who had access to these. Even a gang-lord had to talk to tax officials, the courts and the police. In addition, there were numerous community groups, clergy and political mediators who had access to McGrath. If, during the Troubles, a kid turned up at the probation service and said that the IRA had given him twenty-four hours to get out of the country or he'd be kneecapped, the probation officer had to be able to phone the IRA and check that. That was how much of Northern Irish society still worked. The paramilitaries were illegal gangsters but they had to be deferred to occasionally.

But who would have McGrath's number? Most people would only be able to contact his staff – people like Ig or Aidan, the new press officer. He wondered who would have the hotline to the big man himself. Only those with the most urgent need to sort out problems. Presumably McGrath's sister would have a number for him. She was a nun based in a community house in Andersonstown and helped run a foodbank. But she was hardly going to give it out to him.

Then there were the other paramilitaries, of course. They would need to talk to the republicans occasionally, to defuse tensions. Brankin could call in a favour from Benny Curtis, the loyalist thug who brought him clients. His relationship with Benny went back many years to when Benny had been charged with shooting a Catholic woman and her teenage son as they got off a bus on the Crumlin Road. Terry had helped confuse the court about the identification evidence.

'Mr Brankin, what can I do for you? Toutin' for business? Hey, isn't that a laugh?'

'You never stop, do you, Benny?'

'I always told the lads you were a sound man. I got you plenty of business, didn't I? But that's bad news about your houses, Terry. Nasty. Did you annoy somebody? Probably an occupational hazard with you. I know you really rubbed up some of my boys, but I wouldn't let them do a thing like that to you. You know that, don't you, Terry?'

Terry didn't doubt that Curtis could have ordered the attacks on his homes, but he calculated that he hadn't. It didn't mean that he wouldn't have to be on his guard against him. 'Look, sorry for phoning you so late, but I'm guessing you have a direct line for Dominic McGrath.'

'Ha, you'll get no satisfaction from him. But yeah, I got it off Fr Wright at Clonard. He wanted to be my intermediary, but I said no way: Prods don't trust Jesuits.'

'He's not a Jesuit, Benny. He's a Redemptorist.'

'Same thing. Anyway, you want me to call up Dominic for you and arrange a confab? Sometimes the wee woman answers the phone and I slag her off and say, "Hubby not home yet?" She doesn't like that.'

'Just give me the number.'

'I'll text it over to you and then you'll have to memorise it because it will melt your phone in thirty seconds.'

'No problem. Thanks.'

A minute later his phone beeped with Benny's text and Terry rang the number straight away.

'Yuh?' said McGrath.

Terry spoke quickly. 'I'll keep it brief if you don't hang up. The Cold Case team want me to go down for Magheraloy. That's how it might have to be. Listen, Dom, your secret is safe. Got that? Your secret is safe. Now tell Ig to relax.'

He waited for McGrath to answer. McGrath didn't speak and he didn't hang up.

'That's it,' said Terry.

Still McGrath said nothing and yet didn't hang up. He was playing his wee game: testing Terry to see how cool he really was.

Terry had no choice but to be very cool. So he ended the call himself.

***

The following day in Damascus Street, a police car at Terry Brankin's gate was intriguing the students next door. A constable rang his doorbell while another sat in the car, so it did not seem to be urgent. The students gathered round the car playfully. A girl was trying to persuade the driver to wind down the window and accept a flower. History repeating itself, thought Terry. If '68 be here again, can '69 be far behind?

'Can I help you, constable?' said Terry to the policeman at the door.

'Good afternoon, Mr Brankin. I was just calling to ask you to come into the station at Donegall Pass and take a few queries on your statement about the fires. Nice paint job, I see. You've obviously done a good job here. Not waiting for the insurance money then?' The peeler grinned to show that he had deeper, complex thoughts on the subject which Terry would not like.

Terry couldn't think of any gaps in the statement he had made, but he wasn't going to give this grunt the satisfaction of seeing him ask for clarity. Then he turned to the young people staring at him. He guessed they were wondering if he really had burnt out his own houses, even at the risk of incinerating his wife. Terry turned coldly and studied their faces. They took this as a challenge and scowled back at him. Well, if they thought he was dangerous, he might as well turn that misconception to his own advantage.

'You're allowed music out of that house up to midnight and not a minute after. Are we going to have the bravado first or shall we just agree on that?'

They melted away from him.

***

Terry had often been in interview rooms and knew how deftly the police might usurp his expectations. A suspect who thought he was being invited in to complete a bit of awkward paperwork and was then arrested as soon as he was over the doorstep was going to feel especially vulnerable to life's little surprises. Terry had gone to the desk to introduce himself and had been asked to wait in the musty reception area. After ten minutes – presumably a measured level of annoyance to inflict on him – an unfamiliar young detective came out and said, 'Terence Brankin?'

'Yes?'

'Mr Brankin, I am arresting you on suspicion of arson and attempted murder. You do not have to say anything.' He recited the full legal caution before leading him into the interview room.

Terry sat down and contemplated what might come next. He was certainly going to spend a few days in jail, perhaps just in the police cells, using the ghastly toilet, probably in company. The police would tell the media that a man was helping them with their enquiries into the fires, and he wouldn't put it past them to provide the 'guidance' that the suspect was himself. But why? Mainly just to make it clear that they were focused and busy. One other possibility was that McKeague was throwing his offer of a deal back in his face. The irony was that the greater offence of murder would get him only two years inside because it was covered by the political agreement, while a charge of arson, of burning down his own bloody houses, would erase the next decade from his life. Maybe McKeague preferred that.

The door opened and McKeague came in with the skinny young detective. Neither was in uniform; they might have passed for a couple of insurance salesmen. They didn't speak until they were seated at the table. Then the young detective switched on the recording machine and said, archly, 'April 17, 13:40. Present are Inspector Basil McKeague and Detective Sergeant Caoimhin Ó Conghaile and the suspect, Terence Brankin, who has been properly cautioned. Isn't that right, Mr Brankin?'

Terry could not ask McKeague what his thinking was on the deal he had offered him, since the question would be recorded and might count as evidence – enough perhaps to strip him of all bargaining power.

'That's right,' Terry replied to the young detective.

McKeague said, 'Where is your wife, Mr Brankin?'

'What's that got to do with anything?'

'Where is she?'

'She is in Donegal. We have a cottage there.'

'So she has left the jurisdiction? To evade arrest?'

'Why would she be evading arrest?'

'You are here on suspicion of burning your own property for an insurance claim. We may have questions for her about that too.'

Ó Conghaile said, 'Why did you do it?'

'Do what?'

'Torch five houses and nearly kill as many people, Mr Brankin.'

But Terry didn't think this was about the insurance claim at all. This was just a squeeze on him to confess to the Magheraloy bomb.

McKeague said, 'We have been looking through your recorded accounts. You're not as rich as you look.'

A few days ago, he owned his home with the mortgage cleared and was up to date on repayments on four other properties. He rented his office in town but expected to clear the loans on some of the houses and pay a deposit on that too. And all the rentals were bringing in an income. On top of that, he had a solicitor's practice and plenty of clients. He didn't think that was bad for a man who had started out expecting to give his life for Ireland. But he wasn't going to answer the question. The game now was to be patient and slow. Nothing he said today would get him out earlier, so he pretended to be mulling over this complex question of why he had torched his five houses.

McKeague thumped the table in a rage. 'Have you not had enough of killing? Can you just not be happy unless somebody somewhere is burning?'

That was a strange thing to do. What possible result could McKeague hope to get from such an outburst. Terry had not seen him get hysterical before; it wasn't his style. He wondered if this was the behaviour of a cop who just didn't expect to make a charge stick, and was settling for inflicting damage. Hardly. McKeague might have taken Terry for a killer and many other kinds of low life besides, but surely he had not mistaken him for a frail, uncertain boy whose morale would crumple under a barrage of insults. So this was all for show. Maybe it was simply the good cop, bad cop routine. Just like the old days, he thought. Terry decided that he wouldn't talk at all, not if they kept him a week and beat the shit out of him. 'I suppose', he thought, 'that wee Caoimhin is going to do the good cop bit. Oh spare me.'

McKeague stood up and draped his jacket over the back of the chair. Then he leaned over the table, propped on his fists, and roared at Terry. 'Big fancy solicitor with his big house and fancy wife, and what are you now but some cheap chancer who would toast that same wife and a half dozen others for a few grand out of an insurance company. Well, you needn't think it's going to work this time, mate. I've had every sort of gangster and filth in this room with me, and they all come down to the same thing at the end – human dirt. But you take the biscuit. This town is full of men who think now that they were just sowing their wild oats when they were blowing kids away and shooting peelers on their doorsteps or coming out of church, and that moral and legal reckoning is just an inconvenience. And they put it all behind them, until a time comes in their swanky lives when the old way of doing things might suit them better, and do they stop for a moment to think of others? Let me tell you, Mr Brankin, you should have gone the way of your old comrades – into politics. Then you'd have a little backing. Where you sit now, you have no backing, and you'll not see daylight again until I'm finished with you. Interview terminated. Take him to the cell.'

Young Caoimhin took Terry's elbow as if he was helping an old man to his feet. Terry was barely shaken by the tirade but he saw the logic of it all right. And he now feared that McKeague really did believe he had burnt his houses. That was a complication. Yet he could see the sense in that too. This was a dirty world. He had done dirty things, and if he went down for burning his own houses, even when he hadn't, there would be a certain justice in that too. Then, as he released a long-held tension breath, he turned to the detective for a bit of that 'good cop' stuff – the consolation. Instead, the young man's knee rose sharply. It was like that pain boys get once in a cycling accident when they lose their footing on the pedals and land, groin first, on the bar, and learn never to let that happen again. Terry hardly had time to admire the deftness of the strike before the complex pain suffused him giddily. It was horrible. He felt he might prefer to die now. Only the memory of similar inflictions told him this would pass. There were tears in his eyes. He disappointed himself. He tried to believe he would survive, but felt no reassurance in that moment that his body would ever know comfort again.

***

Cats foul their own patches to warn others to stay away. There is nothing as off-putting as the smell of a stranger's filth. Terry wondered if the police liked the cells to stink. Was it part of the treatment? Or was it just that men held in custody sweated and shat and vomited so much that there was no way to keep the facilities clean. He felt his stomach turn over. Then, seeing the dark slime of the toilet bowl when he bent to it, he clenched to contain himself. It worked for a moment and then out came all his disgust in a flood.

He coughed and spat to clear his mouth of gunk so that he could speak when a constable checked him through the door's shutter. 'I don't suppose you guys have a bottle of disinfectant?' he asked.

'No. We'd be afraid you'd drink it.'

So he flushed the toilet every few minutes in the hope that raw water would carry away enough of the dirt and the smell to allow him to relax and think.

Because he had a tactical mind, Terry tended to attribute intelligence and tactical thinking to others. That could be a mistake, he thought now. As he lay on his bed in the grotty cell, he tried to re-evaluate the behaviour of the two policemen in the interview room, though it had hardly been an interview at all. He saw, on reflection, that Ó Conghaile was the arresting officer in charge of the case. McKeague had probably been invited to sit in, since he was also investigating the Magheraloy cold case. They wouldn't have pulled him off that to investigate the house burnings, but with McKeague's senior rank, Ó Conghaile would have been loath to shut him out.

Terry suspected that McKeague and Ó Conghaile were not working together well. McKeague was using the old methods, Ó Conghaile the new. That explained the malice of the knee in the groin at the end. Ó Conghaile had been trying to learn fast how to be a thug. However, it now seemed apparent that the police really did believe that he had burnt his own houses, even at the risk of incinerating his wife, which was bad. And why would they think he would be happy to kill Kathleen? Because they supposed she was an accomplice, knew the whole plan and would too easily crack, as he never would? He would have preferred they didn't think that. He also knew they wouldn't be able to build a case against him.

They gave him a ghastly lunch on a tray – breaded fish out of the freezer with oven chips and coleslaw – and then they had him in again.

McKeague was sitting at the table and Ó Conghaile was standing behind him.

'I take it you're not going to pretend you don't know who Denis Tatlock is – was.'

Terry said nothing.

'His is another case in my folder.'

Terry said nothing.

'We believe that Tatlock murdered Tom Donnelly all those years ago and that Donnelly had been with your wife on the night he died. She was one of his students. Apparently she was keen on him.'

Terry said nothing but he was thinking hard. 'What the fuck's coming now?'

'We believe that Tatlock was lured to his death by a woman. There was lipstick on his cheek.'

Terry thought this was very likely, but it wasn't Kathleen's.

'Tatlock was a known killer and he was being monitored by Special Branch.'

'Working for them, more likely.'

'We have a recording of a woman's voice calling Tatlock to arrange a meeting. It sounds an awful lot like Kathleen. Voice identification is unreliable from phone calls but we want a sample recording of her voice to compare the two. Why is she in Donegal?'

The only resources that Terry had for dealing with this were the skills he had developed in the IRA. He had left the movement years ago, yet he began to think again as he had then. He had no choice. He had to defend his morale against all assaults, from others and from conscience. He resolved to set aside all considerations of right and wrong. That was the sort of commitment he had to make now. Give the fuckers nothing. But what about the gun? They would search the house in Damascus Street. They might find it. They might not. For now, he would assume that they wouldn't. There was also Ig to consider. McGrath would have told him by now of their phone call, and Terry was not at all sure what Ig would do next.

Fifteen

Ig sat alone at a table in the Dan Breen, with a pint of Guinness in front of him and a wee half-un beside it. All those who might need him knew this was where to find him. But he did not want to be disturbed. This was his thinking time. He had the latest intelligence to mull over.

Terry Brankin had decided to go down for the Magheraloy bomb and he had promised not to bring Dom McGrath down with him. But could he be relied on? He was already in police custody, so things were moving fast. Since Brankin was only going to get two years, he might not even bother about bail and let the time start right away. That's what Ig would do himself, unless he had urgent business to deal with. So it would be an idea to watch closely and see. In the old days, the IRA would have had men in all the prisons and in police stations, and Ig would have had sources to keep him informed. Nowadays, he would need connections among the peelers themselves and, though he had a few, he had none that he could call on today, none inside Donegall Pass police station anyway.

The word was that Brankin had got the wife off-site. It wouldn't be too hard to find her if they needed a little leverage. Or maybe they should just let it go, let him go down and trust him to say nothing about the rest of the organisation. Would the peelers really charge Dominic McGrath, even if they had evidence? Ig knew well that they already had all the details they needed on Dom, and had had it for a long time. Look at the guys who worked for him, who turned out to have been working for the branch or the army or fucking Mossad for all he knew.

Ig had started out in the IRA, thinking that the informer was an occasional traitor, a man of almost inconceivable selfishness. Growing up, for Ig, was discovering that no one could be trusted and that there were more touts than idealists around him. That would perhaps make whacking Brankin and his wife more dangerous than letting them go. It would have to be done as a tight operation that would protect everyone who took part in it. But, then, it being so tight, the police and the media would conclude that it was a high-class paramilitary hit, and there could be political consequences from that. Sometimes it was better to get a mad wee hood to do a job to take the professional look off it, but not this one.

An alternative was to get word to Terry Brankin, tell him that he could go ahead and sink himself if he wanted to, but that if he said anything out of place to the peelers, the wife would get it in the neck. The more Ig thought about it, the more he persuaded himself that was the way to do it. But who would deliver the message? Why, the wife herself of course.

***

Kathleen was at peace now, basking in the silence of the cottage and the surrounding countryside. She stood outside the front door and relished the light breeze in the trees and the sound of the tumbling water of the river nearby. She heard blackbirds and scavenging magpies, the distant yelping of children and, if she concentrated, a car which, by its own solitariness, seemed not to contradict the peace of the place but to confirm it.

She had cooked porridge, poured fresh orange juice and made filter coffee in a jug. She sat out in the early sun and set these at her feet, easing a long tight breath from her chest that she felt she had been holding on to for days.

'Mrs Brankin?'

She was shaken out of her reverie in the sun by the sight of a man coming up the lane. She had on only a T-shirt and shorts and no make-up. Would it be rude to go into the house and fetch a cardigan? She thought that would look a bit frantic and defensive.

'Now,' he said, 'isn't it just beginning to look like summer?'

'It is. What can I do for you?'

'I'm an old friend of Terry's. Well, an old comrade, if you get my drift.'

She scrutinised him warily. She might have to describe him to McKeague or to Terry. He didn't look dangerous. He was not tall or muscular. He was surely in his fifties and he had the patchy redness in his cheeks of someone who drank or had a bad heart.

'You've come at a bad time. Terry's not here.'

'Oh, I know that. Have you heard from him?'

'Not since he left here the other day,' she said. 'You could call him on his mobile if you need him.'

The man laughed. 'Oh, no need, Kathleen. The message is for you. Terry has been arrested. Didn't you know? That's interesting.'

Arrested? That was not what they had expected would happen. They had expected that McKeague would go along with Terry's offer. Had they got evidence on him after all?

'He's being interrogated about the Magheraloy bomb. Now, would you tell him when he calls that he is to say nothing at all about his old friend?'

'I don't think you have anything to worry about,' she said, bracing herself for aggression and wondering how she would deal with it.

The man smiled, the way one would deal with an obtuse child. 'Would you tell him that? That he's not to be saying anything about his old friend? Good. Otherwise, we'll burn down this house and we'll shoot you dead, Kathleen. Will you tell him that too?'

The man was still smiling, as if he had simply told her what time the postman usually called or what the weather was likely to be tomorrow. It was nothing new to him to be scaring people. He enjoyed doing it.

Kathleen was bewildered. These were such unlikely words to hang in the air that she wasn't sure she was hearing them at all.

How was she to find any meaning in them? It appalled her that she lived in a world in which another person might speak so lightly about killing her. Her thoughts were broken by an observation that she was gasping with panic. At first she thought it was the wind. The man might as well have punched her in the face, for she was reeling, confused.

'I ... I don't understand.'

'Oh, I think you do, Kathleen. It could not be simpler. Tell Terry to be very careful what he says about the Magheraloy bomb. Tell him that, to help him concentrate on that need, we have chosen to kill you, should things not work out to our liking. It's just business – nothing personal. I'll not stay for a coffee. You'll be wanting to think that over, won't you?'

She said, 'This doesn't make sense.'

'Oh, I think it does,' he said. 'It gives everyone a chance to avoid getting hurt.'

'That's not what you wanted when you shot at me,' Kathleen replied coldly.

'I didn't shoot at you, Kathleen dear. I shot at a shopping bag. If I'd intended to hit you, I would have done.'

He turned and walked back down the lane, as casually as he had come up it, like a farmer inspecting his ditches. She watched him and tried to breathe. Her breaths came in short clenches. This is terror, she thought, a purely physical reaction with no content. She wondered how he had sneaked up on her so gently. He must have come down the hill behind the cottage, letting the car roll without the engine on. That would be him now driving past the lower meadow. Kathleen sat there until her coffee was cold, until she noticed that she was shivering. Was there any place she could ever feel safe again?

She went into the cottage and sat at the kitchen table in stunned silence. She scrolled through the numbers on her mobile phone, looking for someone who might help. No answer from Terry. There was Nools. But had she the words in her head with which to even start explaining? She texted: 'Call me. ASAP.'

Just a minute later, her phone rang. 'What is it, love?'

'I am in Donegal, Nools. I have just had an IRA man call to say he will kill me.'

'Why? What's going on?'

'It goes back years. The police are questioning Terry about things that happened years ago and the Provos know that. It was them that burnt the houses.'

'Oh, Kathleen.'

'And there's worse, and I can't talk about it.'

'You need to come and stay with me for a while. You'll be safe here.'

'How can I be safe from them anywhere?'

'They're not as dangerous as they make out to be. They have their patch and they don't stray far off it. Some of them are so thick, they wouldn't be able to find our street on a map. Do you know which of them it was that came to you?'

'He didn't leave a card.'

'Describe him.'

'He was a wee podgy man with drinkers' cheeks. I thought he was the plumber or something. But see when he talks, he's scary.'

'I bet you a pound it was that tramp Ig Murray. He's just dirt. He's the one who shot Dinko Tatlock.'

Kathleen had no idea who Dinko Tatlock was or why Nools thought she might.

'He means what he says, doesn't he? And he could do it?'

'Aye, if he'd a stiffener first. He's done a lot of them. He's the lowest of the low, Kathleen. Will you come?'

'I don't know.'

Kathleen's mobile buzzed to let her know that another call was coming through. 'I'll get back to you,' she said.

It was Terry. 'I'm allowed one call. I'm sorry.'

'They're going to kill us! The IRA are going to kill us!'

'No, they're not.'

'They sent Ig Murray here to tell me he would kill me if you told the police that McGrath was involved in Magheraloy.'

'How do you know Ig Murray?'

'Nools said it was Ig Murray.'

'Was she there too?'

'No. Stop asking questions. Listen to me.'

'No', he said, 'you listen. The IRA are not going to kill you or me. They have nothing to gain by doing that.'

'Look, Terry. I'm just telling you what this man said. He said to tell you that if you implicated others in Magheraloy, they would burn down this house and shoot me, and that you had to know that.' She was yelling at him. She did not mean to be yelling at him.

'One thing at a time,' he said. 'I am being held by the police but this is not about Magheraloy. They think I burnt the houses.'

'Oh fuck! Sure, the IRA burnt the houses! They are going to burn this one too. I don't know where to go. At least they can't touch you where you are.'

'Listen, Kathleen. The Provos have done all they intend doing to you – scared you out of your wits. If they harm you, then I'll be free to say anything I like about anybody and they know that. I'll bring down McGrath; they can work that out for themselves. Look, love, I know how they think. They want you scared, not dead. You beat them if you can you manage the fear.'

'Manage the fear? I am in bits here, Terry.'

'Then go for a long drive or something. Stay away from the house tonight. Find a nice hotel. Tomorrow you'll see that the house is still there, just as you left it.'

'What are you going to do?' she asked.

'I can't do anything. I've to wait and see if they charge me. And if they don't, maybe I can make a deal over Magheraloy.'

'Is that it?'

'Can you call my office and tell them I'm in custody. Don't mention Magheraloy. I'll be out soon, so hold on a couple of days and keep your nerve.'

'I wish you were here, Terry.'

'I know, love. I wish I was too. For now though, listen to me very carefully and trust me. The worst that can happen is that you crumple under the pressure. That's how they trained us. If you keep your nerve, everything else becomes manageable. OK?'

***

Each time Terry was taken into the interrogation room, he sat still and said nothing. Ó Conghaile and McKeague betrayed their desperate need for him to speak, and their lack of a case, by the shapeless pattern of their questions and the random attacks they made on him.

'What sort of man would burn his own wife?'

'Was she the real target and the rest a diversion, Terry? What had she done to annoy you, eh?'

Soon, the challenge for them was just to evoke a response. He prepared for these confrontations by imagining the worst they could say or do, so as not to be taken by surprise. Soon he was confident that they had no case against him but their own suppositions and would have to let him go. Then what would they do? Arrest him for Magheraloy and go through the whole thing again?

He was left for hours, uninterrupted, in the dirty cell. He couldn't sleep at night and in the early hours what came back to him was not the horror and the blood, but the night in Heysham – on the barrows, beside the graves of little monks, when the waves were lit like metal by the stars and the light from the power station, when he had crumpled under the weight of remorse.

He didn't think anyone had the right to confront him with his guilt. He despised McKeague and the stupid wee probationer who fired accusations at him. But he could accept accusation from himself, in the dark. He was the one who had said yes, bomb that car, that's the one. He had given the nod and only because it was the right make and he had seen a child in it. Two adults in the front – a man driving, a woman beside him – and a child in the back. He could never justify that mistake.

He would confess to Magheraloy if they would undertake not to screw up his compensation claims for the burnt houses. But they believed he had burnt the houses, so they would not want to do that.

'For crying out loud,' he wanted to say, 'if I'd burnt them for the insurance I wouldn't have made it look like a paramilitary attack, would I?'

Were these people stupid?

It was a weird position to be in – to have to clear his name for the burning of his houses, so that he could confess to blowing up three innocent people.

Sixteen

Terry Brankin was released. He was proud of himself for having kept quiet under pressure for four days. It sent a message to the police that without his co-operation they would not nail him for either the house fires or for the Magheraloy bomb.

The first urgency was that he should not act like a guilty man. The police would be watching him. Others, including the IRA, maybe even the media, would be taking a close interest in his movements. He would have to be very careful. The second urgency was that he should clear his head of the grim days in a cell, and piece together an audit of his problems and an approach to solving them. He still felt contempt for virtually everyone, a hard-edged disdain that had helped him to survive, perhaps a hardening to shield himself from a debilitating remorse. This included a harsh regard for Kathleen and her whimpering about Ig. But that's oul' Provo hard man shite, he told himself. He should think clearly now.

He was looking at two years in prison if his plan worked – he would have to secure himself there and make sure he had backings that others would be wary of. The first option was George Caulfield, the prison warder. It would be strange meeting Nools's husband inside. Would he be an ally or a threat? It was hard to know at this point; he had never got on with him. Benny Curtis? Maybe there were loyalist lifers who, without hope of ever seeing freedom anyway, could be persuaded to look out for him, who'd even enjoy doing it.

He headed to Damascus Street to retrieve his car and gun. It was incredible to him that they hadn't searched his house, or, if they had, had done it so amateurishly. The old RUC would have found the gun in minutes, and they'd have tipped the paint over the kitchen floor too. He drove west to Donegal again. It was an exhilarating trip. Terry was feeling refreshed and emboldened. This feeling of being unafraid and physically solid, focused and in control, was like an old friend he hadn't met in a while. This was how he had been in the 'Ra. Then he had had confidence and courage. Then he had dealt with bigger problems than defending louts like Benny Curtis's sloppy gunmen, who wouldn't have been caught if they had been as professional in their work as he had usually been in his.

Back then, operations were planned methodically. Even that Magheraloy hit. No one would have been embarrassed about it if it had gone well. Back then, his standing in the movement would have been unassailable if he had taken out the Chief Con, even along with his wife and child. Now Terry was in a frame of mind to assert himself again, to be done with shame and the regret. It wasn't he who had started this war. It had come to him, and he had known when he was twenty that he would be humiliated over and over again by army searches and raids on his home and that he would be in danger of sudden death in crossfire anyway, so it made sense to fire back.

And he had done. At first, he thought he would just take out one of the fuckers. It wasn't a single incident that had tipped him over. He had been late among his friends in joining the IRA; he thought they were daft for getting involved. He remembered talking to Peter Carlin one night over a drink in the PDF, a shebeen set up to raise money for supporting prisoners.

Peter had said, 'Keep it q.t., but I've joined. We're not supposed to tell anybody but people get to know pretty quickly.'

'Yeah, if they have seen you squatting in their garden path with a .303.' Terry was contemptuous of the IRA then. It wasn't a well-run organisation. Just as many of them were dying by their own bombs as were getting shot by the army or the loyalists. It was a mess.

A week after this chat, a car blew up on the Westlink with four guys in it and Carlin was one of them. How had that happened?

There was a big military funeral for them and statements issued to the press about young men giving their lives for Ireland, but the truth, when Terry worked it out, was drab. Peter and his team had been sent into town to deliver a bomb. The timer was set for them before they even got into the car. But there had been a royal visit that day. These were never announced in case the IRA would target them. Traffic was rerouted away from the city centre, where some negligible princess and her entourage would be opening a charity shop.

The newspapers speculated that the visit had been leaked and that the bomb had been intended for her. It was the other way round; they had known nothing or they wouldn't have sent the bomb out. And Peter Carlin wouldn't have used up all the time on the clock driving around looking for an alternative target or somewhere to dump the bomb. That was how inept they were. And Terry, standing at the graveside, watching the men in black berets firing shots over the coffin, imagining they were soldiers, thought he could show them how to do it better, how to keep it tight and safe.

He approached Ig in the PDF. Ig was at a table with two other men that Terry took for republicans. They had a double round of drinks in front of them even before nine o'clock. A guitarist was tuning up on the stage and testing his mic. Soon the place would be too noisy for a conversation. Terry was bold about it. He walked up behind Ig and put a hand on his shoulder. The two other men looked grimly at him. Ig didn't turn around. He'd show his nerve by simply reading the situation from the other men, who were more annoyed than startled.

Terry bent to Ig's ear. 'I'd like to talk to you when you have a chance.'

Ig pushed back the chair and stood up. He looked Terry straight in the eye, nodded and led him outside. It was a chilly and dark evening. He felt exposed there in view of passers-by or a possible army patrol, but the IRA had lookouts.

'So, go on,' Ig said.

'I'm thinking of joining.'

'Thinking? Fuck that. Thinking isn't going to get us anywhere.'

He'd thought Ig would be glad of the chance to recruit him and would put some effort into it.

'We don't need you, Terry. But if you need to be part of us, that's up to you.'

'You don't need me? The way your kids are blowing themselves up, you'll soon have nobody left. And you won't be sending me out with a fucking timer nailed into a box. But I could do things.'

'You'd fucking take orders like anybody else, and you're not ready for that, Terry. You're not a soldier.'

Soldier? A drunk scruff like Ig could tell Terry he wasn't a soldier. The fucking cheek of him.

'OK,' Terry said. 'I can walk away and pretend this conversation never happened.'

'Then what?'

He wasn't going to answer that, but he was thinking he could get a rod, learn to use it himself and whack a couple of Brits in his own time, and Ig could go fuck himself.

The two men from the table were now standing at the door.

One of them said, 'Is this fella giving you any gyp, Ig?'

'He says he's thinking of joining the 'Ra.'

'Fuck off, kid. They're queuing up to join and we're turning most of them away.'

'And that,' said Terry, 'is why you've got such a sloppy organisation with most of your people in jail and half the rest of them blowing themselves up.'

'Well, you've got a bit of cheek anyway.'

The man turned to Ig. 'Bring him to Burnsie's tomorrow afternoon and we'll talk about this.'

The two men went back inside and Ig said, 'You'll be picked up tomorrow.'

'Where?'

'Wherever you happen to be.'

Terry went home to his parents' house on Bingnian Drive and slept. When he woke the following morning, he realised he would have to move out of this house so as not to bring the army to his mother's door.

'Busy day, love?' she said over breakfast, trying to penetrate his surliness.

'Usual, Ma.'

When Terry left the house, a man got out of a car parked at the corner of the street and said, 'Get in.'

He got in and was driven, not to Burnsie's, but to meet Packy McGrath, Dom's brother.

Packy was using an office in a community centre. The posters on the wall around him gave advice on benefits and health. He was rough. He sat behind a desk, perpetually sucking at his teeth as if this action was part of his thought process. The driver left the room.

Packy said, 'So you want to volunteer or you don't. Which is it?'

'I want to join.'

'Why?'

'I want to whack some Brits. I'm sick of them sneering at me.'

'Nothing to do with uniting Ireland?'

'Well, to be frank, no. I'm in no hurry for that.'

'You line a shot up at the paras and they'll drop you before you've got your sights straight. They'll probably drop some kid with a skipping rope, two nuns and a pensioner on his bike while they are at it. What fucking use is that?'

'Other guys do it.'

'Other guys do what they're told. They don't come in here announcing what operations they are going to be on before they're even Green-Booked.'

'I am not other guys. I might have something to offer beyond blind obedience. And I'm fucked if I would drive a bomb around town like Carlin looking for a parking space while the timer ticked away. But I may not be the kind of guy you are looking for. In which case, we can forget about this.'

'You know volunteers die and volunteers go to jail. It doesn't matter what type of operations you do, these are likely outcomes. I don't want you to be in denial about that.'

'OK.'

'Right, you're sworn in. You'll be answerable to Ig.'

'Is that it?"

'What do you want, salute the flag or something? We're done.'

While driving to Donegal, Terry was savouring this memory of the day he joined the IRA by eyeballing the hard men and not being humbled by them. They saw the calibre of him. While dwelling on this, he was back in that state of mind again, driving fast over winding and undulating country roads, in control of his big car, snug in the leather bucket seat, pushing and pulling the gearstick almost with blithe contempt. But there were others on the road who were faster, just as there had been challenges in the IRA he had not been equal to. Terry spotted an impatient driver in a pale green Almeira trying to get past him.

'Take your time,' Terry muttered, still mentally swaggering.

But the driver behind him stayed close, looking out for enough space to overtake.

Maybe Almeira man knew the road better than he did and could take it at greater speed if his way was clear, but Terry was not in the mood to be pushed around by anyone, on or off the road. It was a nice day, and he was going to enjoy the journey. He had taken abuse in police custody, endured the humiliation of shitty food in a stinking cell. He had had his few days of being treated like dirt and now he was important again – a 'Ra man planning his moves, and equipped like he had never been in the 'Ra with a decent car that was his own, the freedom to go where he pleased, money and a long-forgotten gun. So he was going to enjoy, in his own bodily ease, the pleasure of taking back control, which, for now, manifested in the feeling of power behind the wheel.

The driver behind nudged close again and then crossed the white line to glance ahead and see if the road was clear, then nipped back into line behind him.

'In my own good time, buster,' said Terry, checking his mirror and seeing the man bunched at his steering wheel, gripping it fretfully.

Round the next corner, a half mile of straight road opened up and the driver behind swung out to take it, but just as he was coming alongside Terry, a car came round the corner ahead, towards them, and he recalculated and dropped back in behind.

'Not so frisky after all?' said Terry.

They reached the bend and the green Almeira sat close behind him through a winding stretch that took them into a small valley. This was annoying Terry. What was the point? Then, over the next rise, with a good half mile clear ahead, the Almeira finally slipped out from behind and charged ahead. And without even thinking about it, on more adrenalin than reason, Terry accelerated, just to annoy Almeira man, just to show who had more poke. Almeira man held his speed and did not drop back, but he needed to get ahead of Terry to be safe. They were racing side by side to the next bend, round which another car might come before they got to it. Terry was laughing, remembering that he still had it in him to be bloody dangerous. Relishing his nerve, he dropped speed and let the Almeira pass him safely just before they reached the corner where an oncoming tractor appeared. The Almeira would have smashed headlong into it if Terry hadn't let him pass. It was then he saw her – in the back seat of the Almeira – the head of a little girl with a ponytail. In the same fleeting moment, he shirked off the horror and the shame.

'Fuck, what did I turn into?'

He stopped the car by the side of the road and waited for composure that was slow to come. Tears threatened, but he thwarted them. Keep it tight. He called Nools, maybe for distraction.

'Are you getting any word from the cops about how serious they are about pinning those fires on me?'

'They think you did it for the insurance.'

'Do you think I did it?'

'Of course not. Where are you?'

'Somewhere past Magherafelt.'

'You coping OK?'

'Not really.'

'Do you want to come here? I'll put the kettle on.'

She opened the door half an hour later to a shrunken and disconsolate man.

'When was the last time you slept?'

'I've just been thinking, thinking and thinking. I'm sick of thinking.'

'Go upstairs and have a bath.'

While he was gone, she cooked a meal, left him alone but trusted the smell of onions and sizzling beef to draw him back down. She opened a bottle of red wine and set it in the middle of the table, turned everything down low when it was almost ready and waited.

He came down in her husband's fluffy blue bathrobe.

'Jesus,' she said, 'now you're confusing me.'

'I feel like a little boy at his auntie's.'

'That's OK. Can't you for once relax and let someone look after you?'

Over dinner he said, 'It's not the first time I had to wear another man's clothes. Operating was all about making use of people and putting up with them. Arriving in the middle of the night, sleeping through the day. When we were in safe houses we had no privacy, sharing a bed with an oul' farmer sometimes, shitting in bags and getting rid of it.'

'You make it sound so romantic.'

'Some of our men thought having a turn with the daughter or even the son was part of the deal. I was back there in an instant once this trouble started, ever since that call from Kathleen when they petrol-bombed the house in Damascus Street. It was like the years in between had never happened. And that is who I am and the rest is just manners.'

'You should have stayed in Lancaster.'

'I know, but I wouldn't have met Kathleen.'

'You'd have met someone else as nice. You're a decent man so another decent woman would have found you.'

'Do you sometimes think you should have stayed there too?'

'Yes, I do, Terry. But I did a good job here. I supported a good man who would have cracked up without me. When your comrades sent him home shaking with panic I held him together. And I was glad to do it – that was my war.'

'And are you a bit burnt out too?'

'I am. And little thanks I got. But life goes on.' Then after a moment's silence she said, 'Do you think the killing is over?'

'You never know for sure. I was done with it.'

'Until now?'

He didn't answer.

'They think you've still got a gun.'

He said nothing.

'Terry, they have a whole history on that gun. If it is ever used again they will only be looking for you. So it's no good to you.'

'Do I look like someone who wants to start the Troubles again?'

Afterwards, she brought bedding, arranged it on the sofa and left him. Ten minutes later, coming down for a glass of water, she checked on him. He was asleep. She kissed him on the forehead and whispered, 'Goodnight.'

She turned to the stairs and heard him say as softly, 'Goodnight, Nuala.'

***

The Sperrins had never looked so solid and radiant. He bypassed Strabane to Clady and the wee stone bridge, with nooks for travellers to step into, out of the way of the oncoming carriage; they had been firing positions once. He felt better when he was over the border where there was less chance of the police taking an interest in him. He could be at peace here.

He parked the car by the side of the road, between Killygordon and Stranorlar. He left the car and walked back along the road for a few hundred yards, relaxing into the feel of the soft breeze and the sound of baying sheep. The familiar fragrance of burning peat was a comfort. He didn't want to be tense when he reached the cottage or he would frighten Kathleen.

She didn't come to the car when he stopped out front. She would have been checking from the window that it was him. She didn't turn around from folding clothes when he walked in. She kept her head down and was uncomfortable with him being there. Her mind was simply too busy with managing fear to be able to dwell on their relationship with each other. She could only focus on things that she could control, could spare no thought for the things that were unresolved. The off-putting cleanness of everything was evidence of that; he could hardly walk across the floor without defiling it. He assumed she intended him to feel that, that she had repossessed the place.

She would have lifted his hopes if she had received him with warmth and concern, hugged him and told him she had been fretting about his suffering in the police cell, but she appeared to have given no thought to what he had been through – and he was used to that. He recognised her moods as clearly as if their names were written on her brow. This one was sullenness. It said, You are nothing but a problem to me.

'I thought you were coming last night.' She didn't wait for an answer but turned to lift a mop in the corner and carry it to the cupboard it belonged in.

He had to provide her with a diversion. This is what a lion tamer does when he enters the cage. He makes no approach but waits for the lion to notice him.

'I have to go in to Donegal Town to buy a couple of jackets.'

'I'd better come with you', she said, recognising that he was making an effort to be pleasant. 'You'll only make a mess of it.'

She sat beside him as he drove towards the coast. At first, she didn't speak and he did not prompt her to. He was willing to endure her worst, trusting that it would pass. She had expected him to explode and storm out earlier; not that she wanted him to do that. She would not have known what to do if he had, other than to indulge the quiet satisfaction of having been right in judging that everything was going wrong.

'Did you tell the police that you would own up to the bombing?'

'I told McKeague that I would make a statement if I was sure that the claims for the houses would go through OK.'

'This is all nonsense. You're asking the police to lie about the burnings. Will they do that?'

'I'm not asking them to lie, just to say they don't know, and that they are confident it wasn't me or the IRA.'

'But it was the IRA.'

'I was in the IRA. Connect the burnings to the IRA and the IRA to me, and we get no money.'

'If they really do think it was you, why would they say it wasn't? Just to get a confession to Magheraloy? They get a bigger pound of flesh out of you if they do you for the fires. You'd go down for a lot longer. That might be what they'd like, Terry.'

Her logic was impeccable. He'd been round those thoughts himself. But there was no way they could get him for the fires because he'd had nothing to do with them.

'Unless,' she said, 'there's another reason to get you to confess to the Magheraloy bombing.'

'McGrath? I've been assuming they don't want him, don't want the political damage. But maybe I should test them on that.'

'Maybe Basil McKeague doesn't care how much political damage he causes,' she said.

Did she have some insight into McKeague's thinking? Had she been talking to him? 'How do you know what he thinks?'

'Who else was I to talk to?'

'Fuck. What did you say to him? What did he say?'

She was not up for an argument about this. She said, 'His bosses might want to spare McGrath, but he's leaving the police and I don't think he would mind pulling him down before he goes. He doesn't care about saving the political process; he despises it.'

'An old bigot, is he? I thought he looked like one.'

'Who cares what his motives are. The only bargaining power you have is to deliver McGrath to him.'

'But if the Provos think they need to kill us both to save McGrath, they'll do it,' Terry replied.

'Best get on with it then.'

'Have you the stomach for this, Kathleen?'

'No. But what choice do I have?'

***

Inspector Basil McKeague was a believer. He liked the instruction to turn the other cheek. He had his own personal interpretation of it that not all theologians would endorse. He read it as leaving the punishment to God. You turn the other cheek, so that the guy will hit you twice and then get a double dose himself of what God gives him. McKeague wasn't interested in the passivity of God; he wanted to see more of His wrath. 'Vengeance is mine,' said the Lord. That's consolation to a copper when he fails to get a conviction.

He needed that reassurance when it was clear that man's justice, which he served, would not get its way. And he had come now to believe that failure was not a problem. He would rather have the likes of Terry Brankin burn in Hell than find his conscience in a cell and beg forgiveness in order to escape that punishment. He had been trying to explain all this to Seamus Lavery, but Lavery was a Catholic: he liked to see punishment in this world, because he thought God was soft.

'God? Are you crazy? He can stand back and watch my whole family blown to bits and yet you rely on him to do right by the men who did it. I don't think so.'

Seamus Lavery made McKeague's living room small. He was a big man of mountain farming stock. His family had survived the recent centuries through hard physical work, and only in this generation had found time to relax and enough wealth to eat well, so he was fatter than nature intended. But he still had the mentality of people who lived by clear decisions and implacable application. The fact he had put that inherited determination into a computer shop would have puzzled his forebears. He had energy and anger to spare.

As a country man, he had little sense of a need to dress himself for the city. Basil presumed that tangled mop of red curls hadn't been combed for years. His teeth were yellow but strong; the sort that could cut string or bite the cap off a beer bottle. Seamus Lavery smiled, for he loved the thought that perverse justice might nail Terry Brankin and put him in jail for a long time for burning his own houses. The joke was almost too good to bear. He lifted the can of stout to his lips again. Basil thought the stuff was evil, but he always had a couple of cans for Seamus when he came.

'And who do you think did burn his houses?' said McKeague, looking intently at him.

'Why, his Provo mates, of course.'

'God forgive me, I should pull you in.'

'I didn't do it!' Lavery shouted.

'Did you fire a shot at his wife?'

'No. Where would I get a gun?'

'I doubt that would be hard for you.'

'I didn't fire a shot at his wife, wouldn't know her to look at.'

McKeague said nothing, unsure if that was one lie or two.

'Maybe Brankin's more use alive if he can bring the big man down,' Lavery said.

'Wishful thinking, Seamus. If Terry Brankin confesses, that won't happen.'

'Why not?'

'If he confesses his own part in the bombing, there will be no trial, no witnesses called, no chance for a barrister to raise McGrath's name in open court. And that's the way Brankin will want it; he won't want to drop his comrades in the shit. He can't be seen to be touting. No, he's going to be a good boy and try to impress his wife by walking into jail alone and taking his two years. I see no way he is going to lead us to McGrath.'

Lavery snarled. 'See, it's all sorted for McGrath. Nobody wants to see that sainted horror punished for what he did.'

***

Kathleen and Terry perused the shops in Donegal Town. The place was crammed with tourists. He bought a couple of tweed jackets that she liked and he talked her into taking a woollen shawl.

'I couldn't wear that in Belfast.'

'Well, wear it at the cottage. It's peasantry chic. We'll get some hens.'

'Do you know, I could live there ... if I knew I was safe.'

She was going to worry about that, whatever he said. They held hands as they strolled along the river, hardly able to believe that real danger could reach them here. Yet this terrain had been sculpted for battle in past centuries. The stonework, the castle, the lovely setting – what were they but the relics of carnage? He'd be as well remembering that.

It was then he started to think more methodically about how to deal with Ig Murray. He could shoot him, but he only had a traceable gun, and anyway, there were plenty of other Igs behind him. It wasn't a man he had to stop, but the whole IRA. The formal ceasefire wouldn't make any difference. They could run him over with a truck, or stab him or blow his head off with a shotgun. All that the ceasefire terms required was a change of style.

Terry's phone rang in the car on their way back to the cottage. It was McKeague.

'Maybe you'd like another conversation.'

'You'll have to extradite me. I'm in Donegal.'

'I could come to Donegal.'

'You're not coming to my home.'

'I'll book into Hyland's in Glenties tomorrow. I might enjoy a little fishing.'

'I'm sure you will.'

'Come and see me in Hyland's tomorrow afternoon, about 3.'

'OK,' said Terry. 'I will.'

Seventeen

Basil McKeague got the room that Meryl Streep had stayed in when *Dancing at Lughnasa* was filmed. That's what a notice on the wall beside the picture said. It meant nothing to him. He unpacked and walked out along a country road into the hills. It always surprised him how quickly he relaxed in the country air. The city was bad for him.

He passed fancy modern bungalows and occasional little cottages, one with a collie dog at the door, eagerly inspecting him. He should have been planning his retirement, but would he be comfortable in a place like this, as an old peeler and a Prod? There wouldn't be much chance of keeping those details to himself. Some of the Provos had claimed this county as their own spiritual home. They even learnt the old language and talked it in the pubs, laced with 'fuckin' and 'cunt' and more of the rough vocabulary that they cherished still, even though it belonged to the hated English. When he was in Special Branch, he had been urged to learn a bit of Irish, to pass himself off as a man who was at home in Fenian bars when he was watching republicans.

What he really wanted was a retirement in which he would not have to think about security or the Troubles. When he looked around at the hills over Glenties, he felt strongly that this was where it should be spent. He felt something like nostalgia for those hills, as if, somehow, they had always been waiting for him.

The phone rang in his pocket. Even here.

'Change of plan,' said Terry. 'Where are you now?'

'I'm not telling you that.'

'It's OK, I can see you. The hotel said you'd gone for a walk.'

Terry Brankin had left the cottage on an old bicycle and taken the hill road over to Glenties. He had packed the pistol in a shoulder bag with the thought that he might get to let off a couple of practice rounds when he was high above everything and miles from any town. He had puffed hard on the bike at first, then recovered and got into a comfortable rhythm in which it had soon become unthinkable that he would violate the peaceful evening. Still, it amused him to be seeing McKeague while he had a gun with him. It would be his own wee joke, enjoyed alone. On the other side of the border, McKeague would be empowered to call in support and have him searched. Not here.

Basil knew he had left himself exposed. Terry Brankin had the physical advantage of bulk and height. He began to calculate the likely gains and dangers for Brankin if he took this chance to be rid of a pesky old peeler. A man like Brankin was trained to seek his best tactical advantage, and would killing a policeman produce that? No, the file on Magheraloy would get handed over to another cop, who would be talking to Brankin next week and who would know that McKeague had met his death in the pursuit of that case.

And, if Terry Brankin still wanted to make a deal, he wasn't going to get much out of a dead body. So, though McKeague had planned that they would have a meeting in a room, in which he would have his own weapon close at hand, and from which Terry Brankin would not be able to run unseen, he grimaced hard and accepted that he was probably as safe here by the gorse blooms as there.

Brankin was standing by the gatepost of a small white cottage of the type that would have had a thatch until the owner decided it was a nuisance to maintain. He was waiting for him, a little canvas camera bag over his shoulder, looking like someone who was just out enjoying himself.

'What the fuck was that nonsense about, arresting me for the houses?'

'Well, if the deal is that we're clearing you of an insurance scam we have to be seen to have looked into it, don't we?'

'I see. You're a bastard but you're a clever bastard.' This raised his hopes. 'Would you not feel safer in Portrush?' Terry said. 'Or is this the fruit of peace – that Donegal is now open to peelers. You spent long enough trying to tell us it was a different country.'

'My mother was from Ardara, and her mother was a native Irish speaker from Doochary.'

'Then how did you end up being in the front line of the defence of Unionism?'

'I never saw that as my job. Isobel Lavery wasn't a unionist.'

'But guys like you didn't advance in the police unless you had the right political credentials and the right handshake.'

'That'll be why I retire as an inspector, will it? Terry, you should know more than this about the country you fought for.'

'Don't throw it in my face that your clique didn't look after you; take it up with them. There was to be nothing for me, if it was left to your lot to run the place.'

'OK, you had a grievance. A smart Catholic boy out of a big Catholic school in 1978 and all the good jobs going to Prods. But your people started out with a smart answer to that – a demand for civil rights and justice and the whole world listening. Where do the bombs come in, Terry? When did it become absolutely essential to your job prospects that people should die?'

'You gave us nothing.'

'After 1972 we had nothing to give. The British took over and all they ever wanted was to end the trouble at any cost.'

'Bloody Sunday?'

'There was never another one, was there? Not after they took over. Are we going to argue politics all day?

'Are you on for a deal?'

'Tell me truthfully ... Oh, don't bother. How would I know if it was the truth?'

'What?'

'Did you burn the houses?'

'No, I did not. On Isobel Lavery's grave, I did not.'

McKeague winced, but he believed him. 'Then here's how I want it. We'll charge you with the Magheraloy bomb, but you will plead not guilty and fight the case.'

This was a surprise turn, and Terry took a moment to think through the logic of it. 'Because you want the story out in public?'

'Yes.'

'And the houses? The government will reckon that I brought the burnings on myself and will give me nothing.'

'We'll say that we believe it was done by an embittered individual.'

'And the Provos get off the hook again.'

'You think it was the Provos?'

'No, no, of course not. Obviously a disgruntled tenant. Thank you.'

Terry looked around at the indifferent hills. What an incongruous place to be having a conversation like this in. 'When are you going to do this?'

'Any time you're in Belfast would suit.'

'And, if I say no?'

'Will you?'

Terry had to laugh, but he saw the logic. On the one hand, the Provos would be assured that he hadn't confessed, but on the other, McKeague would get a trial that would bring out McGrath's name.

'Mind you,' said McKeague. 'It would be a lot easier for us to charge you if you could part with a morsel of evidence.'

'I'll think about it.'

McKeague nodded his goodbye and resumed his walk up the hill. Terry marvelled at the elegance of the plan in which he had been invited to participate. It seemed typical of Northern Irish politics and peacemaking that every constructive move was contaminated by lies. He had never known it any other way. He swung a leg over the old black bicycle and headed back towards the cottage. There was a chill in the air, but the effort of cycling kept him warm and even a little exhilarated. He wasn't sure exactly why he was laughing to himself. Perhaps it was at the prospect of the drama of a trial and the chance to damage McGrath. Perhaps it was to do with a sense that McKeague, having shown himself to be as morally dubious as himself, had absolved him. He had been aching under a fear that what was at stake was his soul; now it was all back to being a game. He enjoyed games.

***

Kathleen at first thought that Terry was back when she heard a car stop at the end of the lane, forgetting that he had gone on the bicycle. She continued to fill the old kettle then set it on the hot plate of the black range, almost by reflex. But a doubt crept up on her. She didn't want to look out to check that those were his footsteps drawing closer now, for she had no way of coping with the danger but by blanking her mind to it. When the dread crossed her that this might be the IRA man coming back to shoot her, she might have run out the back but she would not have got far and the fear would have consumed her before he had even caught up with her; better to try and manage the terror. Better to pretend this might be no one important at all. Then Ig opened the door and stepped inside. She still didn't look round until he spoke. 'Your first instalment, ma'am,' he said.

Kathleen felt fear clutching her gut. She tried not to fall. Ig was dressed in denim dungarees and boots and he wore a skull-hugging woollen cap. He was smiling and he held something at his side that she couldn't make out.

'What do you want?' The heavy iron tongs for the range were hanging within reach. She dismissed a notion that she might fell him.

'I have come to shoot you in the leg,' he said. He raised the gun to show it to her. He held it sideways in an open hand, as if inviting her to admire it. 'He's away out on the bike, isn't he? Sure he'll be back in time to look after you.'

Then she stopped breathing. He read the panic in her expression, the slackening of the lips as in a child about to cry.

'Don't worry. I've done this a hundred times before. I taught Terry how to do it. It never seems to hurt much at first. There is an awkward artery behind the knee, but most times I have managed to avoid it.'

With luck, thought Ig, Terry Brankin would not be back until this was done or he would have to take him down, and her too as the witness of it.

Kathleen found breath to speak angrily. 'Are you ... are you some kind of lunatic?'

'No. We are very practical. We have been thinking about this little problem. It is important to discourage your husband from talking to the police about old friends. Now, if we kill you, as a means of keeping his mouth shut, it's not going to work, is it? He will reckon that he has nothing more to lose and will blab away. Even now, he might be thinking that blabbing first is the way to keep you safe. So the new plan is to shoot you occasionally. In one leg, or an arm, not to kill you, but just to keep reminding him of the need for discretion. Tonight you get your first instalment. Best to get it done quickly so that there is no confusion in Terry's mind about what we intend. He gets so upset sometimes and misreads situations.'

Kathleen started to tremble. She watched him inspecting her body and the room. Her breath was tightening. Her legs were weak. She braced herself. She was close to shitting herself and farted – a quick sequence of soft but audible blurts. Ig said, 'Yes these things can be messy.'

Then his tone became stern. 'Outside,' he said, and when she seemed not even to understand the word, he said, 'Now!' He had calculated that if he laid her down on this stone floor and shot her there, the bullet might ricochet anywhere. Outside was safer, so he grabbed her wrist and pulled her through the door. She had no shoes on.

***

Terry came over the hill towards the cottage, peddling fiercely down the winding road to get the momentum that would carry him halfway up the next hill. He was playing. This was a boreen, so rarely used by cars that grass grew in a line down the middle of it, and he was in danger of veering across that line and skidding. He liked the risk. The old bicycle had only three gears and if he fell back onto the lowest of these, the climb would be slow and tedious. Sometimes his energy and breath were exhausted just when he got to the top of a hill, and then the exertion to keep him moving gently giving way to momentum felt like a gift.

We'll be all right, he thought. He felt almost like announcing his confidence to the hills and valleys, and below him to the glinting sea. He was thinking that life could be good here. They wouldn't need very much. He would be fitter and healthier. They could turn the cottage into a proper home. He began to imagine himself into that life, food from the garden, bits of work here and there, few needs and a lot of free time. Isn't that the life most people really want? Wee buns.

He rolled shakily down the last bend before the cottage, clenching the brakes, and saw the smoke from the chimney. All perfect. They could be done with a lot of worries if they made this their home, and Kathleen would like it because it was so like the life she grew up to, before she went to Queen's. Then he saw her walk out, perhaps to toss a bucket of water or scraps. For a moment this was a beautiful sight to him. It was home. Then he saw Ig walking behind her and he braked sharply and nearly threw himself into a stone wall. There he crouched, stopped and quietened himself.

He watched Ig take Kathleen brusquely by the arm and lead her away from the stony ground at the front. Terry wondered if there were others, out of sight, supporting Ig. He would have to gamble that Ig was alone.

'Lie down on the ground,' said Ig. 'I need to be close to you to get a clean shot. Believe me, love, it's better if we do this right. Lie down.'

'No,' she cried. 'Leave me alone. How can you do this? Please. Please.' She was frantic.

He had her by the wrist and she tugged away at first, and when she found that this was pointless she fell to her knees, begging him, weeping. Her mind was grasping in all directions for ideas of how to appease this horrific man. It was all happening too fast. She had to think. But there was no appeasing the likes of Ig. She knew that. He had clarity of purpose and had stated it plainly. Suddenly it was as if her whole life was trivial. The books she had loved were meaningless. She had lived in the rash and unsustainable assumption that no mad beast would ever come along and destroy her.

She would have been better off as an illiterate beggar in a ditch all her days, if she had at least known how expendable she was, than to have lived as she had, with the laughable fantasy that she was ever safe, and that she really owned anything.

Terry Brankin watched as his wife fell to her knees, her hair loose about her face. He would have to move quickly. Not one ounce of his experience had prepared him for this. As an active paramilitary, the only times you had to plan on the move were when a previous plan had gone wrong, and that should never happen, or when your billet or hideout was exposed and you had to run. When you are the attacker, you always have the option of aborting the operation and coming back another day. He had no experience of fighting apart from tussles in the playground years ago.

He studied the layout of the ground close to him and mapped out a route that would take him closer to them, knowing that Ig might shoot her before he had a chance to take him. He lost sight of them behind an outhouse for one fraught moment. Then he saw Kathleen go down on all fours, looking back at Ig. She wasn't co-operating like the boys he had himself shot, but was turning and writhing and pleading. This was good; it was dragging this out, giving him time.

Kathleen buried her face in her folded arms, her body tight all over. Terry didn't see Ig's gun clearly until he used it to tap the side of Kathleen's knee, to correct her position. He was arched over and shouting at her. She stretched herself out slowly, weeping with resignation, and lay face down, her face in her hands. Ig stroked her inside legs with the pistol to order them apart. He was folding back the hem of her dress, away from the backs of her knees.

Terry saw that Ig had her entirely at his disposal now. He also understood that he intended to shoot her in the legs, not to kill her. He had to contain his anger or he would make a mistake. His Ruger was useless for distance shooting. He had no idea whether it was accurate, zeroed, or whether the shot would tend to one side or the other, for he had only ever used it for kneecappings, that is, up close. He could charge at Ig or call out to him, but either way would give Ig time to shoot Kathleen and then turn around to defend himself with the pistol in his hand.

In films, what would happen at this point was predictable. He would shout out to Ig and Ig would threaten to shoot Kathleen in the head or take her as a hostage, a shield, and try to work his way back to his car. There was no way it would proceed like that in real life. And yet, if left to get on with it, without Terry breaking cover, in the next few seconds he would shoot Kathleen in the legs.

So Terry grabbed his attention. He fired one shot in the air. Ig was startled and glanced in the wrong direction. Even after all these years, he couldn't pinpoint the source of a gunshot in the open. Terry broke cover and ran straight at them. He fired again as he stumbled and hurtled towards them, hardly aiming, hoping that the shock of the shots and his shouting would panic Ig out of a reasoned and tactical response.

Ig spun sharply and ducked. Terry was within a few yards of him before Ig could cock the pistol and get a shot off. He missed. Age and drink had weakened him. Well Terry wasn't sure they hadn't weakened him too as he crashed into him, their heads bumping hard, bundling them together. The sweat of him. The smell. Them tumbling over.

They tripped backwards over Kathleen and rolled on grass and twigs and into the briery ditch, both of them out of control. This would be over in seconds now, one way or the other, and both knew it. It was down to whoever got to a gun first and that was only about luck. They wrestled for everything. Pulling and squirming, trying to back off enough to have space for a punch but not so far as to let the other wrest himself free.

Kathleen was on her feet now but Terry could not read her movements. Then he saw that she had Ig's gun, a Browning 9 mil, in her hand and was fumbling with it, trying to make sense of it. It was cocked, ready to fire.

'Fuck's sake, don't,' he said.

She dropped it as if it was hot.

The two men were gripping each other, one hand at the other's neck, the other with fingers splayed across the other's face. One might get an eye or a good bite, each knowing that whoever lost his grip was finished. Terry was on top. Ig had worked out how to head-butt him while pinned down on his back. Terry took a stunning thud on his brow yet couldn't risk drawing back too far lest his hold on Ig would weaken.

Wrestling to suppress the delirium of terror, Kathleen stepped towards them and dared to put a bare foot onto Ig's face, and Ig, constrained by the force of Terry's weight and his clutch on his arms, turned snarling like a dog. She could not get a firm purchase on him anywhere, then the ball of her foot settled comfortably into his left eye socket and that held the head firm. She pressed harder, feeling the softness of the eye itself yield to her pressure, but again a panic surge freed Ig from her.

'His neck,' said Terry. 'Get his neck.'

'I can't,' she cried. She was almost in a frenzy of indecision and fear. But Ig was weakened and Terry got one hand free and was able to slam his elbow across his cheek.

He yelled at her, 'Give me a fucking gun.'

Kathleen bent to study the ground around her, fretted about and stooped to pick up the Browning.

'The other one,' Terry roared.

She found the Ruger and handled it like a child who had never even played with toy guns: holding it by the barrel as she offered the handle to Terry. It was pointing back directly towards her stomach.

He snatched it from her and shouted, 'Don't look!'

She backed away from him.

Terry pressed into Ig with the weight of his whole body and pushed the gun up under his chin.

'Say hello to Jesus,' he said, and fired.

The press of bodies muffled the sound a little. It was a mess. The whole head burst, though most of the blood followed the bullet away from them. Kathleen stood, wailing in an almost sing-song moan of helplessness. Terry struggled to his feet with eyes only for the bundled and broken filth that was Ig. He braced himself to fire again, for he still had not expended his rage. But there was no need for another bullet and he urged himself to save it, to be calm and to think clearly.

Terry turned his back on Ig's body and reached an arm across Kathleen's shoulders. She was gasping for breath. She slowly looked at him with a hand raised to the side of her face to block her view of Ig. He read that as pleading. He knew her. She was pleading for the impossible, for this to be undone, not to have happened.

'Did he hurt you?'

'No. You?'

'I'm OK.' He was breathless. He could not have kept that up for much longer.

She was pale and dishevelled. Her lower jaw juddered as if she was trying to speak and finding the task beyond her.

'Go back into the house,' he said. 'I have to get rid of him.'

'Shouldn't you call the police?'

'No.'

She accepted for now that he knew best. The little she knew about how to function around this violence had got them nowhere.

Kathleen got up and stood near him with her face away from the body. Her clothes were crumpled and stained. 'Hold me, please.'

He reached his arms around her and said, 'I'm sorry.'

'He said he was going to shoot me in the leg and then come back and shoot me in the arm. I thought he was going to rape me. He could have done anything.'

'You'll be OK. I'll deal with this.'

She walked to the house and closed the door behind her. There the panic would return and she would weep and he would not be with her to console her for he had Ig's body to deal with. Terry picked up the Browning and uncocked it to make it safe. He searched Ig's pockets and found his mobile phone and car keys. As he had expected, Ig had switched off the phone so that his movements could not be traced from it. That helped.

A body is heavy. A dead body is even heavier.

There was an old wheelbarrow in the shed beside the house. The shed itself smelt of turf dust and rotten straw. Over two centuries or more, probably hundreds of animals had used that space to feed, shite, give birth and die in. Terry even considered bringing the body in there, covering it with straw and letting the rats and the flies have it. He took the wheelbarrow down to the meadow. Ig was too heavy and awkward to lift onto the barrow. He tried to stand the barrow beside the body, on its front edge with the handles high and bundle him towards it. Kathleen should have been helping him but he couldn't ask her, yet this was a two person job. In the second attempt, he made it easier for himself by positioning the barrow lower than the body, wrenching half of Ig onto the barrow's edge and then levering the handles down to scoop it up. That got half of him in.

Then Terry hoisted the rest, mostly the legs, with his hands. He wheeled the barrow down the lane. It was off balance for most of the way and Terry struggled to keep it level.

He opened a rear door of Ig's car and parked the wheelbarrow beside it. Then he went to the other side and climbed into the back seat. With more tugging and heaving, he pulled the body halfway in, the broken, blood-wet head against his own stomach. Once he had the centre of gravity on the seat, he got out, went around to tackle the parts that still hung out: the bloody legs and boots. It didn't matter if it wasn't properly set on a seat and slumped half onto the floor. Not yet anyway. Nor did it matter that he was smearing blood all over the furnishings and his clothes, so long as he kept out of sight. When he was finished he would destroy the car.

Terry drove out onto the road and turned towards the coast. He had no plan for disposing of a bloody corpse yet. Ideally he would get rid of the body completely, so thoroughly destroy it that no trace would ever be found, and no evidence from it would point back at him. He thought at first that the best he could probably hope for was to dump it off a cliff, and that it mightn't be found until all forensic traces of Terry and Kathleen were long gone from it. But he wasn't sure yet what to do.

He drove along the promenade at Mount Charles. The tide was out, otherwise he might have been able to borrow a boat and dump Ig into Donegal Bay, with stones in the pockets to keep him down. Even then, this bay was trawled so much by fishermen gathering lobsters that someone was bound to find it in time.

It was such a beautiful evening, the light almost silvery, and there was no wind at all. Sound travelled on a day like this. You might hear a beast in a field snorting at the other side of the bay, too far away to be seen. And dozens, hundreds of people might hear the car, and remember if asked by the police. It was so frustrating to sit looking at the expanse of water that could swallow Ig whole and hide him forever and not to be able to get him into it.

He drove back out onto the main road through Killybegs and Carrick. If he had to stop or got stuck in traffic, anyone might see the body and the blood on the back seat. He took his chances. He knew that people often don't believe what they see; they might rationalise that the body was a drunk. But the streets of Killybegs were quiet.

It was tea time. He thanked God people lived such routine lives. He had often depended on that when he was in the IRA.

Even as he headed out the peninsula, he was in danger of being seen by hillwalkers. Ramblers and tourists would usually have a camera. A farmer might be out checking gates and hedges and have a clear view of him. The road wound up onto the huge hump of Slieve League and took him to the edge of Bunglass, hundreds of feet above the sea and rocks. There, he looked out on the wildness of the western sea and marvelled at the difficulty of disposing of a body when not a human seemed to stir in all that vastness. He couldn't just let the the car run over the cliff and smash below. It wouldn't be carried out by the tide. Within a day or two, a boat would spot it and someone would find a body in the back, with a bullet-shattered head. He had to think this through.

Surely it was possible to get rid of a body in a wild county like Donegal? He could bury it on his own land, of course, but how long would it take one man alone to dig an adequate grave? And people looking for Ig might come to the cottage and sniff around. He had no information on who knew what Ig had planned to do, what back-up he had. It was possible that the Gardaí were tracking Ig and would wonder why the trail that led to Terry Brankin's cottage had ended there. Or there might be an electronic trace on the car, in which case they would be able to extend their search to this very spot. Was he letting his imagination torture him or was he thinking reasonably?

Terry quietened his mind. He knew something of how an IRA man like Ig would work. This car was almost certainly not his own. There was no way an old Provo like Ig would have come out to shoot someone in a car registered in his own name. Therefore, it was likely there was no trace on it, at least not one that led directly to Ig. It was probably stolen, the chassis number erased and the plates changed: a ringer. The same devices that Ig relied on to cover his tracks would serve as well for preserving the secret of his death and disappearance. So all he had to worry about, for now, was the body.

'Think man, think.'

He knew of sandstone caves near Inver, less than a mile from his cottage. They had been excavated for building blocks and cemetery headstones. There were rumoured to be tunnels that had been dug centuries before that no one now went into. But could he find his way deep into one of those caves and conceal a body there? He had been in some of the more accessible tunnels and they were hard enough to negotiate and as cold as a refrigerator. A body would not smell badly there. It would stay fresh. The stink would not arouse suspicion but that suggested another problem. He needed it to decompose or get eaten, or the evidence would linger.

He would have to bury it. He thought of the turf bog on the hill above his cottage where he had cut peat. Often he had stumbled over the brittle heather on the dry bog surface, and once his entire leg had slithered into a hole. He had been amazed at how deep some of the cracks were.

'That's what I'll do.'

He got back into the car and drove, in the near darkness, to the high road between Glenties and Inver, the road he had cycled along just two hours earlier after meeting Basil McKeague. He could imagine how excited McKeague would be to find him now with a dead body and a gun in a stolen car. He was momentarily tempted to stop randomly along the road because, at this time of night, the surrounding terrain seemed like a bog wilderness in which a body thrown out of a car would never be found. But that was daft. He had to leave the body on land that he was assured no one would dig, and that meant it had to be his own.

The body would not necessarily decompose there. Bodies that were thousands of years old had been dug out of the bog, but the shifting surface, almost afloat on the soft peat below, would in time bury Ignatius Murray, where no chance find would expose him to the light of day again.

Terry was able to take the car along the track, deep into the bog, to his own section. He got out to look for a hole or trench.

There were plastic sacks of cut turf in rows along the freshly cut banks, and if anyone from a distance saw him dragging a body, they would easily suppose he was doing the normal work of a cutter on the bog. So he lugged Ig's body from the car and dragged it by the collar of his jacket between two cut banks, into the soggy marsh around his own. He was soon down to his knees in the black oily bog water, with almost no purchase for his feet. The body was a mess now, the blood having blackened, the skin soured and filthy, the clothes torn by stones and bared roots. Even here, Terry would have been able to stretch Ig's body out on the ground with a fair chance that it would never be found under the crisp old heather. But the more inaccessible he wanted the body to be, the more work he would have to do.

The sky was darkening and he was finding his way almost solely by the feel of the terrain. There were occasional trenches from ancient workings that he might trip into. There were folk tales about men disappearing on the bog, tales that he only half-believed, of a lone walker being swallowed by a crack that opened in the shifting bog and closed again. If it was true that a man could fall into one of those and be lost, it would not be hard to hide a body in one. It's just that you never actually find one of these cracks when you are looking for it; it finds you.

He was now about a half a mile from the car, away from the freshly cut turf banks and into the old bog, the part which had not been worked on for decades. He was in a maze of trenches now, mostly covered by dry gnarled ancient heather, so he could not see the ground at his feet.

Terry was exhausted. 'Fuck him! He can lie there.'

When he laid the body down, the heather stalks alone held it up, like a bed. Terry had to press Ig's stiff, dirty corpse through the interweavings, like a child pushing a friend ahead of him through a hedgerow into a forbidden field. At first he was squeamish about the heather scraping Ig's face, or what was left of it, then he shook himself out of such silliness. This wasn't remotely like the body of one who might just be sleeping. It was the ruins of a man. He raised himself and stamped hard on the head and chest and knees. At last, Ig's dead weight carried him through the bed of heather and slithering into the oily stale water below, until only his legs and boots were visible. None of his work would be worth anything if he didn't finish it tidily. There was probably only a drop of about four feet there, but he was confident that no one would find the body by chance, not for a long time. Anyone who smelt the stench of decaying flesh would assume that a sheep had fallen in, for that happened often, and would look no closer.

***

Kathleen's mind was in turmoil. The door was locked and the light was out. She was terrified the night would send new horror to her. She sat in a rocking chair that she had bought to make this cottage feel more traditional and rustic, and she rocked back and forth on it fretfully.

She knew what to expect. She would know when she had wept enough, and convulsed enough, and gasped for enough breath to be able to start relaxing her body; she would know how long to defer thinking. She would have to make some pact with life to survive this, and she would. Waves of panic, which made her shriek and want to rush from the house, into the night, to crouch under some tree and pray, were, to her, like weather that would pass if she framed a clear resolve.

She knew that the windows of her soul had to be open wide to let the storm through, the way you open the windows of a house in the path of a hurricane so that the blast tears your effects to bits and scatters them but leaves the frame standing and the roof intact. She knew how much damage she could sustain short of going completely mad. And if she wasn't sure she could sustain the threat of panic, she at least knew not to succumb straight away. Kathleen hugged her knees and howled.

Terry had been gone for hours. She needed to know he was coming back yet unleashed emotion was something she was best managing by herself; the few times he had seen it had only unnerved him. Better that he was away somewhere, erasing the horror, fighting whatever devils were out there, and giving her time to find sanity somewhere inside herself.

Yet she was taunted by fears that there were more IRA men out there in the hills. Wouldn't there be others supporting Ig, waiting to dispose of the weapon, providing a change of car? Wasn't that how they worked? There was no chance that Terry could be safe. They were bound to have caught up with him. That meant she was alone, that he would not be coming back to protect her, that she had no choice now but to run. But she did not have the energy or clarity of mind to run. She could only curl into herself and wait for what she dreaded, another evil man with another gun.

Peace came slowly. As some composure returned, she thought of calling her mother or Nools. Her mother would simply not comprehend. She didn't know about Terry's IRA past. To her, he was simply the good sensible solicitor who had married her daughter – a man with steady work and a good income. She would never have understood that the real Terry was worth waiting for on such a night. She would have urged her to go to the police, to tell them the whole thing, to be a good citizen, a sensible girl.

Nools would urge Kathleen to rush to her, to move in with her and take shelter there. Nools would be practical and explain the IRA, speaking from insights she had shared before, acquired in circles Kathleen had never moved in. Why shouldn't she do that?

Why? It was simple: Terry needed her.

She was awakened first by raucous crows screeching and scoffing at the dawn, and the softer clamour of smaller birds behind them singing. Maybe they were just clearing their throats.

Then he was standing in front of her, dripping with slime and exhausted. She opened her eyes slowly to the sight of him, unsure she wasn't dreaming up a new horror. She gasped with relief that it was him while almost choking on the fear and disgust. She had never seen him like that, as if he had been bathed in filth, dragged over the earth. He had nothing to say. She didn't want to talk about it anyway.

'Get those things off. I'll run you a bath.' She would have to throw his clothes out. Nothing would ever clean them.

When she came back from the bathroom, he was standing naked by the range, his body pale, scratched, mottled and pathetic.

'Come on.' She led him by the hand, like a frightened child, and he let her soap him in the water and work almost sacramentally over him, to restore his civility and decency, to remind him that he was a good man, with a soul that was entitled to survive, the same man she had loved and married. She kissed him on the head and left him to lie there with his thoughts.

Eighteen

'Yes, Aidan?'

Dominic McGrath had hoped the day was over and he could relax. He had spent the afternoon replying to emails from America and he had yet to update his blog. As a habit from the old days of running from the law, he rarely spent two nights in a row at home. There were party meetings and conferences to attend around the country, pictures to pose for with officials and campaigners, then useful friends to be favoured with the honour of putting him up in their homes and feeding him.

He would be going to Armagh that night to speak at the launch of a book about the local IRA. He had already had his people read it to be sure that there was nothing in it that would embarrass him, but he wondered if he'd get a decent dinner. The last time he had been with that Armagh crowd, they had given him reheated pizza slices in someone's kitchen. He hoped Aidan had made it clear that that just wouldn't do.

He had finished writing the speech and was happy with it. It paid homage to the heroic sacrifices made by the IRA for a just and lasting peace. Every speech was the same but every speech had to be a bit different. He wouldn't do all that work if he didn't enjoy it, but he also needed time to strategise, to think ahead and manage the unexpected. He had a team, but he didn't trust them. He didn't trust anybody.

Aidan looked round the panelled door from his adjoining office, clearly unsure whether or not he should come all the way in. That's what Dominic hated about the boy. He was timid.

'The press are hopping,' Aidan said. 'They've received a statement from Ig Murray through his solicitor. He's outed himself as a tout and done a bunk.'

McGrath just said, 'Read it to me.'

Aidan walked into the office reading with his head down:

> I know this will come as a shock to my comrades in the Republican Movement, but I hope they will understand that I had no choice. Fifteen years ago, I was recruited by British Intelligence, as an informant. They had put me under enormous pressure, after information about my nearest and dearest fell into their hands. I trust my comrades to know how insidious and clever these intelligence agencies are. I swear on the graves of the fallen that I never endangered any of them. My job was to report on the political intelligence available to me. The Brits wanted this, to help them advise the government on its negotiating positions during the peace process. I gave as little as I could, and I assure my friends and comrades in the movement that I often tempered my reports to their best interests and to least damaging effect. I hope the completion of the peace process, to the satisfaction of republicans, proves that I did no harm. I am, however, unable to maintain this secret any longer, and I fear that I cannot go on living in the land we fought for. I have left the land of my birth, to live out the rest of my days in a place where I can bring no taint upon this noble movement and its brave leaders.
>
> My heartfelt apologies for any embarrassment this creates.
>
> Ig Murray.

Devious bastard, thought McGrath. He's trying to finish me. 'How did we get this, Aidan?'

'It came from his solicitor's office. Terry Brankin.'

'Well, isn't that a coincidence?'

'What will we say?'

'Say this is a direct quote from me, and I'll do radio in the morning. "The Republican Movement has been aware for some time that ... no ... has been suspicious for some time that Ig Murray had been compromised by enemies of the peace process.

Unfortunately, the poor man's drink problem made him particularly vulnerable to manipulation. He is in no danger from us."

'Leave it at that for now. If any friendly journalists ask for guidance, tell them off the record that Murray ran most of the disappearances and that his own disappearance now makes it infinitely more difficult for us to give the families what they need. But that's not attributable, OK?'

***

Terry was back in his office where he felt most in control. Here he was surrounded by reminders of his professional life and his achievements. Here he stopped being a 'Ra man and returned to being a lawyer, dressed for the role in a nice new suit with a shirt and tie. This type of clothing felt like armour for him. And he was clean again.

Would McGrath doubt the statement? Terry expected that he would, yet so many of his close associates had turned out to be informers that he might not find it hard to accept that Ig had been one too. People had thought too lightly for years that an informer was someone who had changed sides, but Terry had come to understand that many of them occupied a middle ground between enemies, trying to keep themselves safe and continuing with their war.

Sometimes he wondered if McGrath himself knew for sure whether he was working for the British or the Republican Movement. That routine celebration of the heroism of the IRA was something he could never relax without opening suspicion that he had betrayed them, yet sometimes it also sounded like protesting too much.

Whether McGrath believed the letter from Ig or not, trusted or not that it was genuine, he would want to talk to Terry now. He would have to. It was arranged through Aidan, the press officer. Terry's receptionist rang through when he arrived. 'Mr McGrath is here, with a couple of colleagues.'

Terry had weighed up the possibility that McGrath would send heavies to work him over or even whack him. He had dismissed that as highly unlikely. McGrath came up the narrow staircase into Terry's office with two minders, one in front of him and one behind. Terry didn't know either of them, a fact which in itself reminded him how distant he was from the movement now.

For a man who liked to be well dressed and genial in public spaces, McGrath was disarmingly casual, though the other two looked like knee-breakers. Plainly, he had chosen to come with muscle rather than with brains. That suggested he wasn't confiding his fears to close colleagues. He left the heavies in the waiting area outside, where they could sit and read the *Tatler*, or look at the pictures anyway.

Terry escorted him into a meeting room with a long mahogany table and a photograph of the view across Morecambe Bay on the wall that some clients took to be County Mayo. Terry knew that McGrath would, at least, feel more comfortable in a large room that would be more difficult to bug.

He realised he had never been alone before with McGrath. They had never established how to be fully at ease with each other. Their conversations had always been in offices or at his home with minders at the door, in situations he could control. McGrath had no control at all here, unless he imagined that the two guns in reception were of any practical use to him. They weren't. Having to shoot someone would be failure. So Terry reasoned that he should give McGrath as much as he could spare of the comfort and deference he was used to.

'Always a pleasure to meet you, Dom.'

McGrath frowned. He knew that was a lie for a start. He declined the first seat he was offered and moved closer to the window, through which the sounds of traffic below were clear. He opened the window to increase the noise level. If he was being recorded, the sound would be cluttered. 'Nothing like a bit of fresh air,' he said, and sat down circumspectly, as if the very act of sitting was new to him. 'You've been having a few problems yourself, Terry, old friend.'

'That's right.'

McGrath stroked his chin, as if puzzling over a worrying problem that Terry might help him with. 'What I need to know is if there is any connection between those problems and this ... er ... development.'

'Well we live in difficult and confusing times,' said Terry, who could obfuscate too. 'What connection do you think there could be?'

'I'm wondering about that.'

Terry coughed softly and opened a pink folder in front of him with the documentation relating to Ig Murray.

'Well, Ig, as far as I can see, is playing straight here. He commissioned me to release the statement, to handle media queries and to tie up his affairs, such as they are. He rented his house and owned almost nothing. The police believe he may have been using a wee car that was found burnt out in Larne two nights ago. It wasn't even his own. It was a ringer. Dumping it there suggests that he was getting the ferry. He's gone. I only have occasional calls from him.'

McGrath paused long in order to unnerve Terry. Terry had seen that tactic before. It created a vacuum that he was tempted to fill with more detail, more assertion, all of which would make him look less confident, even a little frantic. He had to sit out the pause.

McGrath said, 'I need a lot more information than that, a chara.'

'Well, you understand the confidentiality requirement which governs my conduct here. I'm afraid that's all I can tell you.'

'Who do you think you are talking to, Terry?'

'I really don't know any more.'

He closed the folder now to signal the completion of his disclosures, though there was nothing in it but the letter from Ig, which he had written himself.

Terry said, 'Ig came to me. He asked if I would release a statement. We discussed the language but only to tidy it up, not to conceal anything. OK, it was my suggestion he include a line about tempering reports to the best interests of comrades. I thought that, for his own sake, he should try to be reassuring.' Terry trusted that he was a good liar and knew that he had to be when dealing with Dom.

McGrath sucked hard. He had habits from when he was a pipe smoker. 'Tell me, what is your take on who burnt your houses? I hear you blamed Ig for that.'

This was dangerous.

McGrath continued. 'You threatened Ig and now he is missing and the only person with anything to offer by way of explanation is you.'

'Look, you know Ig and I were operating a long time and guys who are that close have their rows and still come back to each other and can speak plainly. He says he didn't burn the houses. I don't know what to believe. But who else was he going to go to for a job like this? He wanted someone who was outside the movement but who understood how it worked. At the start of it, I said I would do fuck all for him unless he cleared up the business about the houses and he just sat where you are now and stared blankly at me as if he was in Castlereagh, and he wouldn't budge on it. So I helped him with his statement, and, as far as I know, he went out there and drove to Larne for the boat. I don't even know how I'm going to bill him for the work.'

'Hmmm.' McGrath sat quietly as if savouring these new lies and comparing them with many others he had heard down the years. Then he said, 'I don't believe that Ig Murray was working for the Brits. And if he wasn't, how can I believe that you are working for him? I am left with a huge puzzle. Where is he? Is he alive or dead? Is this a move against me? I don't like the feel of this business at all.'

This was tougher talk from Dom than on the day he had sent Terry off with the nutting squad to be questioned, and they having the option of killing him if they didn't like his answers. His best hope was in his understanding that McGrath scowled when he was helpless and smiled when he was really dangerous. But he also knew McGrath was not that easy to read.

'But you issued a statement of your own to say you had known about Ig all along. Are you thinking of retracting that?'

McGrath looked at him coldly. 'Now you're being smart. What are your plans in relation to the Magheraloy incident?'

'I have no plans,' said Terry. 'I am under investigation. It isn't clear yet whether I will be charged. In any event, you have nothing to worry about. When I was questioned, I said nothing about you.'

'Good,' said McGrath. 'Keep it that way.'

Terry knew what McGrath's best option was now that he feared him: it was to have him killed, if that could be done without political damage. He'd be thinking that one through.

***

Inspector McKeague was sitting quietly in his office, reflecting on the satisfactions of his job. It was a sparsely furnished office, just a swivel chair in front of a computer and some wire mesh paper trays and a stapler at hand. Beside the computer was a little framed photograph of his wedding day, a reminder of a time when he and his wife had liked each other. On his wall, he had a picture of the queen in her youth and, facing it, a large map of Northern Ireland with areas marked in green and orange to designate them as predominantly Catholic or Protestant. Some of his colleagues had hinted that he should not have the portrait of the queen – it might suggest a political affiliation that a cop should not advertise – but he ignored them. No one would formally ask him to remove it.

One of the satisfactions of his job was that it gave structure to his life. He wondered if he would really settle, in a year from now, when he had only his domestic commitments, the service of his wife and his garden to keep him busy. He could give more of his time to the church, but would he enjoy that? He believed in God and Eternal Justice but he winced in the company of men who believed too much, and he didn't want to be one of them. Maybe he would write a book. An old peeler had lots to tell and knew more about most cases than had ever appeared in the newspapers – like the provenance of guns, for example.

His desk phone rang and it was Terry Brankin. McKeague had been hoping to pick the moment for their next inevitable conversation and to derive the sweetest pleasure from its timing.

'Yes, Mr Brankin, you can come to my office.'

It wasn't far from Brankin's own.

It was lunchtime and the bank girls in their uniforms would be lounging in the grounds of the City Hall, to start up the tans they would soon be refining in Greece and Spain. Basil McKeague thought it would be good not to be busy in such weather.

The Cold Case Review team was often happy to meet people in their own homes or in quiet, well-furnished offices in the city, accepting that many of those it dealt with, victims and suspects, would be more candid where they were comfortable. Inspector McKeague was happy to call Terry Brankin into the bowels of the darkest and grimmest police station in town, and would have been happier still if he could call him into the antechamber to Hell – which, for some, is what his office had been.

Terry arrived within fifteen minutes.

'You want a morsel of evidence on the Magheraloy bomb. I have taken your suggestion and modified it,' Terry said.

'Let me hear it then.'

'I am confessing to participation in the bombing,' he said. 'Here is an affidavit, which I will sign, naming Ig Murray and Mick Harkin as the others on the team.'

'Huh.' This wasn't what McKeague had asked for. He wanted a trial and names named. Terry Brankin wasn't offering him that. 'We have nothing to say Ig Murray was there.'

'Take it from me, he was.'

'And that's it?'

'Yes. You want to expose McGrath, you do it by pulling in Murray – if MI5 will let you near him – and putting him in the dock. Failing that, you just issue a warrant, and McGrath will be implicated by association. Ig Murray was his strong-arm, filmed beside him in a thousand news bulletins. McGrath is under big pressure already because his own people are wondering just how many touts he had under him.'

McKeague sighed, venting exasperation. He was thinking this through.

'But I'll sign nothing,' said Terry, 'until the police issue a statement saying that they are looking for an aggrieved individual in connection with the fires at my houses.'

McKeague said, 'Well, we would have you, we would have Murray and we would at least embarrass McGrath. It's a small price, I suppose. Why are you doing this?'

'You are a religious man and you have to ask? I genuinely am sorry. I repent of killing the Laverys.'

'You'll have to do a lot more than that to save your soul, Mr Brankin.'

'Let's call it Purgatory. And another thing – I need a few days to sort things out before I am detained. Give me a week anyway.'

They sorted the whole business out in a few minutes. Terry signed the affidavit and in return a statement was forwarded to the press office, for release to the media, saying that a man was to be charged for the Magheraloy bomb and that an 'embittered individual' was under suspicion for the attacks on Terry Brankin's houses. Brankin would be released on police bail but neither story would make it onto the news. The media would have much bigger concerns by that evening.

***

Kathleen awoke begrudgingly in an unfamiliar bed in the restored Dunluce Avenue flat, close to where Terry was living when they first met. She wished she was back with him in their own home, or even the cottage, with the violence and turmoil behind them. She also had the burden of a huge secret, the killing of Ig Murray, and she couldn't carry that alone. She trusted that Terry was trying to sort things out, and knew that this still entailed dishonesty and crime. She wished she didn't need to know this.

Her flat was nice. Terry's men had erected bookshelves and she now enjoyed buying up copies of her favourites among books she had lost in the fires. She had found some of them second-hand in Bookfinders, the shop she had gone to with Terry the day she met him. Kathleen would have to make a life for herself in this flat, for she would be alone for a couple of years at least when Terry went to jail. He would take his punishment for the Magheraloy bombing and she would stand by him. She felt good about him doing that. He deserved it. She felt cleansed by his admission of guilt, his acceptance of punishment. They wouldn't have to think about that bomb again.

Her phone buzzed beside the bed.

'You're not up? I can hear it in your voice.' It was Nools.

Kathleen immediately erected a guard against her, afraid she would find herself discussing her secrets. Both she and Terry had stayed clear of Nools since their return.

'No harm in that, is there? How are you?'

'I'm grand, love. Just worrying about you and now there's this crazy news about Ig Murray. He was never a tout.'

'I wouldn't know.'

'Can I let you in on a secret?' she said.

'Go ahead.'

'He definitely wasn't a tout. The police are up to high doh over this. They just don't believe it. Have they been to see Terry? He can expect them.'

'Well, I'm sure Terry will just tell them what he told the press. Murray has done a bunk and says he was working for the British.'

'And if the British say he wasn't?'

'Terry can handle it.'

'But, Kathleen. Is Terry being straight with you about this? Think it through. If Ig Murray wasn't a tout and hasn't come out to deny it, that means he's dead. And it also means Terry is up to his neck in that. That's what peelers are saying. They're saying Terry Brankin topped Ig Murray.'

'How do you know what peelers are saying?'

'I know. I'm married to a prison officer. They are friends, neighbours. They come to the house. Look, tell Terry that this is what they're saying.'

Kathleen ended their call and phoned Terry straight away.

'This is madness, Terry. The police are going to get you for this too. And it won't be just two years.'

'Don't worry, love. They won't. They might question me and they might really believe that I killed Ig, but they will never be able to prove it. And there were so many different agencies running spies here, and not talking to each other, that they will never know for sure this isn't genuine. Believe me. The agencies themselves never say who is or isn't working for them. That's their way. Nools knows that too, or she should.'

Terry's gamble was that MI5 wouldn't declare that Ig was not a spy because they wouldn't want to set a precedent of confirming or denying suspicions. A real tout would emerge and they would be expected to disown him too or their silence would be taken as confirmation. They just had to avoid making any comment. Best leave people to work it out for themselves. But he was grateful to Nools for letting him know what the police were thinking.

'And what about McGrath? Does he believe your story?' Kathleen asked.

'No, but what can he do? He has already come out and said that he does believe it, so he can't be seen to change on that.'

'Well, he could have you shot for killing his mate. He's bound to be annoyed.'

'There is unfinished business like that all around him. He'll just leave it. You'll see.'

Kathleen had known Terry for thirty years and she had not expected to be surprised by him. Time alone in the flat thinking, over the past couple of days, had allowed her to see how the violent side of him was intrinsic to the man she knew. She thanked

God that Terry had been able to shoot Ig Murray and save her. She felt no compassion for Murray at all; he was the scariest, most evil man she had ever met. The world was better off without him. Terry would not threaten a woman as coldly, and with such evident relish, as that bastard had done. But he could kill when he reasoned that it was necessary. And he would not be hindered by squeamishness or by moral considerations. He certainly felt that it was for him alone to decide what was just and moral. She could not live her life like that, but she accepted, not just that Terry could, but that he now had to.

She walked through the park and saw boys in shorts playing frisbee and girls on their backs in the grass. Someone in a group near the corner of the green turned a radio's volume up sharply and she heard the distorted sting of the news programme. Her mood lightened, but the sun was no assurance of peace; she had seen awful trouble in the past on days just as lovely as this, times when the whole town was shut down, buildings burning, bombings in the city centre and thousands of people walking home past gridlocked queues of cars.

She hastened towards Damascus Street. Aoife and Ginger were on the step drinking cans of beer and listening to the radio.

'D'ye hear the news?' said Aoife. She looked as if she had been crying. 'They've shot Dom McGrath.'

Kathleen froze, trying rapidly to calculate how this changed things. 'Who shot him?'

'I don't know. I'd say it was his own.'

Ginger nudged her to be quiet.

Kathleen let herself into the house. Terry wasn't home. She tried to call him, but it went straight to voicemail. She turned on the television and watched the pictures coming in from Stormont. McGrath had brought a delegation to the front of the parliament building to lobby for the suspension of plans to mine lignite from land near Lough Neagh. 'We Love Our Lough' said one of the placards. The camera was not on McGrath when the first shot hit him. The microphone picked up the sharp report and the garbled reactions of people in the group. Then there were screams and a scramble round McGrath as he fell. But through the melee, there was a glimpse of his head, his sagging face, a strangely familiar tiredness in his eyes, as if he had been waiting for this. That image was replayed over and over again. By the time the one cameraman there had turned to the gunman, he was surrounded.

The unscripted voice-over from the station presenter said that this was a shocking historic moment, a potential threat to the peace. They were clearly putting the programme together in a panic. Then the report cut to a party press conference, at which the deputy first minister was confirming that his party leader was dead, and was calling for a day of mourning throughout the whole country.

The presenter said, 'There will be a break from our normal programming tonight, for a special report on the life and death of Dominic McGrath. That's at 10.35 tonight. Now we are going over to Downing Street for a statement from the prime minister.'

Kathleen watched that slick, smug young man say, 'Mr McGrath lived by the gun and died by the gun, and whatever symmetry we may be tempted to see in that, we should acknowledge too that he was also one of the great peacemakers of our time. Though he could not undo the grief he had personally brought to many families in Ireland and further afield, he did give his life to ending the conflict and he did lead his people into political reform. Forgive me if I do not give him a soldier's salute, for he was not our soldier, but I do commiserate today with those who have lost a leader and a friend.'

The tone of the prime minister's speech showed he saw no political need to preserve McGrath's reputation. His words signalled to the media that nothing need be spared of the bloody details of McGrath's life. But where was Terry? Kathleen tried his mobile, but only got voicemail again.

'Man Arrested for McGrath Assassination' – the words flashed across the bottom of the screen. There was no name or picture of the man yet.

Fuck, it wouldn't have been Terry, would it? Would he have done that? It would have been one possible answer to the problem, if he could have got away with it. Suddenly she saw that clearly. Of course. The only thing stopping him going to the police and taking the punishment for Magheraloy was the fear that the IRA would try to stop him giving evidence because of the need to protect McGrath. There was a simple solution to that if you didn't care about anything else: shoot McGrath.

She felt sick and she was trembling. The logic settled hard in her. He'd done it, but he'd got caught. But no, he wouldn't have done it that way. He was willing now to take the reduced two-year sentence for Magheraloy. There would be no reduction in the inevitable life term for killing McGrath, or Ig for that matter. He'd have wanted to do it in darkness and to get away. She was in a state of near panic. Why had he brought all this on her? She was furious with him.

Kathleen flicked through the other channels. She paused to hear a woman speaking: 'Such has been the fate of other great peacemakers like Gandhi and Martin Luther King. I am calling on the Irish government to declare a day of national mourning.'

She didn't recognise the speaker but took her for one of the many interchangeable apparatchiks who had surrounded McGrath at press conferences and political rallies down the years.

'Terry, where the fuck are you? Answer your fucking phone!'

There wasn't much Kathleen could do; there was no one she could call for information without having to explain her fears. Then she thought of McKeague. But what if she allowed McKeague to know that she feared it was her husband who had shot McGrath? It was too late to worry about that.

'Inspector McKeague? It's Kathleen Brankin. Have you seen Terry?' She was frantic. 'Someone has just shot McGrath.'

'And you are wondering if it was your husband who shot him? No. We have a man in custody for that. It was Seamus Lavery.'

'Seamus Lavery?'

'Yes.'

She was stumbling through her astonishment to find the words for the question that would clarify this. 'Seamus Lavery, one of the Lavery family? The ones who were in the car at Magheraloy?'

'Yes. That Seamus Lavery.'

'The poor man.'

'Well, he wanted justice, and now he thinks he has it.'

Nineteen

The station sergeant checked the peephole in the door and saw that Seamus Lavery was sitting quietly on the old bed, looking straight at the wall before him. He didn't even look round at him though he'd have heard the little shutter.

'Take as long as you like, Basil. But if he tells his solicitor she'll make a stink about it. Then it's on your head.'

'He won't.'

The sergeant turned the key and opened the door, let Basil in and locked it behind him.'

Still Seamus Lavery hardly moved.

'I'm praying for you,' said Basil.

'Are you, seriously?'

'I am.'

'Don't. I got what I wanted.'

'Seamus, you'll go to jail for a long time. You may need God's comfort to get you through that.'

Seamus turned to face him. 'We'll see. But you'll visit the odd time, won't you?'

'I will.'

'It's what you wanted too though, isn't it?'

'No, Seamus. I wanted to leave it to the Lord.'

'Well the Lord wasn't getting his finger out, was He?'

They sat quietly for a few moments.

Basil said, 'We have the forensic history of the gun. We can link it to half a dozen murders. Some people are saying we should charge you with those killings too, including a peeler and a wee primary school teacher. The gun belonged to the Provos and then to the dissidents. We'll not be announcing that. We don't want a feud.'

Lavery's head slumped into his chest. 'It's a dirty world,' he said.

'Can I suggest we clean it up a bit?'

'How do we do that?'

'Don't plead guilty,' said McKeague.

'I'm proud of what I did.'

'I know. But think it through.'

***

It was late evening when Terry got back to the house in Damascus Street, where Kathleen was waiting.

'You heard the news?' He kissed her lightly on the lips.

'God forgive me, I thought you'd done it.'

'I considered it. I figured his bodyguards would get me. But did you see them scatter? It was actually a wee woman from Toome who brought down the guy with the gun.'

'It was Seamus Lavery,' she said.

'Is that who it was?' Terry didn't unpack that thought any further.

They sat in front of the television, watching the endless stream of reports about the life and death of Dominic McGrath. It shocked Kathleen how brutal the media assessment of him was; she was used to the more reverential treatment he had been given while he was alive. 'They're not giving him credit for anything.'

'I think he humiliated the governments and the media when he could, and they've been saving this up for him.'

There were pictures of McGrath in his black beret as a young IRA man marching in a funeral cortege. He was shown being arrested from his home in a battered anorak, with long hair and a beard. The commentary mocked 'his transition from street fighter and gang leader to slightly crusty-looking politician with ambitions as a poet'.

An intense young academic was saying, 'No, I wouldn't say he had made a significant contribution to the canon of Irish literature as such. Then again, had he devoted more time to his writing, who knows?'

After the news there was a special programme on McGrath's life. Before it started, they heard the television sound echoing, and realised that the students next door were watching it too with the volume up loud. The presenter of the programme was John Carver, a journalist who had fronted serious political programmes and investigative documentaries. It opened with night shots over west Belfast, the street lights and the traffic.

'This is where Dominic McGrath grew up. In his youth, he was a conscientious scholar, but at home, his father inducted him into the ideology of militant republicanism. There was much in young Dominic's own experience that affirmed the need for a struggle against injustice and inequality. There was discrimination against Catholics in the job market, in housing allocation and in the rigging of electoral boundaries.'

The programme cut to the silhouette of a man sitting on a sofa under a portrait of Patrick Pearse. 'The first time he fired a shot? Are youse kidding? Well, I would say it was after rabbits on Black Mountain, when we were about sixteen. We had a wee .22 rifle. I would say it was his da had got that for him, perfectly legal for all I know. Then, later, we both trained in IRA camps on the border, first on old Lee-Enfields and M1 carbines. But the first time, I would say, would have been the rabbit, ha! That wee rabbit should have its place in Irish history.'

The lads next door howled with laughter.

'But Irish history would have taken a different course in the last thirty years if Dominic McGrath had not claimed early leadership of the republican armed struggle in Belfast.' This programme was clearly going to tell the whole story, the story that Terry believed had been glossed over for years to help the peace process.

'Jane McCarroll was a Protestant woman living in the heart of Catholic west Belfast at the start of the Troubles. The Republican Movement believed – and believes still – that she was an informer. And that is why they killed her. But they didn't own up to it at the time. Jane was one of a dozen IRA victims buried secretly, often in marshy bogland, which virtually swallows up the body.'

The programme returned to the silhouetted republican who had known McGrath as a boy.

'I'm not saying Dom pulled the trigger. He didn't. But he didn't exactly stand in the way of it. I remember he said, "I hope it was a clean one, now." Right enough, one shot to the temple did for her while we emptied the chamber into some of the others. Now you'd say, would you not be better doing it when she's not expecting it? But there was religion in the thinking too. Do her when her mind was on God and you were doing her a favour. Fuck, we were as bad as the Taliban in some ways.'

Now the boys next door were angry. One of them was shouting, 'I know that tout. I know that tout. That's fucking toutin', that's what that is.'

One of the others appeared to be trying to calm him, but it made no impression on his ardour: 'You stick with your own. There was a fucking war on. That's toutin', that is. And Dom's not cold in his grave yet. He should be done for that.'

The programme then cut to images of burning buildings in Belfast, and the voice of John Carver said, 'Dominic McGrath was the brains and the energy behind the bombing campaign in the early 1970s.'

Another old republican, also silhouetted, said, 'The first car bomb was an accident. We were sitting up the west, wondering if we'd hear the bang, and suddenly there was this massive harrump! We'd never thought to leave a bomb inside the car before. A car can come in handy. But Jesus, it magnified the blast. It was, like, a new technology. And after that, Dom had wee lads stealing cars all over the place and driving bombs into town in them. Serious.'

'But was there any strategy behind this carnage?' Carver asked. 'By 1972, McGrath had created so much mayhem that the British government had to take over direct rule from the Northern Ireland government. Ministers sought out contacts with the IRA and entered into direct negotiations with Dominic McGrath and his comrades. He was only twenty-four at the time, and files on how previous governments had dealt with Gandhi and Kenyatta were dusted off for clues on how to deal with this smart young man who had a brash revolutionary army at his command.'

Then they cut again to the second republican in silhouette. 'There was no way we were after a settlement at that time. The dander was up. If we'd told the boys we were stopping, they'd have lynched us. But you had to make it look like you were amenable, you know. Not just to tease the Brits, but to appease your own people. Some of them were getting cheesed off with the accidents. A lot of people were saying they didn't want this. So, you had to make it look like we didn't want it either. D'ye hear what I'm saying? Now it's different of course. Everyone wants peace now. But a certain mad anger, like you had then, has to burn itself out – and that can take years.'

'So it was more about youthful energy, getting things out of your system, than actually changing the country?' Carver asked.

'Well, we didn't change it, did we? EasyJet changed our lives more than the IRA ever did. What's the biggest difference the IRA ever made to the lives of the people of the Six Counties? It was stopping the war. That's all. I mean, is that a success story? You fart and then you open the window – well, thanks. Better that you hadn't farted.'

The boys next door were roaring again. Their hero's name was being defiled and they didn't like it.

It went on for a full hour. There were the disaffected republicans who felt betrayed by McGrath's political compromises. There were men who had killed and bombed at his behest, and who now asked what they had got for their bloody investment. Then there were the families of victims. Some said it sickened them to see republicans in government, and others felt left behind but could accept that for the sake of peace. It wasn't all negative. Some politicians spoke of Dominic McGrath's heroic endeavours to bring peace to his country and of the confidence they had had in his genuine determination to complete the protracted peace process.

'He was an OK guy,' said one. 'He made mistakes in his youth. I mean, haven't we all? But he grew into a serious commitment to peace in Ireland, and that is his legacy.'

The lasting impression at the end of the programme, however, was that Dominic McGrath had started the Troubles, and that he had given us peace only by relaxing the violence he had, himself, urged and led.

'That's not fair,' said Kathleen. 'You can't say he was to blame for it all.'

Terry said nothing about the programme.

'What does this mean for us?' she asked him.

'Primarily it means that we are safe. McGrath was behind Ig, and Ig came after us to protect him. Now there is nothing to protect, except perhaps McGrath's good name, and that's being mauled anyway.'

'Do you think his people suspect you of lying about Ig?'

'I think McGrath did, but we don't have to worry about him now. And having covered himself by claiming he already knew that Ig was a tout, he could hardly confide his suspicions, even to his men. I think we're in the clear.'

'Nools says the police think you killed Ig.'

'They're bound to. Don't worry.'

***

Kathleen woke to the sound of the news on the radio: 'The city is preparing for the biggest funeral since George Best's …' She dozed off again and was wakened by the *Nevan Toland Show*: 'Call me if you're disgusted with the coverage of the murder of Dominic McGrath. Do you think it's wrong to speak ill of the dead before they are even buried? Or are you one of those people out there, and there are a lot of them, I can tell you, who think that we are now getting the plain speaking we've waited a long time for? Call me on the biggest show in the province, and tell me what you think. That's our subject for today: Dominic McGrath – peacemaker or pariah?'

This, thought Kathleen, would be fun.

'OK, we have our first call and it's John from Andytown. What's your beef, John?'

'I think it's a disgrace that programme was put out last night. People who hadn't the guts to speak plainly when the poor man was alive are jumping all over him now he's dead. In my book, Dominic McGrath is a martyr for peace, and the smart alecs and the journalists who are sneering at him now aren't fit to tie his shoelaces.'

'Well,' said Nevan, 'Dominic always denied that he was a member of the IRA. You can see why people who didn't believe him would feel more free to say it now when he can't sue them.'

'He wouldn't have sued them. Listen, Dominic McGrath was an IRA leader, and he led the IRA to peace. What's anybody's objection to that?'

'Caller on line two?'

'Come here till I tell you, Dominic McGrath is where he belongs now – in Hell, burning nicely. And knowing that just makes my day.'

The ten o'clock morning news had more: 'There have been scuffles outside Belfast courthouse during a preliminary hearing for Seamus Lavery, who is charged with the murder of the republican leader, Dominic McGrath. Riot police donned helmets and protective gear to face an angry mob of republican supporters. Republican Party councillor Jim Headleigh was with the group.'

They played in Headleigh speaking to the reporter at the scene: 'Already there is a campaign of vilification against Dominic McGrath, and we are here to say that we will tolerate no leniency towards his killer on any pretext that he was motivated by grief over things that Dominic McGrath had nothing to do with, and isn't here to answer for. We will not let this turn into a posthumous trial of Dominic McGrath.'

***

Terry went to the office and worked through the morning, closing files, referring clients to other solicitors, winding everything up. He had not slept well. He had two guns to hide or get rid of before going to jail.

Mid-morning, he took a walk around by the courts and saw the republicans who had picketed the preliminary hearing for Seamus Lavery. Most of them were young and showed no sign of recognising him, though he had known Dominic McGrath during the worst of the Troubles and the most energetic part of the IRA campaign. He couldn't help sneering at what unlikely urban guerrillas these people made, compared to himself and Dominic. He knew details of that man's life that they would not believe.

The city was excited about the assassination. He had known a feeling in the past when you could sense in the air that everyone was worried and aware of danger. Belfast was playing out another drama that would go into the history books. Terry wondered if people here were actually addicted to being at the centre of the news and if they would ever settle down to mundane life.

The assembly and the city council were making plans for the funeral. At this stage, it wasn't clear who was coming. South Africa and the Irish Republic would send representatives. So might Cuba, and maybe even Colombia. Dominic had enjoyed friendships in diverse places. The Palestinians and the Basque separatists would want to be there, but they would have to be kept aside from some of those more committed to the war against terrorism. The great achievement of Dominic McGrath was to be received as a hero by people on different sides: US senators and mujahideen. He had generated international terrorism and exported new skills; he had also brought a terrorist campaign to an end as the price for political power. And now his horrors had been superseded by a new kind of suicidal terrorist who exulted in killing civilians; by contrast, the Provos seemed almost quaint, old-fashioned, squeamish and genteel. Officially, McGrath had become a good guy, but how easy would it be for his supporters to preserve that reputation now that he was dead? Already the strain was showing.

As far as Terry was concerned, the truth was McGrath had been a petty operator, and these pickets, with their demand that he not be tried posthumously, were typical of many of his campaigns, when republicans were demanding the impossible, whinging about how others saw them, incapable of giving any credit to the doubts people had about the cause or their methods.

***

On the morning of the funeral, Terry and Kathleen drove into the west of the city, where they rarely went now. The traffic was thick on the motorway so they avoided it lest they got stuck. He drove up the Grosvenor Road onto the Falls, which had seen huge funerals before. Thousands of people were walking on both footpaths and spilling onto the road itself, all going in the same direction. Though they were still two miles from the church, he preferred to park the car. They walked in the river of people.

The hordes flowed as blithely as if they were going to a football match, without solemnity. They were supervised by republican stewards in hi-vis jackets carrying walkie-talkies. Terry knew their form but he didn't recognise any of the men themselves. This was a new generation which expected to have authority on the road but had never used a gun. Their power was now only in the reputation of their movement. How long would that last?

Terry wondered how many others in the crowd were going to see this funeral out of curiosity, so that they could say they had been there, and out of no particular grief at the loss of Dom McGrath.

Kathleen held his arm. 'I've never been up this far.'

'This is where it all started. This is the heart of it.'

At the bottom of the Whiterock Road a group of men stood and watched. They were slouching as if trying to let everyone see that they were indifferent to this. One, in a blue denim jacket, turned his back on the crowd to joke with his mates, to try to make them laugh. Terry thought he had met the man before. He stood with a slouch. When he spotted the spider-web tattoo, he realised it was Brendan Doris, the first thief and drug dealer he had shot in the leg. One of Doris's friends nodded towards Terry, and Doris turned to boldly confront him.

'Nice one, Mr Brankin. Hell's a bit closer to being full today, isn't it?'

He looked glassily at Terry, with pure contempt. Then he reached in under his denim jacket as if for a pistol, alerting Terry, and withdrew a cheap plastic cigarette lighter. He flicked it into flame and then blew it out. He flicked it again, produced a flame in the breeze and then blew it out.

The message was plain.

'The hoods are on the move, Mr Brankin. We're getting our revenge, and there's more of it coming. You were lucky once, you and the wee missus. Not even singed – imagine that.'

Kathleen urged Terry away from confrontation.

'What does he mean?'

'Bravado,' said Terry. 'He's making out that he burnt the houses.'

'Do you think he did?'

'It's an easy bluff. Could be Ig used him.' Terry would have to think about this.

The funeral Mass for Dominic McGrath was held in St Theresa's on the Glen Road, an old grey stone church with a spire, on the slope of Black Mountain. It was here among these streets where Terry himself had played as a child, gone to school, had had his first kiss and thrown his first petrol bomb, had first burnt a bus and first handled a gun.

Terry and Kathleen didn't intend going into the church; they couldn't have done anyway with such a huge crowd there. The Irish president had sent an aide-de-camp. Though two former Irish prime ministers came, the current one didn't. Intentionally or not, the television programme, broadcast on the night he was shot, had too starkly reminded the country of the early part of the journey that Dominic had made.

The sermon was relayed to thousands standing outside and along the road, though you had to be close to the church to hear it clearly. The priest's voice was garbled by the wind and the cheap speaker system.

'When Dominic McGrath's life is weighed in the balance before the throne of the most high God, it is true there will be much in the reckoning that will count against him. But that is true of us all. What matters is what happens in the heart, and Dominic McGrath was a man who loved his country and loved his family and who could admit towards the end that if he had wronged anyone, he had acted out of that love. This was the same man who had devoted himself heroically to peace. There are those who, even now, want to lay all the grievances of all the victims at his feet, but that is unfair. Dominic – Dom – felt he was called to lead his people through the hard times, not through the easy times. It was not his doing that the people of Northern Ireland were divided against each other. He did not start the war, but he did end it, and for that we owe him our profound gratitude and our prayers. Today a merciful God will hear those prayers.'

At the end of the Mass, the stewards ordered people back from the door of the church to make space for a guard of honour: a dozen men in black military-type jackets and berets. The undertaker, walking backwards down the steps, led the pall bearers: six men of the McGrath family; some of his brothers, some of their sons, his daughter. They moved shakily. Kathleen worried that they would drop the coffin. When they were level again, they lowered the coffin onto the catafalque, a wee folding trolley, and the leader of the colour party stepped forward and unfolded an Irish tricolour on it. On the tricolour he placed a pair of black leather gloves, then stood back, ordered the colour party to attention, and saluted.

Kathleen, holding Terry's arm, felt him stiffen, as if the reflex still worked in him. A lone piper, in a tan kilt and braided green jacket, playing a dirge for a fallen soldier, led the funeral cortege out through the church gates and down the Glen Road to the republican plot in Milltown Cemetery. Half an hour after the hearse had left the church grounds, the road was still filled with people, crammed so tightly that it was impossible to tell which saw themselves as mourners and which as mere bystanders.

Terry and Kathleen weren't able to get to the cemetery in time to hear the oration from a senior IRA member. They would get most of it on television later. Terry could guess what would be said. The speaker might have been Ig Murray if he had still been around. He would say that Dominic McGrath, as a leader of the IRA, had engaged the enemy at arms in combat and in political negotiation and had brought the conflict to an end, having retired from the field of battle undefeated. Well, that would be true – to a degree. There had been a brief spell at the start of the Troubles when it had been possible to snipe at the soldiers on patrol and even exchange fire with them and survive, but those days passed quickly. Dominic's war had been a war of car bombs and doorstep shootings. The word 'combat' hardly described it.

'Do you know this area?' Terry asked Kathleen. 'I can show you the school I went to if you like.' There was no point in trying to get to their car until the huge crowd had cleared.

'OK.'

They walked back up the Glen Road across the side of the mountain and he pointed out the places he had known as a child and the things that had changed in the past decades: where the convent had been, the boys' home and the brewery. There were two schools on opposite sides of the road, one originally for boys who had passed the eleven-plus and one for those who had failed.

'I failed mine. Dominic McGrath passed his, though.'

'So it wasn't just the boys who failed who joined the IRA?'

'No. Not at all.'

They walked further out the road. 'When I was a child this was all countryside,' Terry said. 'There was a lake called the Half-Moon Lake, where kids occasionally drowned. God knows where it is now. And we would scramble through the fields up the mountain to the quarry and from there you could point out your own house and shout as loud as you liked. And there was a pub that we used to sneak to out of school.'

'Had you any idea that the Troubles were coming?'

'I don't think so. We knew that the unionists were in charge and that there were some jobs a Catholic would not go for. But out here you saw very few Protestants and you didn't fight with them.'

'So you didn't grow up with some raging sense of injustice?'

'No. Maybe others did. I can't imagine Dominic did, though, either. No. When I first went on a civil rights march, I had to ask somebody what the issues were.'

'What was it made you want to kill people?'

'It was about being a man, I suppose. It's hard to remember what it was at first because it changed so fast. We thought we were the aggrieved ones and we had a right to go to war. But we didn't think anyone had the right to fight back at us.'

'And children died.'

'Do you know, it was mostly children? We were children and the people we killed were children, well under twenty a lot of them. And wee small kids were killed too by ricochets and bombs. The Troubles ended when the children who started them became middle-aged men and didn't want to do it anymore.'

They walked in silence for a while.

'Here, let me show you Colin Glen.' He led her through a narrow gate into a wood. 'This is where we brought the girls for a wee lumber.'

'A what?'

'A wee lumber. That's what we called a snog.'

'That's disgusting.'

It was like stepping into another world. Suddenly they were off the dusty road, away from the traffic, and on the banks of a broad shallow river surrounded by high trees, and they were wading through ferns.

'It's a long time since we had sex in the open air,' he said with a smile.

'And it will be at least as long again,' she laughed. But she kissed him and took his hand. 'How are you?' she said.

'I'm coping, love. This will soon be over.'

'I have nightmares, Terry. Sometimes I dream I am trying to wake you up and he is coming closer and closer.'

'And is it any comfort to know that he is dead?'

'Oh yes,' she said. 'That's what gets me through the night.'

Twenty

Brendan Doris was aglow with a mix of dazzies and Buckfast as he walked past the cemetery wall on the Whiterock Road. Terry watched his unsteady meandering from a hundred yards behind him and gained on him slowly. There was no point in saying anything to Doris; the rationale was plain. A man who had tried to kill him and Kathleen might try again. Simple.

Terry would make this quick. He had no backings and only one gun: Ig's 9 mil. There was no point in even scaring the guy. He didn't want to see his terror or hear his pleadings; he only wanted to remove a problem. He remembered his training and Ig saying, 'You're there to erase him, no need to give him something to remember you by.'

But he had to do it right. It would have been easier with the Ruger. A 9 mil bullet can bounce back at you off a heavy coat, even ricochet from a thick skull.

On that stretch of downhill road between the Whiterock and the Falls, there were no others walking. There were houses on the other side of the street, but their blinds were drawn. Some would hear the shots, but experience told Terry that few if any would think of coming after him. He quickened his pace and then bound nimbly to right behind Doris without alerting him, the cocked pistol in his hand. The guy was out of his head anyway. He was about to die happy. Then Terry reached high and as close as he could to the side of Doris, almost like a dancer enfolding him, to get a precise aim, angled towards the side of his head, almost his upper neck, just under the ear. Doris moved groggily, sensing movement beside him, but he was too bleary to register danger.

Terry shot once up into him. The impact slung the head sideways and Doris went down. There wasn't much blood, which probably meant the bullet was still in the skull, had bounced around and pureed the brain. Ig had told him that happened sometimes. He liked that shot. He called it a rattler. And it was enough, but Terry put two more bullets – Crack! Crack! – into the back of the punctured skull, enough to be sure of finishing him while saving a few rounds, just in case he met trouble getting away. And Christ it felt good to be in control again.

Then he scrambled up onto and over the cemetery wall, though messing up his clothes enough to rouse suspicion if the police saw him. He ran through the graves to the park beyond, and across the park onto side streets that led down to the Glen Road and to his car. When he got back to Damascus Street, he took off all his clothes. He burnt his jacket and trousers in a bucket in the back yard and put everything else in the washing machine and then had a thorough shower. Cleansed and drying himself, his phone on the toilet seat beeped. It was Kathleen: 'Night love, XXX'. She'd never know what he had just done for her.

***

Benny Curtis looked at Terry across his desk as if he thought he was mad.

'You'll never practise as a solicitor again.'

'I was getting tired of it anyway.'

Terry opened a drawer and took out the Ruger, wrapped in a hand towel, and pushed it across to him. 'You're confident you can get that into Maghaberry?'

'Wouldn't even try. And what kind of protection would it be to nut somebody *after* he'd jumped you? No, I'll keep this, but in return I'll have a few heavy boys hovering near you in there. People will know that if they mess with you they'll get a broken arm or an eye thumbed through. We owe you that.'

'Thanks.'

'But it'll be like fucking Super Mario in there, you know. Space Invaders. Think of the people you've needled over the years and the most likely place for them all to be. Jail. They'll be coming at you from all directions. Yet you could have beaten this easy.'

'I don't want to. I'm sorry I killed that child, sorry I killed anybody; sorry I'm stuck with probably having to kill again.'

'I thought you were harder than that, Terry.'

'You're not sorry for anything?'

'I never give it a thought,' said Curtis.

***

One big change in Belfast since the Troubles ended was that there were more places to get a nice meal. But on the last night, Terry brought Kathleen to one of the older cafés they had known during their university years, one of those that had taken its chances against the bombing campaign.

The tables were constructed out of old sewing-machine stands. Each had a candle melting over an empty wine bottle it plugged. The artworks on the wall, by the woman who ran the place, were garish caricatures of slim women in exotic locations. He liked them.

They had remembered to bring their own wine and Terry filled Kathleen's glass. While she studied the chalked-up specials on a blackboard by the counter, he thought she was achingly beautiful. Everything was working out. They had painful times ahead but they were all planned for.

She said, 'Did you see on the news there was a guy shot dead up the Whiterock?'

'Looks like a falling out between drug dealers. That's what the police are saying anyway.'

More cheerfully, they assessed the money that would be coming to them, in compensation for damage to five properties. Their home had been destroyed, so had two of the flats. Two other properties had been restored, and they would expect the full cost of that work to be repaid. They would be able to sell all five sites.

'OK, prices are half what they were,' said Terry, 'but I would hope we will still have a pot of a million and a half.'

'And if we don't get the insurance?'

'Negative equity all round. Selling the sites wouldn't even clear the mortgages. I don't know. Perhaps just! But don't worry. It's in the bag.'

That night they stayed together in Kathleen's flat. She turned to him in bed and said, 'Will you be all right without me?'

He touched her leg. She kissed his nose. He felt under her nightdress and rested his hand on her bare hip.

'Ah – ha.'

And they made love, fully engaged in each other. He kissed her neck. She arched her body to wrench as much pleasure for herself as she could give to him. And they did not disengage when they were spent and weary, but held each other close.

***

Kathleen accompanied him to court because she was proud of him. He should have worn a good suit, she said, but he had argued that whatever clothes he wore would spend two years in prison stores and look like rags when he got them back.

They sat in the public gallery to watch the case before theirs: a woman charged with shoplifting. When his turn came, he squeezed her hand and stepped into the dock.

The charge of triple murder was put to him. He pleaded guilty. The judge remanded him in custody and reserved sentence to a later date, but everyone in court knew that whatever number of life sentences he arrived at, Terry Brankin would be free again in two years.

***

Kathleen felt more alone that night than ever before, wondering how prison would change Terry. She sat with the television off and unable to concentrate on reading. She thought she might run a bath and soak herself in warm suds for an hour, but she could not rouse herself to that effort either. I have little right to be depressed, she thought.

Then the phone rang.

'Hello, this is Henry McKillop of the *Belfast Mail*.'

Kathleen interjected. 'You have a statement from my husband's office. I have nothing to add to that.'

'But I wonder if you have any comment to make on the news that Seamus Lavery has been charged with burning your family home and several other properties belonging to you.'

'I hadn't heard that.'

'The police announced this evening that they are charging a man with the fires and they are briefing that it's Lavery. Would it surprise you if he had burnt your houses?'

Kathleen had enough sense to hang up at that point, but she would now have to find someone else who could tell her what was going on and what this meant. She fretted through the night. Her morning radio told her more than she needed to know:

'Belfast solicitor Terry Brankin is in jail this morning after his surprise confession to the Magheraloy bombing, which killed three members of the Lavery family. And now the police have charged Seamus Lavery with recent attacks on several properties owned by Mr Brankin. That's the same Seamus Lavery who has been charged with the murder of republican leader Dominic McGrath. So what's the connection between Dominic McGrath and Terry Brankin? To unravel this complex story, let's hear from our security correspondent Brian Dingle. Well, Brian?'

'Well, as we say in the trade, this one is getting complicateder and complicateder. It was only last week that the police issued a statement saying that they were looking for an individual responsible for a series of arson attacks on Terry Brankin's home and several other houses owned by him. This was read at the time as good news for Mr Brankin on a bad day, for it lifted from him the suspicion that he had started the fires himself, to reap the insurance money. This coincided with Mr Brankin being charged in connection with the Magheraloy bomb. The prominent Belfast solicitor has confessed to having been a member of the IRA bomb team which detonated a roadside device under the Laverys' car as they drove back north after a visit to the Republic.'

'Well,' said the interviewer, 'is there a possibility that Lavery had specific intelligence on the bomb which would have connected Terry Brankin to it?'

'Well, it is hard to see how he could have had such intelligence, since no one in the media had it. It came as a total surprise to us that Terry Brankin, a respected solicitor, had been in the IRA at all.'

***

Kathleen had breakfast in a nearby café and read the newspaper stories about Terry and the bomb. The coverage was embarrassingly extensive. There was a photograph of herself walking from the court building with a folded newspaper ineffectually raised to hide her face. The local morning papers had inside page features recalling the Magheraloy bomb, along with pictures of the dead. One cartoonist speculated on the first meeting between Seamus Lavery and Terry Brankin in prison with the caption: 'Hello, I'm the guy who killed your mum and dad.'

Besides that, a more analytical piece described the measures usually taken by the Prison Service to protect dangerous prisoners from each other. A member of the prison officers' union said, 'Sometimes you spend so much time watching the hard guys that you have to withdraw men from other services, like education.'

One article was a profile of Terry: 'This Belfast solicitor now admits he was an IRA killer.' The paper had dug up cases that Terry Brankin had worked on, and drew out the irony of his having, at times, represented victims and even loyalists.

Her phone beeped. It was yet another text from Nools. Just: 'Holy fuck!'

Kathleen keyed in a reply: 'We killed Ig Murray. Be grateful for that!'

She had more sense than to actually send it.

Life, she realised, would not be easy with Terry locked away, and now she would have no privacy. Everywhere she went, people would know that she was the wife of a famous bomber.

***

Terry Brankin had an uncomfortable first night in Maghaberry prison. He had a cell to himself but other prisoners played music; some played Tamla Motown, others hard rock or even rebel songs. Two years of this, he thought, would drive him mad. He had imagined a life in which he would catch up on his reading and get physically fit. The governor, a trim Englishman, had met him when he arrived and told him that Seamus Lavery would be kept apart from him on another wing.

'You are not to try and contact him or send any messages to him and I expect you to let me know if he tries to get in touch with you. Is that clear?'

Lavery would spend much of his time in solitary confinement for protection from republicans who would want to avenge McGrath's assassination, and from ordinary gangsters who would seek to ingratiate themselves with the Republican Movement by delivering his scalp to them.

Twenty-One

Seamus Lavery stood proudly in the dock of the clean modern courtroom, listening to the charges against him. He stood with a countryman's slouch, unimpressed by the polished pine, the symbols and the wigs. After long years of smouldering, he had finally done something about those who had killed his parents and his sister, and he was pleased with himself. Now he was going to be a bloody nuisance to everybody by denying that he killed McGrath though dozens of people had seen him do it. He had received nearly a hundred letters congratulating him on his direct action. And now he could do more.

The bewigged judge looked down, peering over his sheaves of paper, and eyeballed Lavery. He had all the authority that his position gave him, yet Lavery imagined that if he met him in his shop or on the street, he would look like just another middle-aged tubby man with reddened cheeks, one of the many he met every day who would be dead in a decade.

'And in relation to the charge that you did murder Dominic McGrath, how do you plead?'

'Not guilty, your honour.'

The judge betrayed his contempt for that plea with only a half-smirk. 'And in relation to the charge that you did commit acts of arson against five properties owned by Mr Terence Brankin, how do you plead?'

'Guilty, your honour.'

'And on the several charges of attempted murder?'

'Not guilty, your honour.'

None of this would make the slightest difference to Lavery. He would do life for murdering McGrath. But dragging out the trial would enable the fullest telling of his story.

The prosecuting lawyer stood up. Aibhlin McConaghy was a large woman whose black legal robes draped round her like curtains.

She said, 'Your Lordship, the prosecution will seek to establish that the defendant is guilty of both the murder of Dominic McGrath and the attempted murder of Kathleen and Terence Brankin, Gillian McDonald, Thomas McCoy and the several residents of properties owned by Mr and Mrs Brankin. We will seek to demonstrate to the court that he was motivated by a desire for revenge against the IRA for the destruction of his family in a bomb attack at Magheraloy. We will establish that he firmly believed that Terence Brankin was a member of the bomb team. That team had intended to blow up the car of the Chief Constable. Mr Lavery also acted in the belief that Dominic McGrath was a member of the IRA Army Council, which ordered that attack.

'On the first charge of shooting and killing Mr McGrath we will call witnesses who will say that they were present and had a clear view of the defendant firing the fatal shot. We will also produce in evidence the pistol used, a Glock 17.

'On the second charge of burning several properties belonging to Mr Brankin, Mr Lavery has pleaded guilty. It falls to us only to prove the third charge that his intention in these attacks was to take life – indeed, many lives.'

For days, Terry Brankin would be cross-examined by Lavery's defence council, seeking to establish mitigation in the minds of the jury.

'You killed Mr Lavery's family, didn't you?'

'Yes.'

'Speak up please.'

'I have confessed to the bombing that killed his parents and his sister. It is common knowledge.'

'Thank you.'

The barrister paused to give the jury time to reflect on that, reaching down to sort papers with one hand.

'And why was Mrs Brankin staying at the house in Damascus Street on the night of the fires?'

'We were going through a bad patch.'

'And why was that?'

'Is that really relevant?' asked the judge.

'I believe it is, your honour.'

'She had just learnt about the bombing,' said Brankin.

'Speak up please.'

'We had had a visit from the police to enquire into the Magheraloy bomb. That was when my wife learnt of my part in it.'

'It was not easy for her to accept that her husband was a murderer, was it?'

'No.'

'But she has come round to it now?'

The judge intervened again. 'Enough of this. I see no way in which this line of questioning advances the case we are hearing.'

The barrister conceded with a smile. He had said enough to get a story onto the front pages.

Seamus Lavery sat in the dock scowling at Terry and turning often to stare at Kathleen. This woman had done what no one else had done; she had forgiven the killer of his mother, his father and his sister.

Kathleen faced the photographers and television cameras again when she stepped out into the rain. She knew not to say a word but to keep walking through them. Journalists would stand in front of her but they would have to move if she ploughed on. They had no right to bar her way. 'You love your husband, don't you?' a young woman said to her. The headline on the paper next day was: 'I Love my Killer Husband'. She had no recollection of having answered the reporter. Perhaps she had nodded some kind of assent.

Terry was back in the dock next day.

'Who planned the Magheraloy bomb?' asked Lavery's defence.

Terry had been happy to implicate Ig Murray and Mick Harken. He had made no mention of anyone else. 'I don't know,' he said. 'It had all been worked out before it was put to me.'

'Who put it to you?'

'Ig Murray. He was the one who ordered most of the operations I was on.'

'Did you know Dominic McGrath as an officer in the IRA?'

'I know since his funeral that he was an IRA officer. That's now in the public domain.'

'You are trifling with me, Mr Brankin. Was Dominic McGrath involved in the plan to bomb a target in a car at Magheraloy?'

'I don't know.'

'I suspect you know fine rightly, Mr Brankin. Has it not been common knowledge throughout this society for decades that Mr McGrath was an IRA leader?'

'He always denied it.'

Kathleen watched and wished Terry had said plainly what he knew, what he had told her, that he wouldn't play games. And she was learning to anticipate which lines from the trial would resound through the papers. This time it would probably be: 'Penitent Provo Still Covering for IRA Leader'.

'Enough of this,' said the judge.

'I think it will be clear to the jury, your honour, that it was politically inconvenient to press charges against those responsible for killing Mr Lavery's father, mother and sister, and that it was understandable, if not justifiable, that he took action on his own account. That is the point I am seeking to illustrate.'

Then Seamus Lavery was questioned. The thick Derry accent brought back to Terry a clear memory of his interview with Finian, the funeral, the tensions in that family. He had a strange feeling of knowing him better than he was entitled to.

'Did you know that Terry Brankin was the bomber who killed your parents and your sister?'

'I did surely.'

'How did you know that?'

'Peelers told me.'

'Police officers had told you that he was a suspect?'

'No, they told me 'twas him that done it.'

'Who specifically told you?'

'Don't know.'

'Can you recall the occasion?'

'No.'

'You're not being very helpful here, are you?'

'Everybody knew, sure, 'twas him. People know these things. That's how it is.'

'Did you attack Mr Brankin's home on the night of—'

'Nobody else was doing anything about it.'

Again, the papers led mostly on Terry and the Magheraloy bombing. It was as if it was Terry who was on trial.

***

Basil McKeague was familiar with the layout of the visiting area of Maghaberry prison and had marvelled before at how quickly a prisoner might come to look relaxed and at home there. Seamus Lavery moved with the easy slouch of a man who had no expectation of leaving here for a long time. The seating round a little table was rigidly bolted to the ends of a cross-shaped frame. Prison officers walked among the tables, to check that neither side was handing over contraband and that they could hear the conversations.

'You've dragged it out far enough,' said Basil.

'I'm enjoying it, seeing Brankin and especially that bitch of a wife of his squirming. They think they are good people, you know. I've looked in their eyes and seen that much in them. They have no notion that they are the scum of the earth. He kills my father and my mother and my sister, and still he can sit there looking aggrieved and put upon, as if some dreadful misfortune has befallen him. And she's sitting their gazing over at him all the time, doting on him in a place like that! And every time someone says anything against him she winces as if she'd had a needle stuck in her. No, I'm getting value out of this.'

***

The judge, in his summing up, said, 'Mr Lavery will of course attract a great deal of sympathy, given what he has suffered. He has known since he was a child that his parents and sister were murdered by the IRA, and the two names that he was led by some errant police officers to associate with that attack were those of Mr Dominic McGrath and Mr Terence Brankin; the latter has confessed to his part in the crime. Let no one say, however, that Mr Lavery was right to attack either man. It is particularly odious that he was content to endanger the lives of other people in the service of vengeance, including those of Mrs Brankin and several of the Brankins' tenants. This court remains highly suspicious that Mr Lavery did not act alone in the fire-bombings of the Brankin houses. It defies our own experience of this type of attack in the past that one person could have been so effective in such a short period.'

He sentenced Lavery to twenty years, imprisonment. Addressing him personally, the judge said, 'Mr Lavery, I do not believe that you are an evil man. I do not believe that there has been any evidence before this court to suggest that you would have lifted a hand in harm to any man alive if you had not yourself been cruelly wronged. Nevertheless, the law is to be obeyed, and if this court was to show any leniency or any relaxation of that vital principle, it would be in danger of licensing revenge by many thousands of others in this afflicted society who have suffered as you have done, to a greater or lesser degree.'

***

The letter to Kathleen from the insurance company said: 'We advise you that the judge's conclusion that several people were involved in the attack on your houses brings it within the scope of the Northern Ireland Office's package of compensation measures for damage to property caused by paramilitary organisations. We refer you to paragraph 17 clause c in your policy, which stipulates that, in the event that the Criminal Injuries Compensation

Authority is held to be responsible for paying damages, no claim can be made through the insurer.'

The letter outlined her right of appeal but she took that as a formality. The company was confident it could refuse her.

The letter from the Northern Ireland Office said: 'After due deliberation on the conviction of Seamus Lavery and the comments of the judge, we have decided that you are not entitled to compensation for the damage to your properties in so far as the past actions of Mr Brankin drew those attacks upon you. It is not the policy of this office to compensate past or present members of paramilitary organisations for violence inflicted upon them that has arisen from their membership of those organisations and their activities within them. We can only advise you to seek redress through your insurance company.'

These were hard times for Kathleen Brankin. She had sat in court watching Terry looking paler and thinner every time he was called to give evidence. Now she would have to sell their burnt-out houses for the value of the sites they were built on. The NIO did agree to cover the cost of damage to the property of tenants, so at least she was not liable for that.

Twenty-Two

Kathleen was bored and anxious. She had appointed an estate agent to sell their properties. Her application for Jobseekers' Allowance was complicated by her theoretical wealth. But she needed an income. She couldn't even do the simplest work, like tutoring pupils for English or marking papers without first updating herself on the curriculum. So she read books and lounged about the flat and went out for walks that she found tedious, just to get the exercise.

She knew that if she made new friends, they would recognise her in time as the wife of the Magheraloy bomber, the woman who had told the tabloids how much she loved him. Even if she joined a night class, people would stare at her and whisper behind her back. No, it was better to stay at home on her sofa and get a little drunk.

Sunday was always the most difficult day for her. She needed to get out of the small flat. On a weekday morning, she could go and sit in a local café and read the paper; on Sundays half the population of the new peace-time Belfast seemed to have breakfast with friends, ordering coffees in formulae and permutations she couldn't interpret. If she went late to the café, she would find a queue at the door waiting for tables, and if she went early and took a table for herself, she would feel guilty about holding up a whole table for one person when the crowds came. If the sun was out she could walk in the park. If it was raining she might sit in and talk to no one the whole day. That's what that Sunday was like: grim, demoralising.

If the phone rang, it was usually an Indian guy called Roy or Paul to tell her that her internet had been hacked or was about to be cut off or to offer her a package that included a mobile phone and Netflix. Sometimes she was even tempted to stay on the line to have someone to talk to. Or it was Nools. Nools phoned every few days to check that she was OK, to suggest meeting for coffee or to update her on what was happening in the prison. George was approaching retirement so he had a flexitime package that allowed him to ease himself out gently and, in theory, adapt himself to full-time home life.

'He says Terry is in big demand; everybody wants legal advice. I'd say it's doing his head in.'

Nools knew more about what was happening in the prison than Kathleen learnt from her visits.

She said, 'There's a journalist called Finian Hardwick who goes in to teach creative writing classes. I asked George if he was concerned that he'd do the inside story. He says there is no inside story, except that prison is boring. You'd think he nearly preferred the old days when they were throwing parcels of shite at the screws.'

Kathleen said, 'You know, I found it very hard to stand by Terry after hearing what he did. I couldn't have stayed with him if he hadn't gone down for this.' She had braved danger and disgrace, faced cold reality in the need to kill Ig, and yet she retained a superstitious sense that Terry had cost them the right to have a child of their own. 'There is justice in it.'

Nools said, 'I'm married to one of those men myself you know, a good man who did bad things. He doesn't cope so well. I have to look after him. But I don't think too much about the brutality in that job, torturing prisoners in the old days, beating them up. They used to put them in cold baths and scrub them with a yard brush. He still comes home at night to the horrors. He says I don't know the half of it and I'm sure that's right.

'And why don't I leave him for an easier life? Because he needs me.'

Kathleen said, 'Do you think Terry needs me?'

'He's paying a high price to keep you. I think you keep him right. Out there on his own – what might he not do? He's taking his punishment for you. He'd hardly have agreed to do that if he was on his own. He'd have taken his chances, owned up to nothing and out-bluffed them all. But even then, it would never have gone away and in ten years from now there'd be another cop at your door, maybe this time with evidence. It's good what he's done.'

'But you said they suspect he killed Ig Murray. Might they come after him for that?'

She said, 'No, I don't think so. I think they are sure Ig is dead, and they are happy about that. Maybe if he really was a tout they'd care more. Funny, isn't it?'

Nools often came to visit and Kathleen shared with her the fear that life would never be normal again, that she was wary of going into company because her face had been on television and in the newspapers, the face of the woman who forgave a child killer.

Nools said to her, 'You have to walk confidently. People will know who you are but that's for them to deal with. Many will meet you not with contempt but with curiosity. They will say, "She a nice woman; not a devil at all." And they will reason that if someone nice like you is loyal to Terry, then Terry can't be all bad, there must be some good in him. But if you give up, they will say, "she was a saint putting up with him but in the end even she couldn't stick him."

'You see, he will have no life to come back to unless you go out there and act perfectly normal and disarm every sneer, not with a smile or a reply, but just by ignoring it and acting as if you had every right to shop in Sainsbury's or go to a night class without being stared at.'

On another visit, Nools told her, 'The police are searching for Ig's body. In Larne. They're discussing whether or not to demolish new houses to see if he was buried in the foundations. They got a call from somebody.'

Kathleen listened with interest and said nothing.

'That's it,' said Nools. 'You're getting the hang of it.'

'Of what?'

'Of the secret life.'

Once, Kathleen was walking through Corn Market when a man reached her a religious tract. He had it right in front of her before they recognised each other. It was Basil McKeague. She took it in her hand and read the legend over a picture of Jesus by the shores of Galilee: 'The One Who Sees Into All Hearts'.

'I wonder what he sees in yours,' she said.

'Ah, Mrs Brankin. Let me assure you, prayer never hurt anybody. You should try it.'

'Have you retired?'

'No, but I get days off and I try to use my time as best I can, that's by spreading the Lord's word.'

'Really?'

'Yes, really.'

'You must have a pretty dire home life.'

The road out to Maghaberry prison was bleak and barren in winter, and often the hills were frosted in the mornings. Sometimes Kathleen saw familiar faces among the visitors. Once a loyalist leader called Benny Curtis smiled at her and she winced. She had seen him on television. She thought she saw Basil McKeague in the car park, but she wasn't sure. The man was dressed more casually than McKeague had ever been in her company. And when she looked for him in the visiting area, there was no sign of him. She wondered what he'd be doing there. How safe was Terry from this man's ploys, or indeed from Seamus Lavery?

The visits were arduous. She could lodge some money for Terry at a desk in the prison entrance, after identifying herself by pressing her finger onto a granulated red light. She had to leave her handbag in a locker before her first search. In a little hallway, she joined a queue of other visitors instructed, in turn, to stand still on a circle marked on the floor so that a large black Labrador might sniff their crotches for contraband, drugs or explosives that might be concealed there. Once she saw a young woman taken aside when the dog wagged his tail frenziedly and nuzzled into her enthusiastically to signal a find. The embarrassed woman protested, but she was refused her visit and sent home. Kathleen wondered why, if the prison authorities were confident she was carrying drugs or explosives, they didn't detain her and summon the police.

Finally, she would enter a large hall like a school canteen, indeed more like a children's creche. Every table had plastic chairs in primary colours. Around the walls hung the paintings of prisoners, some of them neat and competent, some garish and suggestive of fire and blood.

Terry was always seated before her and would stand to kiss her while a prison officer in a white shirt with black epaulettes stood close by to supervise, that being the moment they would be close enough to pass something between them. He always wore a dull brown sweater over an open-neck shirt. He'd be washed and shaved but often wouldn't have combed his hair. And they would start out by trying to be excited while knowing that little had changed since the last visit, or that if it had, he could have phoned her.

Terry looked almost relaxed at the visiting table and that annoyed her. He had the look of a feckless son who had torn himself away from a pool game to eat his dinner.

'I think I am just turning into a beast in here. It is the only way to survive.'

'Well, remember that you have a life to go back to, unlike some of them.' She looked around her at men who were slouched and sullen, young ones with tattoos, older ones who looked more tired than anything else. They all had the manner of men wasting their time, like the louts you would see hanging round a pub, waiting for it to open, only here there were dozens of them.

'The flat's nice,' she said. 'I've put my name down for subbing in schools and put an ad in the shop window offering to tutor for English A-Level.'

He apologised for her having to make these efforts to maintain herself but she insisted that she was enjoying it. She tried not to betray exasperation that they had lost so much.

'What is the point in talking about the money,' he said, 'when there is nothing I can do in here?' He even joked about the way they had been ensnared into losing their compensation rights. 'Can you imagine how Nevan Toland and the rest would have howled if we'd got compo while I was sitting in here doing time for murder? We hear that programme every day in here, it's a gas.'

She told him that she had seen Basil McKeague, thinking that would awaken his senses.

'He comes in to see Lavery. Perhaps has some notion of saving his soul.'

'Do you think he put Lavery up to attacking the houses?'

'Lavery didn't burn the houses. But McKeague would have told him to confess and make sure we didn't get the compensation. Dirty bastard. And he'll have told him to plead not guilty to shooting McGrath, and then get me called as a witness and the whole thing aired in court.'

'Well, who did burn the houses?' said Kathleen.

'It was that wee hood we saw on the day of Dom's funeral. Remember the one with the lighter.'

'Can he not be charged?'

'Not now. Remember the drug dealer who was shot on the Whiterock. That was him.'

'Jesus, Terry. This place does my head in. You live and breathe in a world in which you know these things, expect to know them. I don't and I don't want to.'

'You know about Ig. Not many people know about Ig.'

'I can live with that. Good riddance to him.'

'Well, that's how it starts, love, with the first discovery that some problems don't take care of themselves.'

'I just hope we can live without more problems of that kind. I'm afraid that when you start it just gets deeper.'

'I think the loose ends are all tidied up now. We'll get through this and start again when I get out.'

For Christmas Kathleen gave Terry a clutch of new novels and he gave her a card.

The spring brought memories of happier times, the way it always does. The hills broke out in yellow gorse and then the hedgerows in hawthorn blossom. A year had passed since McKeague had called at their door with questions about the past.

Once a social worker stopped Kathleen on the way out of the prison and asked for a quick chat. She was a large woman with jet black hair turning grey. Kathleen didn't want her to think she was spurning her so she agreed to listen.

'It's very hard, isn't it? I wonder, would you be interested in asking for conjugal visits? I think the governor would be amenable.'

It took a moment for Kathleen to grasp that she was being offered sex with her husband. 'That's very kind of you,' said Kathleen, 'but don't they put something in his tea?'

'No. Everyone thinks that,' said the woman, 'but you give that some consideration, and call me any time. I'm here to help.'

***

One evening George Caulfield came to see Terry in his cell. Terry was stretched out on his bed reading a newspaper. George was past expecting any respect from prisoners. Terry wasn't going to leap off the bed and stand erect and attentive before him. And Terry had never been sure of whether George was an ally or an enemy, even though he had bought a house off him. He feared George was jealous of his friendship with Nools, was never confident there was only friendship between them.

George closed the cell door and sat down. He had all the bearing of a man who was totally fed up with his job but unsure he'd be any happier anywhere else. 'I'm here to say we are a bit concerned about your security.'

'Something changed?'

'Maybe nothing. You never know for sure how many enemies you have, do you? Not in this bloody country.'

'No.'

'Just take care and we'll do our best for you.'

Terry thanked him sincerely for the heads-up.

In the canteen the next day, Terry looked around to see if anyone was staring at him. He tried to put a number on the types that might come after him: the hoods he had kneecapped, or their friends; chucky-heads who saw him as a defector, including some who might seriously be wondering what happened to Ig, not buying the story about him being a tout; not Seamus Lavery, who was never allowed near him, but friends he might have made inside; loyalists who just saw him as an old Provo, an easy target now that the movement wasn't backing him; loyalists who had worked out that Terry must have had something to do with the nutting of Dinko; loyalists who saw him as a lawyer who had let them down because they shouldn't have put their faith in a fucking Fenian lawyer in the first place. And – who knows – maybe any lout who wanted to make a name for himself?

While he was studying faces for signs of danger a large man with no hair and a lot of tattoos on both arms eased into the seat beside him. Terry read the tattoos: loyalist flags and symbols – this guy wasn't shy about his allegiances.

'Benny asked me to look out for you,' he said.

'And how are you going to do that?'

'I'm going to stick so close to you that if I was any closer I'd be up your hole.'

'Does Benny know something?'

'He knows that smart fellas like you don't shower alone. My brief is to spot the hassle when it comes and crush it so hard the one after that will think twice. Any problems with that? Trying to stay on the right side of Jesus or anything?'

'No,' said Terry.

'Good. Just being seen talking to me will help.'

The move, when it came, was a spanner dropped from an upper wing, deftly enough to pass through the squares in the wire mesh. The bald man with the tattoos bounced Terry out of the way and took the impact on his own chest and went down with a cracked sternum. Next morning, Bo Tatlock, Dinko's brother, was found in his cell, dead from a broken neck.

The killing would never stop.